'It's a girl,' said the Queen anxiously, 'and the sweetest little — '

'*I'm* the best judge of that,' said the uninvited fairy, and she hooked the baby out of its satin cradle. 'Well, let's have a look at you.'

All very traditional, you might think, but you'd have no earthly chance of predicting the rest of the story of the Parrot Pirate Princess, for originality ought to be Joan Aiken's middle name, and this traditional beginning is just the jumping-off ground for a fairy story totally *un*like anything else you have ever read.

Tragic romance seems as sad with her between a lonely farmer and his swan bride as between all the princes and princesses you've ever met; even with her ghosts: the worst problem in dealing with them isn't fear but hurting their feelings; and her kings may be unexpectedly diffident and considerate like the King who stood all night before his coronation.

Anyway, it's all good fun, and more than that – except when it's sad, or beautiful or thoughtful as well, and there hardly *could* be more delight and entertainment packed into one book. Three of the stories, *All You've Ever Wanted, The Parrot Pirate Princess* and *Yes, But Today is Tuesday,* were the first stories Joan Aiken sold. They were written when she was 17.

Her other books in Puffins are *The Wolves of Willoughby Chase, Black Hearts in Battersea, Night Birds on Nantucket, The Whispering Mountain* and *The Cuckoo Tree,* besides two other collections of short stories, *A Small Pinch of Weather* and *The Kingdom Under the Sea.*

For readers of nine and over.

JOAN AIKEN

All But a Few

ILLUSTRATED FROM
DRAWINGS BY
PAT MARRIOTT

PUFFIN BOOKS

Puffin Books, a Division of Penguin Books Ltd,
Harmondsworth, Middlesex, England
Penguin Books Australia Ltd, Ringwood, Victoria, Australia
Penguin Books Canada Ltd, 41 Steelcase Road West, Markham, Ontario, Canada

—

The stories published in this Puffin edition are a selection of those which appeared
in the collection *All and More*, published by Jonathan Cape Ltd, 1971, by
Joan Aiken. The stories first appeared in *All You've Ever Wanted*
(first published in 1953) and *More Than You Bargained For*
(first published in 1955).

—

Published in Puffin Books 1974

—

This edition copyright © Joan Aiken, 1974
Illustrations copyright © Jonathan Cape Ltd, 1971
Made and printed in Great Britain by
Hazell Watson & Viney Ltd, Aylesbury, Bucks
Set in Monotype Garamond

Contents

For
DAVID
*who used to listen to them on walks,
and had the P.P.P. as a
birthday present*

All You've Ever Wanted

MATILDA, you will agree, was a most unfortunate child. Not only had she three names each worse than the others – Matilda, Eliza and Agatha – but her father and mother died shortly after she was born, and she was brought up exclusively by her six aunts. These were all energetic women, and so on Monday Matilda was taught Algebra and Arithmetic by her Aunt Aggie, on Tuesday, Biology by her Aunt Beattie, on Wednesday Classics by her Aunt Cissie, on Thursday Dancing and Deportment by her Aunt Dorrie, on Friday Essentials by her Aunt Effie, and on Saturday French by her Aunt Florrie. Friday was the most alarming day, as Matilda never knew beforehand what Aunt Effie would decide on as the day's Essentials – sometimes it was cooking, or revolver practice, or washing, or boiler-making ('For you never know what a girl may need nowadays' as Aunt Effie rightly observed).

So that by Sunday, Matilda was often worn out, and thanked her stars that her seventh aunt, Gertie, had left for foreign parts many years before, and never threatened to come back and teach her Geology or Grammar on the only day when she was able to do as she liked.

However, poor Matilda was not entirely free from her Aunt Gertie, for on her seventh birthday, and each one after it, she received a little poem wishing her well, written on pink paper, decorated with silver flowers, and signed 'Gertrude Isabel Jones, to her niece, with much affection'. And the terrible disadvantage of the poems, pretty though they were, was that the wishes in them invariably came true. For instance the one on her eighth birthday read:

> Now you are eight Matilda dear
> May shining gifts your place adorn

> And each day through the coming year
> Awake you with a rosy morn.

The shining gifts were all very well – they consisted of a torch, a luminous watch, pins, needles, a steel soapbox and a useful little silver brooch which said 'Matilda' in case she ever forgot her name – but the rosy morns were a great mistake. As you know, a red sky in the morning is the shepherd's warning, and the fatal results of Aunt Gertie's wellmeaning verse was that it rained every day for the entire year.

Another one read:

> Each morning make another friend
> Who'll be with you till light doth end,
> Cheery and frolicsome and gay,
> To pass the sunny hours away.

For the rest of her life Matilda was overwhelmed by the number of friends she made in the course of that year – three hundred and sixty-five of them. Every morning she found another of them, anxious to cheer her and frolic with her, and the aunts complained that her lessons were being constantly interrupted. The worst of it was that she did not really like all the friends – some of them were so *very* cheery and frolicsome, and insisted on pillow-fights when she had toothache, or sometimes twenty-one of them would get together and make her play hockey, which she hated. She was not even consoled by the fact that all her hours were sunny, because she was so busy in passing them away that she had no time to enjoy them.

> Long miles and weary though you stray
> Your friends are never far away,
> And every day though you may roam,
> Yet night will find you back at home

was another inconvenient wish. Matilda found herself forced to go for long, tiresome walks in all weathers, and it was no comfort to know that her friends were never far away, for although they often passed her on bicycles or in cars, they never gave her lifts.

However, as she grew older, the poems became less troublesome, and she began to enjoy bluebirds twittering in the garden, and endless vases of roses on her window-sill. Nobody knew where Aunt Gertie lived, and she never put in an address with her birthday greetings. It was therefore impossible to write and thank her for her varied good wishes, or hint that they might have been more carefully worded. But Matilda looked forward to meeting her one day, and thought that she must be a most interesting person.

'You never knew what Gertrude would be up to next,' said Aunt Cissie. 'She was a thoughtless girl, and got into endless scrapes, but I will say for her, she was very good-hearted.'

When Matilda was nineteen she took a job in the Ministry of Alarm and Despondency, a very cheerful place where, instead of typewriter ribbon, they used red tape, and there was a large laundry basket near the main entrance labelled The Usual Channels where all the letters were put which people did not want to answer themselves. Once every three months the letters were re-sorted and dealt out afresh to different people.

Matilda got on very well here and was perfectly happy. She went to see her six aunts on Sundays, and had almost forgotten the seventh by the time that her twentieth birthday had arrived. Her aunt, however, had not forgotten.

On the morning of her birthday Matilda woke very late, and had to rush off to work cramming her letters unopened into her pocket, to be read later on in the morning. She had no time to read them until ten minutes to eleven, but that, she told herself, was as it should be, since, as she had been born at eleven in the morning, her birthday did not really begin till then.

Most of the letters were from her 365 friends, but the usual pink and silver envelope was there, and she opened it with the usual feeling of slight uncertainty.

> May all your leisure hours be blest
> Your work prove full of interest,
> Your life hold many happy hours
> And all your way be strewn with flowers

said the pink and silver slip in her fingers. 'From your affectionate Aunt Gertrude.'

Matilda was still pondering this when a gong sounded in the passage outside. This was the signal for everyone to leave their work and dash down the passage to a trolley which sold them buns and coffee. Matilda left her letters and dashed with the rest. Sipping her coffee and gossiping with her friends, she had forgotten the poem, when the voice of the Minister of Alarm and Despondency himself came down the corridor.

'What is all this? What does this mean?' he was saying.

The group round the trolley turned to see what he was talking about. And then Matilda flushed scarlet and spilt some of her coffee on the floor. For all along the respectable brown carpeting of the passage were growing flowers in the most riotous profusion – daisies, campanulas, crocuses, mimosa, foxgloves, tulips and lotuses. In some places the passage looked more like a jungle than anything else. Out of this jungle the little red-faced figure of the Minister fought its way.

'Who did it?' he said. But nobody answered.

Matilda went quietly away from the chattering group and pushed through the vegetation to her room, leaving a trail of buttercups and rhododendrons across the floor to her desk.

'I can't keep this quiet,' she thought desperately. And she was quite right. Mr Willoughby, who presided over the General Gloom Division, noticed almost immediately that when his secretary came in to his room, there was something unusual about her.

'Miss Jones,' he said, 'I don't like to be personal, but have you noticed that wherever you go, you leave a trail of mixed flowers?'

Poor Matilda burst into tears.

'I know, I don't know *what* I shall do about it,' she sobbed.

Mr Willoughby was not used to secretaries who burst into tears, let alone ones who left lobelias, primroses and the rarer forms of cactus behind them when they entered the room.

'It's very pretty,' he said. 'But not very practical. Already it's almost impossible to get along the passage, and I shudder to think what this room will be like when these have grown a bit higher. I really don't think you can go on with it, Miss Jones.'

'You don't think I do it on purpose, do you,' said Matilda sniffing into her handkerchief. 'I can't stop it. They just keep on coming.'

'In that case I am afraid,' replied Mr Willoughby, 'that you will not be able to keep on coming. We really cannot have the Ministry overgrown in this way. I shall be very sorry to lose you, Miss Jones. You have been most efficient. What caused this unfortunate disability, may I ask?'

'It's a kind of spell,' Matilda said, shaking the damp out of her handkerchief on to a fine polyanthus.

'But my dear girl,' Mr Willoughby exclaimed testily, 'you have a National Magic Insurance card, haven't you? Good heavens – why don't you go to the Public Magician?'

'I never thought of that,' she confessed. 'I'll go at lunch-time.'

Fortunately for Matilda the Public Magician's office lay just across the square from where she worked, so that she did not cause too much disturbance, though the Borough Council could never account for the rare and exotic flowers which suddenly sprang up in the middle of their dusty lawns.

The Public Magician received her briskly, examined her with an occultiscope, and asked her to state particulars of her trouble.

'It's a spell,' said Matilda, looking down at a pink Christmas rose growing unseasonably beside her chair.

'In that case we can soon help you. Fill in that form, *if* you please.' He pushed a printed slip at her across the table.

It said: 'To be filled in by persons suffering from spells, incantations, philtres, Evil Eye, etc.'

Matilda filled in name and address of patient, nature of spell, and date, but when she came to name and address of person by whom spell was cast, she paused.

'I don't know her address,' she said.

'Then I'm afraid you'll have to find it. Can't do anything without an address,' the Public Magician replied.

Matilda went out into the street very disheartened. The

Public Magician could do nothing better than advise her to put an advertisement into *The Times* and the *International Sorcerers' Bulletin*, which she accordingly did:

AUNT GERTRUDE PLEASE COMMUNICATE
MATILDA MUCH DISTRESSED BY LAST POEM

While she was in the Post Office sending off her advertisements (and causing a good deal of confusion by the number of forget-me-nots she left about), she wrote and posted her resignation to Mr Willoughby, and then went sadly to the nearest Underground Station.

'Aintcher left something behind?' a man said to her at the top of the escalator. She looked back at the trail of daffodils across the station entrance and hurried anxiously down the stairs. As she ran round a corner at the bottom angry shouts told her that blooming lilies had interfered with the works and the escalator had stopped.

She tried to hide in the gloom at the far end of the platform, but a furious station official found her.

'Wotcher mean by it?' he said, shaking her elbow. 'It'll take three days to put the station right, and look at my platform!'

The stone slabs were split and pushed aside by vast peonies, which kept growing, and threatened to block the line.

'It isn't my fault – really it isn't,' poor Matilda stammered.

'The Company can sue you for this, you know,' he began, when a train came in. Pushing past him, she squeezed into the nearest door.

She began to thank her stars for the escape, but it was too soon. A powerful and penetrating smell of onions rose round her feet where the white flowers of wild garlic had sprung.

When Aunt Gertie finally read the advertisement in a ten-months-old copy of the *International Sorcerers' Bulletin*, she packed her luggage and took the next aeroplane back to England. For she was still just as Aunt Cissie had described her – thoughtless, but very good-hearted.

'Where is the poor child?' she asked Aunt Aggie.

'I should say she was poor,' her sister replied tartly. 'It's a pity you didn't come home before, instead of making her life a misery for twelve years. You'll find her out in the summer-house.'

Matilda had been living out there ever since she left the Ministry of Alarm and Despondency, because her aunts kindly but firmly, and quite reasonably, said that they could not have the house filled with vegetation.

She had an axe, with which she cut down the worst growths every evening, and for the rest of the time she kept as still as she could, and earned some money by doing odd jobs of typing and sewing.

'My poor dear child,' Aunt Gertie said breathlessly, 'I had no idea that my little verses would have this sort of effect. What ever shall we do?'

'Please do something,' Matilda implored her, sniffing. This time it was not tears, but a cold she had caught from living in perpetual draughts.

'My dear, there isn't anything I can do. It's bound to last till the end of the year – that sort of spell is completely un-alterable.'

'Well, at least can you stop sending me the verses?' asked Matilda. 'I don't want to sound ungrateful . . .'

'Even that I can't do,' her aunt said gloomily. 'It's a banker's order at the Magician's Bank. One a year from seven to twenty-one. Oh, dear, and I thought it would be such *fun* for you. At least you only have one more, though.'

'Yes, but heaven knows what that'll be.' Matilda sneezed despondently and put another sheet of paper into her type-writer. There seemed to be nothing to do but wait. However, they did decide that it might be a good thing to go and see the Public Magician on the morning of Matilda's twenty-first birthday.

Aunt Gertie paid the taxi-driver and tipped him heavily not to grumble about the mass of delphiniums sprouting out of the mat of his cab.

'Good heavens, if it isn't Gertrude Jones!' the Public Magician exclaimed. 'Haven't seen you since we were at college together. How are you? Same old irresponsible Gertie? Remember that hospital you endowed with endless beds and the trouble it caused? And the row with the cigarette manufacturers over the extra million boxes of cigarettes for the soldiers?'

When the situation was explained to him he laughed heartily. 'Just like you, Gertie. Well-meaning isn't the word.'

At eleven promptly, Matilda opened her pink envelope.

Matilda, now you're twenty-one,
May you have every sort of fun;
May you have all you've ever wanted,
And every future wish be granted.

'Every future wish be granted – then I wish Aunt Gertie would lose her power of wishing,' cried Matilda; and immediately Aunt Gertie did.

But as Aunt Gertie with her usual thoughtlessness had said, 'May you have all you've *ever wanted*', Matilda had quite a lot of rather inconvenient things to dispose of, including a lion cub and a baby hippopotamus.

Yes, But Today is Tuesday

MONDAY was the day on which unusual things were allowed, and even expected to happen at the Armitages. For on Mondays Papa Armitage went up to London to see that the office was managing all right without him, and Mamma, of course, was out most of the time doing the National Savings. And that left the children alone in the house with Agnes, though more often than not, Mrs Epis would come up to keep her company.

It was on a Monday, for instance, that two Knights of the Round Table came and had a combat on the lawn, because they insisted that nowhere else was smooth and flat enough. And on another Monday, two albatrosses nested on the roof, laid three eggs, and knocked off most of the tiles. And on yet another Monday, all the potatoes in a sack in the larder turned into the most beautiful Venetian glass apples, and Mrs Epis sold them to a rag and bone man for a shilling. So the Armitages were quite prepared for surprises on a Monday, and when Papa and Mamma came home in the evening, they were apt to open the front door rather cautiously, in case a dromedary should charge at them, a thing which had happened on that famous Monday before Christmas. Then they would go very quietly and carefully into the drawing-room and sit down, and fortify themselves with sherry before Mark and Harriet came in and told them precisely *what* had happened in the course of the day.

You will see, therefore, that this story is all the more remarkable because it happened on a Tuesday.

It began at breakfast time, when Mark came into the dining-room and announced that there was a unicorn in the garden.

'Nonsense,' said Papa. 'Today is Tuesday.'

'I can't help it,' said Mark. 'Just you go and look. It's

17

standing out among the peonies, and it's a beauty, I can tell you.'

Harriet started to her feet, but Mamma was firm. 'Finish your shredded wheat first, Harriet. After all, today *is* Tuesday.'

So Harriet very unwillingly finished her shredded wheat and gulped down her coffee, and then she rushed into the garden. There, sure enough, knee deep in the great clump of peonies at the end of the lawn, stood a unicorn, looking about rather inquiringly. It was a most lovely creature – snow-white all over, with shining green eyes and a twisted mother-of-pearl horn in the middle of its forehead. Harriet noticed with interest that this horn, and the creature's hooves, had a sort of greenish gleam to them, as if they were slightly transparent and lit up from within. It seemed quite pleased to see Harriet, and she rubbed its velvety nose for a minute or two. Then it turned away and took a large mouthful of peony blossom. But almost at once it spat them out again and looked at her reproachfully with its lustrous green eyes.

Harriet reflected. Then she saw Mark coming out, and went towards him. 'I think it's hungry,' she remarked. 'What do you suppose unicorns like to eat?'

'Do you think perhaps honey-comb?' Mark suggested. So they went secretly to the larder by the back door, and took a large honey-comb out on a platter. Mark held it out to the unicorn, first rolling up his sleeves so that the creature should not dribble honey on to him. It sniffed the honey in a cautious manner, and finally crunched it up in two mouthfuls and looked pleased.

'Now do you suppose,' said Harriet, 'that it would like a drink of milk?' and she fetched it some milk in a blue bowl. The unicorn snuffled it up gratefully.

'I think it must have been travelling all night, don't you?' said Mark. 'Look, it's got burrs all tangled up in its tail. I'll comb them out.'

At this moment Papa came out into the garden for his after-breakfast stroll. At the sight of the unicorn he paused, stared at it, and finally remarked:

'Nonsense. Today is *Tuesday*. It must have got left over from last night. It was very careless of you not to have noticed it, Harriet.' The unicorn looked at him amiably and began to wash itself like a cat. Mark went off to hunt for a large comb.

'Do you think we could ride it?' Harriet asked her father.

'Not at the moment,' he answered, as the unicorn achieved a particularly graceful twist, and began licking the middle of its back. 'If you ask me, I should think it would be like riding the sea-serpent. But of course you're welcome to try, when it has finished washing.'

Mrs Epis came out into the garden. It was not her usual day for coming to the Armitages, but her mother had gone to Brighton for the day, and she felt lonely at home, and had come up to give Agnes the benefit of her company and advice.

'There's a policeman at the door,' she told Papa, 'and Mrs Armitage says will you come and deal with him, please.'

'A policeman,' Harriet observed to herself. 'They don't usually come on a Tuesday.' She followed her father to the front door.

This policeman was different from the usual one. Harriet could not remember ever seeing him before. He looked at a piece of paper in his hand and said:

'I have an inquiry to make about a unicorn. Is it true that you are keeping one without a licence?'

'I don't know about keeping it,' said Mr Armitage. 'There's certainly one in the garden, but it's only just arrived. We hadn't really decided to keep it yet. I must say, you're very prompt about looking us up.'

'Please let's pay the licence and keep it,' whispered Harriet very urgently.

'Well, how much is this precious licence, before we go any further?' asked Papa.

The policeman consulted his piece of paper again. 'Ten thousand gold pieces,' he read out.

'But that's absurd. Today is Tuesday!' exclaimed Mr Armitage. 'Besides we haven't got that in the house. As a matter of fact I doubt if we've got so much as one gold piece in the house.'

Harriet did not wait to hear what happened after that. She went out to where the unicorn was standing patiently in the middle of the lawn, with two large tears in her eyes.

'Why do you have to have such an enormous licence?' she asked it. 'You might have known we couldn't keep you.' A large green drop of water the size of a plum dropped down on to her hand. It was the unicorn's tear.

Mark came across the lawn with a comb. Harriet felt too sad to tell him that they couldn't afford the unicorn. She watched him begin slowly and carefully combing the long tail. The unicorn looked round to see what was happening, and then gave an approving grunt and stood very upright and still.

'Good heavens!' said Mark. 'Look what's fallen out of its tail. A gold piece! And here's another!' At every sweep of the comb gold pieces tumbled out on to the grass, and soon there was a considerable pile of them.

'They'll do for the licence!' exclaimed Harriet. 'Quick, Mark, go on combing. We want ten thousand of them. Here are Papa and the policeman coming to inspect it.' She began feverishly counting the coins and sorting them into heaps of ten.

'It's going to take a terrible time,' she remarked. 'We might as well ask the policeman to check them.'

The two men seemed rather astonished to see what was going on. Harriet had a feeling that the policeman was not altogether pleased. However, he knelt down and began helping to count out the coins. Just as Agnes came out to tell the children that their eleven o'clock bread-and-dripping was on the kitchen table, they finished the counting. The policeman gave Mr Armitage a receipt and took himself off with the money in a bag over his shoulder. And Mr Armitage looked at his watch and exclaimed that it was high time that he did some work, and went indoors.

Mark and Harriet sat on the lawn, munching their bread-and-dripping and looking at the unicorn, which was smelling a rose with evident satisfaction.

'I wonder if it ought to be shod?' murmured Mark, looking at its greenish hooves. 'If we're going to ride it, I mean.'

They went over and examined the hooves at close quarters. They looked rather worn and sore.

'I don't suppose it's used to stones and hard roads like ours,' said Harriet. 'You can see it's a foreign animal by the surprised look it has on its face all the time.'

Mark agreed. 'Would you like to be shod?' he asked the creature. It nodded intelligently. 'Well, if that isn't good enough, I don't know what is.' They made a halter out of a green dressing-gown cord of Harriet's, and led the unicorn down to the forge, where Mr Ellis, the blacksmith, was against a wall in the sun, reading the paper.

'Please, will you shoe our unicorn for us?' asked Harriet.

'What, you two again!' exclaimed Mr Ellis. 'I thought today was Tuesday. First it's dromedaries, then unicorns. Thank 'eavens they've got 'ooves of a normal shape. Well, you lead 'im in, Master Mark. I'm not pining to have that there spike of his sticking into me breakfast.'

The unicorn was beautifully shod, with light, small, silvery shoes, and seemed very pleased with them.

'How much will that be?' Harriet asked.

'I'll have to look up in my list, if you'll excuse me,' said Mr Ellis. 'I can't remember what it is offhand, for a unicorn. Cor, you won't 'alf have a time at the Toll Bridge at Potter's End, if you ever takes 'im that way.' He went into the back of the forge, where the great bellows were, and found a grubby list. 'Quagga, reindeer – no – further on we want,' and he ran his finger down to the end and started up. 'Zebra, yak, wildebeest, waterbuck, unicorn. Twelve pieces of gold, please, Miss Harriet.' Fortunately Mark had put the comb in his pocket, so there was no difficulty about combing twelve pieces out of the unicorn's tail. Then they started back home, fairly slowly, giving him time to get accustomed to the feel of his new shoes. He lifted his feet gingerly at first, as if they felt heavy, but soon he seemed to be used to them.

Back on the lawn he became quite lively, and pranced about kicking up his heels.

'We haven't thought of a name for him,' said Harriet. 'What about Candleberry?'

'Why not?' said Mark, '...and *now* I am going to ride him.'

The unicorn took very kindly to having riders on his back, except for an absent-minded habit of tossing his head, which on one occasion nearly impaled Harriet on his horn. They noticed that when he galloped he could remain off the ground for quite long stretches at a time.

'He can very nearly fly,' said Harriet.

'Perhaps the air where he comes from is thicker,' suggested Mark ingeniously. 'Like the difference between salt and fresh water, you know.'

And then, just as they were deciding to rig up a jump and see how high he would go, they saw a little old man in a red cloak standing on the lawn and watching them. Candleberry stood stock still and shivered all over, as if his skin had suddenly gone goosey.

'Good morning,' said Harriet politely. 'Do you want to speak to Mr Armitage?'

But the little man had his eyes fixed on Candleberry. 'How dare you steal one of my unicorns,' he said fiercely.

'I like that!' exclaimed Mark. 'It came of its own accord. We never stole it.'

'You will return it at once, or it will be the worse for you.'

'After we've paid for its licence, too,' chimed in Harriet. 'I never heard such cheek. We shouldn't dream of returning it. Obviously it ran away from you because it was unhappy. You can't have treated it properly.'

'What!' almost shrieked the old man. 'You accuse *me* of not knowing how to treat a unicorn!' He seemed nearly bursting with rage. 'If you won't give it back, I'll make you. I'll cast a spell over it.'

'Hold on,' said Harriet. 'We've had it shod. You haven't any power over it any more.' Even she knew that.

At these words a terrible look crossed over the old man's face. 'You'll discover what it is to interfere with me,' he said ominously, and struck his staff on the ground. Mark and Harriet with one accord grabbed hold of Candleberry's bridle. The whole place became pitch dark, and thunder rolled dreadfully overhead. A great wind whistled through the trees. Candleberry stamped and shivered. Then the gale caught up all three of them and they were whisked away through the air. 'Hang on to the bridle,' shrieked Mark in Harriet's ear. 'I can see the sea coming,' she shrieked back. Indeed, down below them, and coming nearer every minute, was a raging sea with black waves as big as houses.

When the storm burst, Mamma and Papa Armitage were inside the house.

'I hope the children have the sense to shelter somewhere,' said Mamma. Papa looked out at the weather and gave a shriek of dismay.

'All my young peas and beans! They'll be blown as flat as pancakes,' he cried in agony, and rushed out into the garden. But as he went out the wind dropped and the sun shone again. Papa walked over the lawn, his eyes starting in horror from his head. For all about the garden were one hundred unicorns!

He went back into the house in a state of collapse and told Mamma.

'It's those children,' she said indignantly. 'They've no business to. They know perfectly well that today is Tuesday.'

'My garden will be trampled to pieces,' moaned Mr Armitage. 'How will we ever get rid of them?'

'Perhaps Mark and Harriet will have some ideas, the little wretches,' suggested Mrs Armitage. But Mark and Harriet were nowhere to be found. Mrs Epis was having hysterics in the kitchen. 'It's not decent,' was all she could say. She had come upon the unicorns unexpectedly, as she was hanging some tea cloths on the line.

Agnes, oddly enough, was the one who had a practical idea.

'If you please, sir,' she said. 'I think my dad wouldn't mind three or four of those to use as plough horses. Someone told me that once you've got them trained, they're very cheap to feed.'

So her father, Mr Monks, came along, looked over the herd, and picked out five likely ones as farm horses. 'And thank you kindly,' he said.

'You don't know anyone else who'd be glad of a few, do you?' asked Papa hopefully. 'As you can see, we've got rather more than we know what to do with.'

'I wouldn't be surprised but what old Farmer Meade could take some in. I'll ask him,' Mr Monks volunteered. 'And there's old Gilbert the carter, and I believe as how someone said the milkman was looking for a new pony.'

'Do ask them all,' said Mr Armitage desperately. 'And look – stick this up on the village notice-board as you go past.' He hastily scribbled a notice:

'Unicorns given away. Quiet to ride or drive,' which he handed to Mr Monks.

The rest of that day the Armitages were fully occupied in giving away unicorns to all applicants. 'It's worse than trying to get rid of a family of kittens,' said Mrs Armitage. 'And if they don't turn out well, we shall have to move away from the village. Oh, there's the artist who lives up on Pennington Hill. I'm sure he'd like a unicorn to carry his paints about for him.'

All day there was no sign of Mark or Harriet, and the parents began to worry. 'If it were Monday, now, it would be all right,' they said, 'but where can they be?'

Late in the evening, after they had disposed of the last unicorn to the baker's boy, and he had gone rejoicing along to Mr Ellis (who was nearly at his wits' end by this time) to have it shod, Mark and Harriet trailed in, looking exhausted but content.

'Where *have* you been? And what *have* you done to your clothes?'

'It wasn't our fault,' Harriet said drowsily. 'We were bewitched. We were blown over the sea, and we fell in. We would have been drowned, only a submarine rose up under us and took us in to Brighton.'

'And why didn't you come home straight off, pray?'

'Well, we had to earn some money for our bus fares. They won't take unicorn-gold in Brighton, I don't know why. So we organized a show with Candleberry on the beach and

All about the garden were one hundred unicorns

earned an awful lot. And then we had a huge tea, and Mark caught the bus, and I followed along by the side on Candleberry. He's terribly fast. He's asleep in the greenhouse now. We thought that would be a good place for him. What's the matter with the garden? It looks terribly trampled.'

Harriet's voice was trailing away with sleep.

'You two,' said Mrs Armitage, 'are going straight to bed.'

'But we *always* stay up to supper on Mondays,' complained Mark in the middle of a vast yawn.

'Yes,' said his father, 'but today, as it happens, is Tuesday.'

The Ghostly Governess

THE house stood a little way above the town, on the side of a hill. The front windows looked out on a great bare expanse of downs, stretching into the distance. From the pantry, and the bathroom, and the window half-way up the stairs, you could see down the river valley to Lynchbourne, the smoky port two miles away, and beyond its roofs, masts, and funnels, was the silver line of the sea.

The children approved of the house at once; it was old and full of unexpected corners, with a smell of polished floors and lavender and old carpets. The family had taken it furnished for the summer.

'I asked the agent and he said we could use the piano,' said Mrs Armitage, 'so you'll be able to keep up with your practising.'

But Mark and Harriet made secret faces at each other. They preferred the idea of hide-and-seek in the unexplored cupboards or picnics on the downs, or taking a boat down the river to the sea. They also explored the town – it was hardly more than a village – below the house. The thing they liked best was a cottage down by the river. The paths in its gardens were all paved with oyster shells, and there were two great carved dolphins on either side of the door.

'I wonder who lives there,' said Mark, 'I bet they've got some lovely things inside.'

But the cottage seemed to be unoccupied. The windows were all closed and curtained, and no smoke came from the chimney. They found out that it belonged to an Admiral, so it seemed probable that he was at sea.

By the end of a week they felt as if they had been there all their lives. Every day they asked if they could take out a picnic lunch, and the Armitage parents declared that they had never known such peace; they hardly saw the children from breakfast till supper time.

'But I'm glad to find that you're keeping up your practising,' said Mrs Armitage. 'I heard you playing that little German tune – what is it? – "Du Lieber Augustin" – very nicely the other evening.'

'Oh yes,' said Harriet, and looked blank. The conversation turned on other things. Afterwards when she compared notes with Mark they agreed that neither of them had ever played 'Lieber Augustin'.

'Do you suppose Father might have?'

'He never plays anything but Bach and Beethoven.'

'Well, someone must have played it, because I was humming it this morning, so I must have heard it somewhere.'

'Maybe it was on the wireless. Let's take our bikes down to Lynchbourne and see if there's a new ship in.'

They forgot about the incident, but later Harriet had cause to remember it. She woke in the night very thirsty, and found that her glass was empty. Coming back from the bathroom she thought she heard a noise downstairs and paused. Could someone be playing the piano at half past one in the morning? Harriet was not at all timid, and she resolved to go and see. She stole down the stairs in her slippers. Yes, there it was again – a faint thread of melody. She pushed the drawing-room door open and looked in.

The moon was setting and threw long level stripes of light across the floor and the polished lid of the grand piano. There was nobody in the room. But as Harriet stood in the doorway she heard faint tinkling music which sounded more like a cottage piano than a Bechstein, and after a moment a quavering old voice was lifted in song.

> 'Ach, du lieber Augustin, Weib ist hin, Gold ist hin,
> Ach, du lieber Augustin, alles ist hin.'

The piano keys were moving up and down by themselves.

Harriet ought to have been terribly frightened, but she was not. The quavering voice sounded too harmless. She stood in fascination, watching the keys move and wondering how long it would go on, and if, perhaps, she was dreaming.

Presently the music stopped and there was the sound of the stool being pushed back. Harriet took a step backward. On the edge of the patch of moonlight she saw a little, frail old woman, dressed in a long grey skirt, white starched blouse, and a grey shawl over her shoulders.

'Ah,' she said in a brisk, but kind voice, 'you don't know me yet, child, I am your new governess. Come, come, where are your manners? I should see a nice curtsey.'

'How do you do,' said Harriet, curtseying automatically.

'I hope we shall get along very well,' the old lady continued. 'Strict but kind is my motto, and *always* lady-like behaviour. If you want an example of *that*, you have only to look up to our dear Queen, who is such a pattern of all the virtues.'

'Yes,' said Harriet absently, looking at her enormous cameo brooch, velvet neckband and elastic-sided boots. The governess reminded her of the old yellow photographs in her grandmother's house.

'But now, child,' said the old lady, 'you must be going for your afternoon rest. It is nearly two o'clock. Later we shall begin to know each other better. By the way, I have not yet told you my name. It is Miss Allison. Now run along, and don't let me find you chattering to your brother during the rest hour.'

'No, Miss Allison,' said Harriet mechanically, and such was the governess's spell over her that she turned round and did indeed go straight back to bed and to sleep.

Next morning at breakfast Harriet was silent as if stunned. However, her father and brother talked all the time, and it was not noticed.

Later, when she and Mark were sitting in a quarry, eating the eleven o'clock instalment of their lunch (chocolate and buns) Mark said:

'What's happened to you? Toothache?'

'No. Mark,' said Harriet unexpectedly, 'do you remember the other day when Mother said something about my practising "Lieber Augustin", and I hadn't, and we thought it must have been the wireless?'

'Yes.'

'Well, I think we've got a ghost in the house.' And she told him the story of her last night's adventure.

Odd events were not uncommon in the Armitage family – there had been the occasion when they found a unicorn in the garden, and other such happenings, so Mark did not, as many brothers would have done, say 'Rot, you're trying to pull my leg'. He sat reflecting for a while. Then he said:

'What did you say her name was?'

'Miss Allison.'

'And she was dressed in a sort of Victorian costume?'

'Yes. I don't know what sort of time exactly – it might be any time from 1840 to 1900 I should think,' said Harriet vaguely, 'but, oh yes, she did say something about looking up to our dear Queen as a pattern of propriety. It sounded like Queen Victoria.'

'I do hope we see her again,' said Mark. 'It sounds as if her day and night were the exact opposite of ours, if she told you to go and rest at two in the morning.'

Harriet agreed with this. 'And another thing,' she said, 'I believe she's only visible in the complete dark. Because at first she was sitting in the moonlight playing the piano – at least I suppose she was – and I couldn't see her at all till she stepped out of the light into the darkness.'

'Well, well, we'll have to start picketing her. I suppose she gets up when it gets dark.'

'Nonsense,' said Harriet, 'that wouldn't be till after ten. You never heard of a governess getting up at ten, did you? No, I bet she gets up in the *light*, just as we get up in the dark in winter.'

'Anyway we'll have to have one of us watching for her at night,' Mark went on. 'We'll have to do it in shifts and get some sleep in the day-time. We'd better start now.'

'Let's have lunch first.'

On the edge of the patch of moonlight she saw a little, frail old woman

So they ate their picnic and then dutifully lay back on the springy turf and closed their eyes. But it was not a great success, for one or other of them kept bouncing up with brilliant ideas on ghost-governesses. They agreed that it would be best if they both watched together the first night in case she turned out not to be the mild inoffensive creature that she had appeared to Harriet. They also agreed to take pencils and notebooks with them in case she took advantage of her governess-hood and starting teaching. Besides, they might learn something interesting.

At last they did achieve an intermittent doze, in the hot sun and the silence, and lay there for a couple of hours. Then they picked an enormous basket-full of cowslips and started home for a late tea.

That night they listened carefully until the parents had gone to bed, and then slipped downstairs into the drawing-room. As before, the moonlight lay across the floor, but much further round. Everything was silent, and all they could hear was their own breathing. Harriet began to have a dreadful feeling of disappointment.

'Perhaps she won't come again,' she whispered gloomily.

'Nonsense,' said Mark, 'we've hardly been here any time. If your feet are cold, sit in the armchair and tuck them under you.'

Harriet thought this a good idea. They sat on, and now they could hear the grandfather clock ticking in the hall, and the lonely lowing of a cow somewhere below in the valley.

All of a sudden a quiet voice said:

'Ah! Children. There you are. I've been looking for you everywhere. This, Harriet, is your brother Mark, I presume?'

Harriet's heart gave a violent jump, and then began beating very quickly. Miss Allison was standing, as she had been yesterday, on the edge of the pool of moonlight. She held a ruler in her hand and looked benevolent, but just slightly impatient.

Harriet got up and curtsied, and then she introduced Mark, who was standing with his mouth open, but otherwise looked fairly collected.

'Now we will go to the schoolroom,' said the governess, 'and that is where I should like you to wait for me in future. We will only come to the drawing-room for music lessons, on Tuesdays and Fridays.'

The children cast anxious glances at each other, but followed her upstairs meekly enough, watching with interest as she twinkled in and out of patches of moonlight in the corridor, and wondering which room she had decided to use as the schoolroom. They found that it was Mark's bedroom, which was very convenient, as Harriet whispered to him.

'Don't whisper, Harriet dear,' said Miss Allison, who had her back turned, 'it's unpardonably rude.' She was doing something which looked like writing on an invisible blackboard. 'There, that's finished. Now, Harriet, will you bring your back-board out of that corner and lie on it. I wish to see you on it for at least half an hour every day, to give you a lady-like and erect deportment.'

Harriet had a look in the corner but saw nothing except Mark's tennis racket and a box of balls.

'I don't see it,' she said unhappily.

'Nonsense, dear. Your left foot is on it at the moment. Try to be observant.'

As Harriet's left foot was resting firmly on the floor, she felt rather injured, but, catching the governess's eye, she hastily stooped, picked up an imaginary back-board with both hands, and carried it to the middle of the room.

'It would help,' she said to herself, 'if I knew what the dratted thing looked like. But I suppose it's as long as I am.'

'That's right. Now lie on it. Flat on your back, arms at your sides, eyes looking at the ceiling.'

Harriet lay down on the floor, looking at Miss Allison doubtfully, and was rewarded by a nod.

'Now Mark,' said the governess briskly, 'I have written on the blackboard a list of Latin prepositions followed by the ablative case. You will occupy yourself in learning them while I write out an exercise for you both. Harriet, you can be trying to think of twenty wild flowers beginning with the letter L.'

She sat down at an invisible table and began briskly writing on nothing. Mark looked gloomily at the empty space where the blackboard was supposed to be, and wondered how he could learn a list of words he couldn't see. This adventure, it seemed to him, was a bit too much like real life. He wished Miss Allison was a more conventional ghost with clanking chains.

Harriet gave him a grin, and then, as Miss Allison looked particularly preoccupied, she whispered:

'A, ab, absque, coram, de . . .'

Mark's face cleared. Of course, now he remembered the words. Thank goodness he had learned them at school. He thought for a moment anxiously of what would happen when they didn't know what she had written on the blackboard, but anyway, that was in the future. No use worrying about it now.

At the end of what was presumably half an hour, Miss Allison turned round.

'Well!' she said. 'Harriet, you may put away your board. Mark, let me hear you recite. You should have it by rote now.'

'A, ab, absque,' he began.

'Never let me see you recite like that, Mark. Hands behind your back, feet in the first position, head up.' Mark obeyed peevishly.

'Now begin again.'

> 'A, ab, absque, coram, de,
> Palam, clam, cum, ex and e
> Tenus, sine, pro, in, prae
> Ablative with these we spy.'

'Very good, Mark, though your pronunciation is a little modern,' she said. 'You may open that blue tin and have a carraway biscuit.'

Mark looked about for a blue tin, saw none, and opened an imaginary one.

Harriet did rather badly over her wild flowers beginning with L. Half the ones she thought of, such as Lady's Smock, Lady's Slipper, Lady's Tresses, Lords and Ladies, and all the

34

Lesser Stitchworts and Lesser Chickweeds were disqualified, leaving her with a very poor list. She got no carraway biscuit. However, as Mark's had been imaginary, she did not greatly mind.

After this, they had to do embroidery. It also was totally imaginary. They held invisible pieces of linen, threaded invisible needles, and sometimes for the fun of the thing stuck them into their fingers and squeaked with imaginary pain. It was all very amusing. It soon appeared that even if they couldn't see their work, Miss Allison could. She kept up a running fire of comment, from which they gathered that Mark's was bad and Harriet's fairly good. This seemed reasonable enough. Mark was rather indignant at being expected to do embroidery, but after a while the governess began to read aloud to them a fascinating book called *Improving Tales* all about some good children and some bad ones, so he just stuck his needle in and out and listened.

'There,' said Miss Allison finally, 'that will do for today. For your preparation you will both turn to page two hundred in your Latin grammars and learn the list of words beginning:

> Amnis, axis, caulis, collis,
> Clunis, crinis, fascis, follis –

and you will also each write me a composition entitled "Devotion to Duty".'

'Please,' said Harriet, 'which is our Latin grammar?'

'Why, Crosby, of course. The blue book. Now run along, dears. You will want to get ready for your walk.'

Mark wanted to go to bed, but she gave him such an extremely firm look that he went out with Harriet.

'You'll have to sleep on the sofa in my room,' she whispered, 'and creep back as soon as it's light. I wouldn't dare try to disobey her.'

'Nor me,' he whispered back. 'She looks much firmer than any of the masters at school.'

Luckily it was very warm, and there were some spare blankets in Harriet's room, so he was quite comfortable and slept well.

They were both rather silent and sleepy at breakfast, but afterwards on the river-bank they discussed things.

'What are we going to do about those wretched essays?' asked Mark sourly. 'I'm blowed if I write about devotion to duty.'

'Oh, that's all right,' Harriet replied. 'Don't you see, the composition will be just like the embroidery. We'll show up an imaginary one.'

'I don't quite understand that,' said Mark, screwing up his eyes and throwing stones into the mudbank; the tide was rapidly running out.

'Nor do I,' agreed Harriet candidly, 'but I *think* it's something like this: you see she must have taught hundreds of children when she was alive, and I expect she made them all do embroidery and write about devotion to duty. So when we give her our imaginary things she thinks about the ones she remembers. See what I mean?'

'Well, almost.'

'No, what *I'm* worried about,' Harriet went on, 'is if she asks us to learn things and recite. Because if we haven't got the books to learn them from – like this wretched Crosby – we're stumped. Have you ever heard of Crosby?'

'No, we use Kennedy at school.'

'So do we. Well, maybe we could ask to write them down from memory instead of reciting them. It'll be all right, of course, if she asks us to learn something like the *Ancient Mariner.*'

'I dunno,' said Mark, 'all this sounds a bit too much like work to me.'

'It is a bit. Still, not many people have learned Latin prepositions from a ghost. That's something.'

'I tell you,' said Mark, 'the attic.'

'What about it?'

'There are hundreds of old boxes there with things in them that belong to the house. I was up there one day looking for secret passages. Maybe if we looked in them we'd find some old lesson books that belonged to the people who were here before.'

'That's an idea. We might find something about Miss Allison, too – a diary or something. Let's go now.'

'Anyway,' Harriet pointed out as they walked back to the house, 'if it does get too much of a good thing we can always just stay in bed at night and not go to her.'

'All right for you,' said Mark, 'but I expect she's in my room all the time. She'll probably just haul me out of bed at ten o'clock.'

The lunch bell rang as they came up the garden, so they had to put off their search in the attic.

It was a dark, cool room, lit only by green glass tiles in the roof. Harriet sat for a while pensively on a box while Mark rummaged about, turning out with everything little piles of thickish yellow powder smelling of pine-needles.

'That's for the moths,' she said. Then she began folding the things and putting them back as he went on. They were mostly clothes folded in tissue paper, and old rush baskets pressed flat, large women's hats with draggled bunches of feathers, and pairs of kid gloves.

'People wore things like these in the last war,' said Harriet. 'Look, here's a newspaper. January 1919. This is too modern.'

'Half a sec.,' said Mark, 'over here they seem to be older.' He pulled out an enormous flounced ball-dress of fawn-coloured satin; some shawls; a pair of satin slippers; a little woven basket with a lid containing brightly coloured glass bracelets and necklaces of glass beads; a large flat box full of fans – ivory, with pink flowers, satinwood, and wonderful plumy feathers.

'I wish there were some letters or books or something,' Mark murmured discontentedly. Harriet was exclaiming to herself over the fans before laying them back in the box.

'This one's very heavy,' said Mark tugging at a chest. The lid came up unwillingly. Underneath was a gorgeous Chinese hanging of stiff silk, folded square. He lifted it out.

'Aha!' A heavy, old-fashioned bible lay on the tissue paper. 'Harriet, look here!'

Harriet came across and read over her brother's shoulder the inscription in a beautiful copperplate handwriting:

'To my dear daughter Georgiana Lucy Allison from her affectionate Mother, Christmas 1831.'

'Well!' they breathed at each other. Mark flipped through the leaves, but there was nothing else, except for a faded pansy.

'Let's see what else there is in the box.'

Underneath the tissue paper were more books.

'Lesson books,' said Harriet ecstatically. '*Primer of Geography*. Mason's *Manual of Arithmetic*. Look! Here's Crosby's *Latin Grammar Made Easy*.'

Besides the lesson books there were children's books – *Improving Tales for the Young*, *Tales for Little Folks*, *Good Deeds in a Bad World*, *Tales from the Gospel*, and a number of others, all improving. Several of them also had Miss Allison's name in them. Others had children's names – 'John, from his affec. Governess', 'Lucy, from Mamma', and in a large stumbling script 'Lucy, from Isabel'.

'We'd better take down all the lesson books,' said Harriet. 'They can live in the bookshelf in your room – there's plenty of empty space.'

They had a further search in the other boxes, but found nothing else interesting except some children's clothes – sailor suits, dresses and pantalettes, which Harriet would have liked to try on. 'But they look so fragile,' she said with a sigh, 'I'd probably tear them.' So everything was replaced, and they went downstairs, each with an armful of books.

Later that evening Harriet's mother found her sprawled on the drawing-room sofa looking at a book and then shutting it and muttering to herself.

'You look as if you were learning poetry,' said Mrs Armitage, glancing over her shoulder. 'What, *Latin*! Good heavens, I have got diligent children. Incidentally I wish you'd find another tune to practise on the piano. I find myself singing that "Lieber Augustin" all day long.'

That night when Harriet went along to Mark's room at about midnight, she found him already hard at work reciting the principle parts of Latin verbs.

'Mark knows his list of words very well, Harriet. I trust that you will also be able to earn your carraway biscuit,' remarked Miss Allison and then, while Harriet lay on her imaginary back-board she read them a long, boring chapter about the Wars of the Roses.

'I generally start my pupils at the *beginning* of history, with William the Conqueror,' explained the governess, 'but your dear mother expressed a wish for you to study this period particularly.'

Afterwards Harriet recited her Latin and also earned a carraway biscuit. Then they showed her their invisible essay on Duty, and Harriet's point was proved. She obviously saw them, even if the children didn't, and peevishly pointed out several spelling mistakes.

'Mark, you will write out the word "ceiling" fifty times,' she said. 'That will be all for this morning, dears. Harriet, will you ask Anne to run up with a duster and I will dust my room myself. And tell her that she forgot to sweep under the bed yesterday, though I reminded her particularly.'

'Mother,' said Mark one morning, 'can I change my bedroom? I'd much rather sleep in the room next to Harriet.'

'Well, if you do,' said his mother, looking at him acutely, 'you must promise not to be popping in and out of each other's rooms all night. I thought I heard something last night.' But they gazed at her so innocently that she agreed and said they could change the things over themselves.

'Just as well,' said Mark, when they were carrying sheets along the passage. 'Do you know she hauled me out of bed last night and asked me what I thought I was doing sleeping on the schoolroom sofa.'

'She *is* queer,' Harriet remarked thoughtfully. 'I sometimes wonder if she really *sees* us at all. She obviously doesn't see the same furniture as we do, because sometimes she uses tables and chairs that aren't there, and when she talks about our parents she doesn't mean Mother and Father, because they never said anything to her about the Wars of the Roses.'

'And there's all this business about Anne and Cook, too. I suppose she sort of sees them all round. Poor old thing,' said

Mark, tucking in a lump of blanket, 'I'm getting quite fond of her.'

'You know I'm sure she has something on her mind. She looks so worried at times, as if she was trying to remember things.'

It soon appeared that the children had something on their minds too.

'You both of you look dreadfully tired nowadays,' remarked Mrs Armitage. 'You aren't sickening for measles, are you? And don't you think you're overdoing this holiday work a bit? Surely you don't need to do all that Latin and History. The other night, Mark, I came into your room and you were muttering the dates of the Kings of England in your sleep. Take a bit of rest from it. By the way, there's an Admiral Lecacheur coming to tea this afternoon – he lives in that little house on the river you've taken such a fancy to. If you want to get invited to have a look round it you'd better put in an appearance.'

'Lecacheur?' said Mark vaguely, 'I seem to know that name.'

'Yes, it's the family who lived here before. He's the owner of this house, actually, but he's mostly away, so he prefers to let it and live in the cottage.'

Lecacheur! Of course it was the name written in the lesson books! Mark and Harriet exchanged a swift excited look.

'Is he an old man?' asked Mark carelessly.

'About sixty, I believe. Now I must fly, I've masses to do. Be good, children.'

'If he's about sixty,' said Harriet, when they were alone, 'he must have been born in 1885. I *wish* we knew when Miss Allison died.'

'Well, we know she was alive in 1831 because of the bible. I wonder how old she was when she was given that?'

'Say she was about ten,' said Harriet, counting on her fingers, 'that makes her sixty-five when the Admiral was born. Well, that's quite possible. She looks more than that. He may easily have known her. We'll have to draw him out, somehow.'

'Maybe, if he knew her, he'd know what it is she worries about,' said Harriet hopefully. 'You know, I believe if we could find out what's on her mind and – and help her, she'd vanish. That's the sort of thing ghosts do.'

'Well, I'm not sure I'd be sorry,' said Mark, puffing out a deep breath. 'I'd like a night's sleep for once. Remember when we didn't wake up, how cross she was next night? And I've had just about enough Latin verbs. *And* the Kings of England.'

Harriet agreed. 'And the parents are beginning to think that there's something funny going on. Father started whistling "Lieber Augustin" the other day, and then he turned and gave me an *awfully* queer look. It's all because she will play it in the middle of the night.'

Admiral Lecacheur turned out to be a pleasant man, large, jovial, and grey-haired. It was not difficult for the children to get an invitation from him to go and look at his cottage.

As he showed them the stuffed shark, and the model ships in bottles, Harriet summoned up the courage to speak.

'Admiral,' she finally said timidly, 'did you ever know a Miss Georgiana Lucy Allison?'

'God bless my soul, yes,' he said, turning round and smiling at her, 'she was our family governess. Is there some stuff of hers still knocking about the house?'

'Yes, there are some books of hers. And a bible.'

'Old Allie,' he said reminiscently. 'She was a wonderful old girl. Must have been with our family for fifty years. She taught three generations of us. I was the last.'

'Did she teach you?'

'I remember her very well,' he went on, without noticing the interruption, 'though she died, I suppose, when I was about five. That would be around 1890. But she'd already taught me to read, and some of the multiplication tables, and the Kings of England. She was great on learning things by heart. Not like the modern education you get now, I daresay. "Cedric," she used to say, "how will you ever get on in life if you don't know these things?" Ah well. Here I am an Admiral, and I dare say if she'd taught me longer I should have been Admiral of the Fleet. But there! she must have died more than fifty years ago.'

He smiled at their serious faces and said, 'Now here's a thing you ought to like. Just look at the size of that!' and he handed Harriet a shell the size of a dinner plate.

'Well, we still don't know what's on her mind,' said Mark, as they walked homewards.

'No, but we couldn't ask him all at once. Another time we'll jolly well pump him.'

But as things turned out they didn't need to. That night when Mark was reciting the dates of the Kings of England, he absent-mindedly followed William-and-Mary by 'Queen Anne, 1700'.

There was an ominous pause, and Miss Allison suddenly burst into tears.

'Cedric, you wicked boy,' she sobbed, 'will you *never* get it right? How can you expect to be a success in life, if you don't know your dates? And you going into the Navy, too.' She hid her face in her hands, but through them they could hear her say, 'I'm getting so old. How can I die happy if that boy doesn't know the date of Queen Anne? All the others learned it.'

'Please don't cry,' said Mark awkwardly, patting her shoulder. 'It was only a mistake. I do know it. Really I do. It's 1702, isn't it?'

But she went on sobbing 'Cedric! Cedric!' and after a minute Harriet touched his arm and pulled him softly out of the room.

'Let's go to bed,' she whispered. 'We can't do anything about her. And I've got a brilliant idea. Tell you in the morning.'

Next day she dragged him down to Dolphin Cottage. The Admiral was surprised to see them. 'What, you again so early? You're just in time to help me syringe my greenfly.'

'Admiral,' said Harriet, fixing her eyes on him earnestly, 'will you tell me something terribly important?'

'What is it?' he said, very much astonished.

'Tell me when Queen Anne came to the throne.'

He burst into a great roar of laughter, slapping his knees. 'Well, I'm blessed! Do you know, it's funny you should ask me that, because it's the one date I never have been able to remember. Miss Allison used to get wild about it. "I shan't die happy till you know that date, Cedric," she used to say. But she did die, poor old soul, and I don't know it to this day.'

'Come and sit down,' said Harriet, dragging him to a garden seat. One on each side, she and Mark told him the whole story. When he heard how Miss Allison made their nights a burden he shouted with laughter.

'That's just like her, bless her,' he exclaimed.

'So you see, it really has got to stop,' Harriet explained. 'We're getting worn out, and I'm sure she is – after all she must be about a hundred and twenty, far too old to be teaching. And she's so miserable, poor dear. I think you can help us.'

She told him their plan, and after some hesitation the Admiral agreed. 'But if you're pulling my leg,' he threatened, 'you'll never forget it, the pair of you.'

'Now you've got to learn it,' said Harriet, 'write it on a bit of paper somewhere – here, I'll do it for you. Now stick it up where you'll be able to see it all day. And we'll meet you at the garden gate tonight at midnight.'

'What your parents would say if they caught us – ' he exclaimed, but he agreed. The children went home very hopeful.

The meeting came off as arranged. They let him in by the garden door and took him quietly up the back stairs into the school-room, where Miss Allison was pacing up and down looking very impatient.

'What time – ' she began, and then suddenly she saw who was with them. 'Why, *Cedric*!'

'Allie!' he exclaimed.

'You wicked boy! Where have you been all this time?'

'I'm sorry,' he said meekly, looking more like a small boy than a grey-haired man of sixty.

'Just you tell me one thing,' she said, drawing herself up

43

and giving him a piercing look. 'When did Queen Anne come to the throne?'

The children gazed at him anxiously, but they need not have worried. He had learned his lesson this time.

'Seventeen-two,' he said promptly, and they sighed with relief.

Miss Allison burst into tears of joy.

'I might have known it,' she sobbed. 'My good boy. Why, now you know that, you might even become an Admiral, and I can die happy.'

And as they watched her, suddenly, flick! like a candle, she had gone out, and there was no one in the room but their three selves.

'Well, I'm blessed,' said the Admiral, not for the first time. 'Old Allie.' He walked quietly from the room. Mark saw him down to the garden gate. When he came back he found Harriet dabbing at her eyes with a handkerchief.

'You know, I'm going to miss her,' she said. 'Oh, well, let's go to bed.'

They never saw Miss Allison again.

'DADDY, have we really got a fairy godmother?' asked Harriet, dropping her basket full of holly leaves in a corner of the room and coming over to the fire, where tea was laid on a little table.

'Possibly, possibly,' he replied, without coming out of his evening paper.

'No, but really?' she persisted. 'A rather silly-looking lady, with popping eyes and a lot of necklaces?'

'Oh, yes, now I remember,' said Mr Armitage, putting down his paper and starting to laugh. 'She was the one who dropped you in the font. Your mother never took to her much. And right away after the christening she tried to interest me in a scheme for supplying old fairy ladies with needlework patterns.'

'Goodness, can't they make their own?'

'Apparently not. Yes, of course, she was going to give you each a wish for your christening presents, but your Ma pointed out that if you had it then you'd only wish for your lunch and it might be better to wait for a few years.'

'Yes, well that's just it,' explained Mark, 'we met her just now in Farthing Wood and she offered us a wish each, so we said could we think it over and tell her tomorrow; you know how it is on the spur of the moment, you can never think of anything sensible.'

'Very prudent of you,' murmured his father. 'Try not to wish for anything that needs *upkeep*, will you, like racehorses or aeroplanes. You know what the price of petrol is now.'

Here Mrs Armitage came in and started pouring tea.

'Children, I'm afraid I've a disappointing message for you from Mr Pontwell. He says he's very sorry but he doesn't think he *can* have you in the carol choir.'

'Not have us in the choir? But Mr Willingdon always did.'

'Well, I suppose he's more particular about voices. He says he wants the singing to be specially good this year. And you know I don't mean to be unkind, but you can neither of you sing in tune at all.'

'Yes, the other day,' agreed Mr Armitage, 'I wondered who could possibly be sawing wood in the bathroom, only to find –'

'Oh, he is a mean man,' said Harriet, taking no notice. '*Nobody* ever minds about keeping in tune in carols. And I do love carol-singing too. Oh, why did Mr Willingdon have to go and get made a canon?'

'Couldn't we go along with them and keep quiet?' suggested Mark.

'No, I thought of that, but he said, "You know how effervescent Mark and Harriet are, there's no knowing what they'd do." I think he's afraid of you.'

'Well, I think that's most unkind of him. We'll just have to go out by ourselves, that's all.'

'No, no,' said Harriet, 'don't you see what we can do? What about our fairy godmother and the wishes?'

Next day they met the pop-eyed lady as arranged in Farthing Wood.

'Well, dears,' she beamed at them. 'Thought of a good wish?'

'Yes, please,' said Mark, 'we'd both like to have simply wonderful voices – to sing with, I mean.'

The lady looked a little blank. '*Voices?* Are you sure you wouldn't like a nice box of chocolates each? Or a pony?'

'No, thank you very much. We have a unicorn already, you see. But we really do need good voices so that we can get into the carol choir.'

'Well,' she said doubtfully. 'That's rather a difficult wish. I don't think I could arrange it for you *permanently*. But perhaps for a week or two, I *might* be able to manage it –'

'Oh, please do try.' They both looked at her imploringly.

'Very well, dears, since it means such a lot to you.' She shut her eyes and clenched her fists with an appearance of terrific concentration. The children waited breathlessly.

'Now then,' she said after a moment or two. 'Try to sing a few notes.'

They were rather embarrassed and looked at each other for encouragement.

'What shall we sing? "Good King Wenceslas"?' They sang the first few lines rather timidly and were much disconcerted by the notes which boomed out – Harriet's voice had become a terrific contralto which would not have disgraced a twelve-stone prima donna, and Mark's was a deep and reverend bass.

'I say, I hate to seem ungrateful, but couldn't we be soprano and treble – it would be more natural, don't you think?'

'Perhaps you are right, petty,' said the lady, and closed her eyes again, looking a shade martyred. Oh dear, we are giving her a lot of trouble, Harriet thought.

This time the result was more satisfactory, and they thanked her with heartfelt gratitude.

'How long will it last?' asked Mark.

'Thirteen days. You will find that it wears off at midnight.'

'Like Cinderella,' said Harriet, nodding.

'So remember not to give a performance just at that time. Well, dears, I am *so* pleased to have met you again, and please remember me to your dear Mamma.'

'Oh yes, she said do drop in to tea whenever you are passing. Goodbye, and thank you *so* much – you *are* kind –'

When they had left her they dashed straight to the Vicarage and inquired for Mr Pontwell, but were told that he was round at the church.

The new Vicar was a red-faced rather pompous looking man. He seemed slightly embarrassed at meeting Mark and Harriet.

'Oh – er, hullo, my dear children. What can I do for you?'

'Well, sir, it's about our being in the carol choir,' Mark plunged.

He frowned. 'Dear me, I thought I had made that perfectly plain to your dear mother. I am afraid I cannot see my way –'

'No but,' said Harriet, 'we feel sure that you are acting

under a wrong impression of our voices. You probably heard us on some occasion when Mark had a cold, and I was, um, suffering from my laryngitis, and of course you had quite a mistaken idea of what we could do. We just want you to be *very* kind and hear us again.'

'Well, really, my dear children, I don't think that is the case, and there hardly seems much point in reopening the question – however, if you insist – '

'Oh, we do insist,' agreed Mark. 'What shall we sing, Harriet, "Oh for the wings of a dove"?'

They were much more confident this time, and opened their mouths to their widest extent.

> 'Oh, for the weengs, for the weengs of a dove –
> *Far* away, far away would I rove'

When Mr Pontwell heard their exquisite treble voices soaring about among the rafters of the church his eyes nearly dropped out of his head, and he sat down suddenly in a nearby pew.

'Good gracious,' he said, 'I had no idea – of course you were quite right to come. My *dear* children – gracious me, what an extraordinary thing. I had quite thought – but there, it only shows how mistaken one can be. You will indeed be an addition to the choir.'

He went on saying things like this as they walked through the churchyard.

'You will come to the practices on Wednesdays and Saturdays, will you?'

'Of course,' said Harriet anxiously, 'and when are we going out singing?'

'Monday evening the nineteenth.' Mark and Harriet did some rapid calculation. Monday the nineteenth would be the last day of their thirteen, which seemed cutting it rather fine.

'I suppose it couldn't *possibly* be any earlier?' said Harriet. 'You see, rather odd things sometimes happen in our family on Mondays – rather *unaccountable* things – and it would be so awful if we were late or prevented from coming, or anything.'

She was thinking of the day when their house had suddenly turned to a castle on the Rhine for twelve hours.

'No, my dear, I am afraid the date cannot be changed, as I have already made several arrangements for the evening, including a visit of the choir to Gramercy Chase. Sir Leicester will be *most* interested to hear you sing, so I do trust that you will not let any of these, er, unaccountable things happen during the day, *or* while you are out with the choir.' He looked at them sternly.

'So you're really in the choir?' said Mr Armitage that evening. 'And going to Gramercy Chase. Well, well, it's a good thing it will be dark.'

'Why?'

'It's the most hideous house between here and Birmingham. Sir Leicester always says he wishes he had a good excuse to pull it down. It was entirely rebuilt, you know, in nineteenth-century gothic, except for the haunted terrace.'

'Haunted?' said Harriet. 'Oh good. What by? That's where we're going to sing.'

'Oh, some bird, called King William's Raven (don't ask me why) who only appears to foretell bad tidings to the house of Gramercy. The last time was just before the current baronet was killed at Waterloo. He flies along the terrace lighting torches in the brackets – of course they've put in electric lighting now, so I don't know how he'd manage – '

Harriet and Mark had a somewhat difficult time at the choir practices, as all their village friends were only too familiar with their usual voices, and they had to face a considerable amount of chaff and a lot of astonishment at this sudden development of flute-like tones.

'Been keeping quiet all these years, eh? Didn't want to waste yourselves on us, I suppose?'

'Ah,' said Lily, the blacksmith's daughter, 'they've heard as how Mr Pontwell's going to have a recording made on Monday night.'

In fact there was a general rumour going round that Mr Pontwell had something special up his sleeve, and that was why he was so particular about the singers and the practices;

though whether he was having the singing recorded, os royalty was going to be there, or some great impresario war staying at Gramercy Chase to hear them, was not known.

Mr Pontwell made a particular point of asking them to wear tidy dark clothes and rubber-soled shoes so that they should not squeak on people's gravel.

'What a fusser he is,' Mark complained to Harriet.

'Never mind,' she replied, 'at least we're going to be *there*.'

Nothing untoward happened to Mark and Harriet on Monday the nineteenth. Indeed the day was suspiciously quiet and they both of them became slightly anxious as evening approached. However, they got away safely from home and met the other carol-singers in the vicarage at eight o'clock, as had been arranged. The vicar was handing out torches and carol-books.

'Now, are we all assembled? Excellent, excellent. I suggest we start off with a good rousing "Adeste Fideles" outside the church, just to get our lungs in, then through the village as far as Little Foldings (should take a couple of hours) where Mrs Noakes has very kindly promised us hot drinks, and Sir Leicester is sending the shooting brake to collect us all there. We are expected at Gramercy Chase round about eleven o'clock.'

As they were starting on their first carol, Mark felt a cold nose pushed down his neck, and turned his head to look into the reproachful green eyes of Candleberry, their unicorn.

'Goodness! I thought you were shut up for the night. Go home, bad unicorn,' he said crossly, but Candleberry shook his head.

'Dear me, is that a *unicorn*?' said Mr Pontwell, at the end of 'Adeste Fideles'. 'He shouldn't really be here, you know.'

'I'm very sorry,' said Mark. 'I can't think how he got out. But he's extremely well-trained. He won't interrupt, and he could carry anyone who got tired.'

'Very well,' said Mr Pontwell. 'He certainly makes a picturesque addition. But if there's the least sign of trouble, mind, you'll have to take him home.'

However, there was no trouble; though they had so many

requests for encores that they arrived at Little Foldings very much behind schedule, and had to gulp down their drinks and hurry out to the shooting brake, which sped away through the dark across Gramercy Wold, with the unicorn easily keeping pace beside it. Even so they arrived at the Chase well after half-past eleven.

Sir Leicester welcomed them, and hurried them at once round to the terrace where they were to sing. Mark and Harriet tried to get a look at the hideousness of the house as they walked past it, but only received a general impression of a lot of pinnacles and gargoyles. The terrace was enormous – at least half a mile long and twenty yards wide, extending to a low wall, which was topped by a series of lamp posts, now fitted with electric lamps.

The singers, hot and panting from their hurry, flung down coats and mufflers on the wall, and clustered together opposite the orangery door, where they were to sing. As they were finding their places for the first carol there was a prodigious clattering of hooves and Candleberry arrived, galloping down the terrace like a Grand National winner. Mark went to meet him and quiet him down. When he returned he muttered to Harriet:

'Now I know what all the fuss was about. There are some blokes over there in the shade with a television camera. That's why Mr Pontwell's been taking such a lot of trouble.'

'Well, do keep an eye on Candleberry,' she muttered back. 'Oh, look, here comes Mr Pontwell. Thank goodness, now we can start before I get nervous.'

They were half-way through their first carol when Mark noticed that Candleberry seemed very uneasy; he was shivering, stamping his feet and looking over his shoulder a great deal. Mark himself glanced rather fearfully down the long, dark expanse of terrace.

At the same time, Harriet heard something in her ear which sounded like a ratchet screwdriver being painstakingly worked into granite. She turned her head to listen and realized that it was Mark singing. She caught hold of his hand and tapped his watch.

'Hey,' she whispered under cover of the singing, 'it's midnight and we've lost our voices. Better pipe low. Bang goes our chance of charming thousands of listeners.'

Mr Pontwell was energetically conducting 'The Holly and the Ivy' when an unpleasant scent invaded his nostrils. He sniffed again – yes, it was the smell of burning clothes. Could it be that dratted unicorn, with its incandescent horn? Had it set fire to somebody's cap? He glanced about angrily, and then saw a flame leap up on the terrace wall.

'I say,' called a voice through the singing, 'someone's set fire to our coats!'

In fact the pile of coats and scarves was now blazing up in a positive bonfire.

Instantly there was a clamour of angry voices and the singing died away.

'Ladies – gentlemen – my dear friends,' cried Mr Pontwell in anguish, 'please – the evening will be ruined –'

'It's that perishing unicorn,' someone exclaimed furiously, 'never ought to have been allowed to come –'

But at that moment Candleberry came galloping in hot pursuit of something which was flying along the terrace carrying a light. As they passed through the illumination of the bonfire this was seen to be an enormous dark bird carrying a lighted candle, the flame of which streamed over its shoulder.

'Good heavens,' cried Sir Leicester, who had gone very pale, 'it's the family raven.'

'Please, my dear singers,' implored Mr Pontwell, who thought of nothing but his performance, 'let us have a little order. What do a few coats and scarves matter? Or a little natural fauna. Let me hear a nice spirited rendering of "We Three Kings".'

But at that moment a man dashed towards them from the television camera, crying: 'Bring that unicorn back. It's miraculous! A real unicorn, chasing a ghostly raven – good lord, this will be the television scoop of the century! Stand back, will you! Who owns the unicorn? You sir? Can you get him to come this way?'

Mark called Candleberry and he galloped back, driving the

Candleberry came galloping in hot pursuit of something

raven in front of him. It was still crossly looking for something to light with its candle. It had been foiled by the electric lamps and had to fall back on the heap of coats. At last with a croak of decision it swooped down and set fire to somebody's carol-book.

'Stop it, stop it,' shrieked Mr Pontwell, but the TV expert at the same moment shouted 'Hold it, hold it. Stand aside, you others. Hold out your books. This is wonderful, wonderful!'

Only Mr Pontwell was not pleased with the evening's work. Everyone else was warmed and exhilarated by the fire, and informed that their fees as television performers would amply cover the loss of coats and carol books. Sir Leicester himself seemed to have disappeared, but his chauffeur drove the choir back, cheerful and chattering, at about three in the morning.

'Poor man,' said Harriet to Mark, 'I expect he's worrying about what dreadful doom is going to fall on the house of Gramercy. After all, it's not so funny for him.'

At breakfast next morning the telephone rang. Mr Armitage answered it, and after listening for a few minutes, began to laugh.

'It was Sir Leicester,' he said, returning to the table. 'He's had his dreadful doom. The architect's report on Gramercy Chase has come in, and he's learned that the whole place is riddled with dry-rot. It's all got to come down. He's simply delighted. He rang up to ask if I knew of a comfortable cottage for sale.'

The Frozen Cuckoo

THERE was a good deal of trouble at breakfast. To begin with, Mr Armitage was late, and that made Mrs Armitage cross, as she always liked to have the meal over quickly on Mondays, so that the dining-room could be turned out. Then she began reading her letters, and suddenly inquired:

'What is the date today?'

'The second,' said Harriet.

'I thought so. Then that means she is coming today. How very inconsiderate.'

'Who is coming today?'

'Your cousin Sarah.'

'Oh no!' said Mark and Harriet together, in deep dismay. It is dreadful to have to say it of anybody, but their cousin Sarah was really a horrible girl. The only thing she seemed to enjoy was playing practical jokes, which she did the whole time. Nobody minds an occasional joke, but an endless course of sand in the brown-sugar bowl, grease on the stairs, and plastic spiders on the pillow-cases soon becomes tiresome.

'It'll be apple-pie beds, apple-pie beds all the way,' said Mark gloomily. 'Can't you put her off?'

'No, Aunt Rachel has to go into hospital for an operation, so I'm afraid you'll just have to bear with her. She's coming at lunch time.'

Here Mr Armitage arrived, and sat down rubbing his hands and saying: 'The Christmas roses will be out any minute now.'

'Your bacon's cold,' said his wife crossly. 'Here are your letters.'

He opened a long, important-looking one which had a lot of printed headings on it, and instantly began to puff and blow with rage. 'Evicted? Requisitioned? What's this? Notice to quit forthwith, before 11 a.m., December 2nd. Who the dickens is this from?'

'Good gracious my dear,' said his wife, 'what have you got there?'

'It's from the Board of Incantation,' he replied, throwing the letter to her. 'They've requisitioned this house, if you please, to make a seminary for young magicians, and we have notice to quit immediately.'

'A. Whizzard,' murmured Mrs Armitage, looking at the signature. 'Wasn't that the name of the man whose book you were so rude about in your review?'

'Yes, of course. I knew the name seemed familiar. A shockingly bad book on spells and runes.'

'Oh dear,' sighed Mrs Armitage. 'I do wish you'd learn to be more tactful. Now we have to find somewhere else to live, and just before Christmas, too. It really is too bad.'

'Do we really have to be out by eleven o'clock?' asked Mark, who with Harriet had been listening round-eyed.

'I shall contest it,' said his father. 'It's the most monstrous tyranny. They needn't think they can ride over me rough-shod.'

However, Mrs Armitage who was a quiet but practical person, at once sent Harriet along the village to ask if they could borrow the house of Mrs Foster, who was going off to the south of France, while they looked around for somewhere else to live. Then with the help of Mrs Epis she packed up all their clothes and put them in the car. Mr Armitage refused to leave with the rest of the family, and remained behind to tackle the invaders.

Sharp at eleven o'clock several men who looked like builders' labourers arrived. They rode on rather battered, paint-stained old broomsticks, and carried hammers, saws, and large sheets of beaver-board.

'Morning, Guvner,' said one who seemed to be the foreman, advancing up the front steps.

Mr Armitage stood in the way with his arms folded. 'I protest against this unseemly intrusion!' he cried. 'It is entirely contrary to the British Constitution.'

'Ah,' said the foreman, waving a screwdriver at him in a pitying manner, 'you're cuckoo.' At once Mr Armitage vanished, and in his place a large bird flapped in a dazed manner round the front door.

Just then an enormous, sleek black car rolled silently up to the gate, and a tall, sleek, dark man stepped out and came up the steps, swinging an elegant umbrella.

'Excellent, Wantage, excellent. I see you have arrived,' he said, glancing about. 'I trust you have had no trouble?'

'Only a little, sir,' said the foreman, respectfully, indicating the bird, which let out a hoarse and indignant 'Cuckoo'!

'Dear me,' said the sleek gentleman. 'Can this be my unfortunate friend Mr Armitage? Such a pleasant person – perhaps just a *little* hot-tempered, just a *little* unkind in his reviews? However it would certainly be unkind to wrest him from his old home; we must find some accommodation for him. Hawkins!' The chauffeur's head looked out from the car. 'Bring the case, will you.'

A large glass dome was brought, of the kind which is placed over skeleton clocks, with the hours and minutes marked on one side.

'There,' said the gentleman, tucking Mr Armitage under one arm. 'Now, in the study, perhaps? On one's desk, for inspiration. When I place the bird in position, Hawkins, pray cover him with the case. Thank you. A most tasteful ornament, I flatter myself, and perhaps in time we may even teach him to announce the hours.'

'Your father's being a long time,' said Mrs Armitage rather anxiously to the children. 'I do hope he isn't getting into trouble.'

'Oh, I don't suppose it's worth expecting him before lunch,' said Mark. 'He'll argue with everybody and then probably go for a walk and start drafting a letter to *The Times*.'

So they sat down to lunch in Mrs Foster's house, but just as they were raising the first bites to their mouths, Harriet gave a little squeak and said:

'Goodness! We've forgotten all about Sarah! She'll arrive at the house and won't know what's happened to us.'

'Oh, she's sure to see Father somewhere around, and he'll bring her along,' Mark pointed out. 'I wouldn't worry. We can go along afterwards and see, if they don't turn up soon.'

At this moment Sarah was walking onward to her doom. She found the front door of the Armitage house open, and nobody about. This seemed to her a good moment to plant some of her practical jokes, so she opened her suitcase and stole into the dining-room. The long table was already set for tea. There were thirteen places, which puzzled her, but she supposed her aunt and uncle must be giving a party. Some plates of sandwiches and cakes covered with damp napkins were standing on a side table, so she doctored them with sneezing powder, and placed Fizz-bangs in some of the tea-cups.

She was surprised to see that the rooms had been split in two by partitions of beaver-board, and wondered where the family were, and what was going on. Hearing hammering upstairs she decided to tiptoe up and surprise them. Feeling around in her suitcase again, she dug out her water pistol, and charged it from a jug which stood on the sideboard. Then she went softly up the stairs.

The door facing the top of the stairs was open, and she stole through it. This was Mr Armitage's study, which Mr Whizzard had decided should be his private office. Just now, however, he was out having his lunch, and the room was empty. Sarah went to work at once. She laid a few drawing-pins carefully on what she supposed to be her uncle's chair, and was just attaching a neat little contrivance to the telephone, when there came an interruption. The huge black cat, Walrus, who had stayed behind when the family left, had strolled into the study after Sarah, and taken a deep interest in the dejected-looking cuckoo sitting under the glass dome. While Sarah was busy laying the drawing-pins he leapt on to the desk, and after a moment's reflection, knocked the glass case off the desk with one sweep of his powerful paw.

The huge black cat, Walrus, leapt on to the desk

'Sarah!' cried Mr Armitage in terror. 'Save me from this murdering beast!'

Completely startled, thinking that her uncle must have come in unheard while her back was turned, Sarah spun round and let fly with her water pistol. The jet caught the unfortunate bird in mid-air, and at once (for the weather was very cold) he turned to a solid block of ice, and fell to the ground with a heavy thud. The cat pounced at once, but his teeth simply grated on the ice, and he sprang back with a hiss of dismay.

At that moment Mr Whizzard returned from lunch.

'Dear me!' he said peevishly. 'What is all this? Cats? Little girls? And who has been meddling with my cuckoo?' But when he saw Mr Armitage's frozen condition he began to laugh uncontrollably.

'Warlock! Warlock! Come and look at this,' he shouted, and another man came in, wearing a mortarboard and magician's gown.

'The lads have just arrived in the dragon-bus,' he said. 'I told them to go straight in to tea, as the workmen haven't quite finished dividing up the classrooms. What have you got there?'

'Poor Armitage has become quite seized up,' said Mr Whizzard. 'If we had a deep-freeze –'

Before he could finish, several young student-magicians dashed into the room, with cries of complaint. They were all sneezing.

'Really it's too bad, when we're all tired from our journey! Sneezing powder in everything, and tea all over the floor. A joke's a joke, but this is going too far. Someone ought to get the sack for this.'

'What is the matter, my lads?' inquired Mr Whizzard.

'Someone's been playing a lot of rotten practical jokes.'

Sarah quailed, and would gladly have slipped away, but she was jammed in a corner. She tried to squeeze past the desk, but one of the drawers was open and caught her suitcase. A small bomb fell out and exploded on the carpet, amid yelps of terror from the students.

'Seize that child,' commanded Mr Whizzard. Two of them unwillingly did so, and stood her before him. He cast his eye over the diabolical contents of her suitcase, and then the label attracted his attention.

'Armitage. Ah, just so, this is plainly an attempt at sabotage from the evicted family. They shall pay dearly for it. Nightshade, fetch an electric fire, will you. There's one in the front hall.'

While they were waiting, Mr Whizzard sat down in his chair, but shot up again at once, with a murderous look at Sarah.

Nightshade returned with the fire, and plugged it in.

'Good. Now place the bird before it, in this pencil tray, so as not to damp the carpet. The cat sits at hand on this chair, ready for when the thawing process commences. It should not be long, I fancy. Now my young friends, you may return to your interrupted meal, and as for you,' with a savage glance at Sarah, 'a little solitary confinement will do you no harm, while I reflect on how to dispose of you.'

Sarah was dragged away and locked into a beaver-board cell, which had once been part of Harriet's bedroom.

'Now I think we deserve a quiet cup of tea, after all this excitement,' said Mr Whizzard to Mr Warlock, when they were left alone. 'We can sip it as we watch poor Armitage melt. I'll ring down to the kitchen.' He lifted the telephone, and instantly a flood of ink poured into his ear.

Meanwhile Mark and Harriet had decided to come in search of their father and cousin.

'It might be wise not to go in the front way, don't you think,' said Harriet. 'After all, it's rather odd that we haven't heard *something* of them by now. I feel there must have been some trouble.'

So they went stealthily round through the shrubbery, and climbed up the wistaria to Harriet's window. The first thing they saw when they looked in was Sarah, pacing up and down in a distracted manner.

'Good gracious – ' Harriet began, but Sarah made frantic gestures to silence her. They climbed in as quietly as they could.

'Thank heaven you've come,' she whispered. 'Uncle Armitage is being roasted to death in the study, or else eaten by Walrus. You must rescue him at once.' They listened in horror, as she explained the position, and then hurriedly climbed out again. Sarah was no climber, so she hung out anxiously watching them, and thinking of the many times her uncle had given her half-crowns and pats on the head.

Harriet ran to the back door, where the cat's tin plate still lay, and began to rattle it, calling 'Walrus, Walrus, Walrus! Dinner! Walrus! Fish!'

Mark climbed along the wistaria to the study window, to wait for the result of this move.

He saw the cat Walrus, who was still sitting on the chair, attentively watching the melting process, suddenly prick up his ears and look towards the door. Then as Harriet's voice came faintly again he shot out of it and disappeared.

'Confound that animal!' exclaimed Mr Whizzard. 'Catch him, Warlock!' They both ran out of the door, looking to right and left. Mark wasted no time. He clambered through the window, grabbed the cuckoo, and was out again before the two men returned, frustrated and angry.

'Good heavens, now the bird's gone,' cried Mr Warlock. 'What a fool you were to leave the window open. It must have flown out.'

'Impossible! This is some more of that wretched child's doing. I'm going along to see her, right away.'

He burst in on Sarah, looking so ferocious that she instinctively caught up the first weapon she could see, to defend herself. It was a screwdriver, left lying on the floor by one of the workmen.

'What have you done with the cuckoo?' Mr Whizzard demanded.

'I haven't touched it,' Sarah truthfully replied.

'Nonsense. Do you deny that you enticed the cat away by black arts, and then kidnapped the cuckoo?' He approached her threateningly.

Sarah retreated as far as she could and clutched the screwdriver. 'You're crackers,' she said. 'I tell you I haven't – '

Her mouth dropped open in astonishment. For where Mr Whizzard had been standing there was nothing but a large white cardboard box, with a red and blue picture on the lid. At this moment Mark and Harriet came climbing back through the window.

Downstairs in the dining-room the young wizards, having cleared away tea, were enjoying a sing-song.

> 'Ha, ha ha, he he he,' they sang,
> 'Little broom stick, how I love thee.'

They were interrupted by Mr Warlock.

'Have any of you boys seen Mr Whizzard?' he inquired. 'He went to interview the young female prisoner, and I haven't seen him since.'

'No, sir, he hasn't been in here,' the eldest one said. 'Won't you come and play for us, Mr Warlock? You do play so beautifully.'

'Well, just for five minutes, if you insist.' They began to sing again,

> 'Necromancers come away, come away, come come away,
> This is wizards' holiday,'

when suddenly they were aware of the three children, Mark, Harriet, and Sarah, standing inside the door, holding red and blue crackers in their hands.

'What is the meaning of this?' said Mr Warlock severely. 'You are trespassing on private property.'

'Yes,' said Mark. '*Our* property. This is our house, and we would like you to get out of it at once.'

'Vacate it,' whispered Harriet.

'Vacate it at once.'

'We shall do no such thing.'

'Very well then. Do you know what we have here?' he held up one of the crackers. 'Your Mr Whizzard. And if you don't get out – vacate – at once, we shall *pull* them. So you'd better hurry up.'

The wizards looked at each other in consternation, and then, slowly at first, but with gathering speed, began to put their things together and take them out to the dragon coach. The children watched them, holding their crackers firmly.

'And you must take down all that beaver-board partitioning,' said Harriet firmly. 'I don't know *what* Mummy would say if she saw it.'

'The workmen have all gone home.' .

'Then you must manage on your own.'

The house began to resound with amateurish bangs and squeaks. 'O, Nightshade, you clumsy clot, you dropped that board on my toe.' 'Well get out of the way then, you nitwit necromancer.'

At last it was all done, and at the front gate the children handed over the twelve red-and-blue parts of Mr Whizzard.

'And it's more than you deserve,' said Harriet, 'seeing how you were going to treat our poor Pa.'

'We should also like that screwdriver, with which I perceive you have armed yourself, or we shall not be able to restore our Director to his proper shape,' said Mr Warlock coldly.

'Oh, dear me, no. You're nuts if you think we're going to let you get away with that,' said Sarah. 'We shall want it in case of any further trouble. Besides, what about poor uncle – oh dear – ' she stopped in dismay. For Mr Warlock had disappeared, and his place had been taken by a sack of coconuts.

'Oh, never mind,' said Harriet. 'You didn't mean to do it. Here, do for goodness' sake hurry up and go.' She shoved the sack into the arms of Nightshade, and bundled him into the coach, which slowly rolled off. 'We must simply dash along to Mrs Foster's. I'm sure Mummy will be worrying.'

They burst in on Mrs Armitage with their story. 'And where is your Father?' she said immediately.

'Oh goodness.' Mark looked guilty. 'I'd forgotten all about him.' He carefully extracted the half-stifled looking cuckoo from his trouser pocket.

'Out with the screwdriver, Sarah.'

Sarah obediently pointed it at him and said, 'You're Uncle' and he was restored to himself once more, but looking much rumpled and tattered. He glared at them all.

'I must say, that's a fine respectful way to treat your Father. Carried in your trouser pocket, indeed . . .'

'Well, I hope this will cure you once and for all of writing those unkind reviews,' said Mrs Armitage coldly. 'Now we have all the trouble of moving back again, and just when I was beginning to feel settled.'

'And talking of cures,' said Mr Armitage, turning on his niece, 'we won't say anything *this* time, seeing it's all turned out for the best, but if ever I catch you playing any of your practical pranks again – '

'Oh, I never, never will,' Sarah assured him. 'I only thought people enjoyed them.'

'Not in this family,' said Mark.

The Parrot Pirate Princess

THE King and Queen were quarrelling fiercely over what the baby Princess was to be called when the fairy Grisel dropped in. Grisel, that is to say, did not drop in – to be more accurate, she popped out of one of the vases on the mantelpiece, looked round, saw the baby and said:

'What's this?'

'Oh, good afternoon,' said the King uncomfortably.

'We were just putting you on the list of people to be invited to the christening,' said the Queen, hastily doing so. She had presence of mind.

'Mmmmm,' said Grisel. 'Is it a boy or a girl?'

'It's a girl, and the sweetest little –'

'*I'm* the best judge of that,' interrupted the fairy, and she hooked the baby out of its satin cradle. 'Well, let's have a look at you.'

The baby was a calm creature, and did not, as the Queen had dreaded, burst into loud shrieks at the sight of Grisel's wizened old face. She merely cooed.

'Well, you can't say she's very handsome, can you? Takes too much after both of you,' Grisel said cheerfully. The baby laughed. 'What are you going to call her?'

'We were just wondering when you came in,' the Queen said despairingly. She knew that Grisel had a fondness for suggesting impossible names, and then being extremely angry if the suggestions were not taken. Worse – she might want the baby called after herself.

'Then I'll tell you what,' said Grisel, eagerly leaning forward. 'Call it –'

But here she was interrupted, for the baby, which she still held, hit her a fearful whack on the front teeth with its heavy silver rattle.

There was a terrible scene. The King and Queen were far too well-bred to laugh, but they looked as if they would have liked to. The Queen snatched the baby from Grisel, who was stamping up and down the room, pale with rage, and using the most unlady-like language.

'That's right – laugh when I've had the best part of my teeth knocked down my throat,' she snarled. 'And as for you – you – ' She turned to the baby who was chuckling in the Queen's arms.

'Goo goo,' the baby replied affably.

'Goo goo, indeed. I'll teach you to repeat what I say,' the fairy said furiously. And before the horrified Queen could make a move, the baby had turned into a large grey parrot and flown out of the window.

Grisel smiled maliciously round the room and said: 'You can take me off the christening list now.'

She went, leaving the King and Queen silent.

The Parrot turned naturally to the south, hunting for an island with palm trees, or at least a couple of coconuts to eat. After some time she came to the sea. She was disconcerted. She did not feel that she could face flying all the way over that cold grey-looking water to find an island that would suit her. So she sat down on the edge to think. The edge where she sat happened to be a quay, and presently a sailor came along, said 'Hullo, a parrot,' and picked her up.

She did not struggle. She looked up at him and said in a hoarse, rasping voice: 'Hullo, a parrot.'

The sailor was delighted. He took her on board his ship, which sailed that evening for the South Seas.

This was no ordinary ship. It was owned by the most terrible pirate then in business, who frightened all the ships off the seas. And so fairly soon the parrot saw some surprising things.

The pirates were quite kind to her. They called her Jake, and took a lot of interest in her education. She was a quick learner, and before the end of the voyage she knew the most shocking collection of swear words and nautical phrases that ever parrot spoke. She also knew all about walking the plank and the effects of rum. When the pirates had captured a particularly fine ship they would all drink gallons of rum and make her drink it, too, whereupon the undignified old fowl would lurch about all over the deck and in the rigging, singing 'Fifteen men on a dead man's chest, Yo, ho, ho and a bottle of rum,' and the pirates would shout with laughter.

One day they arrived at the island where they kept their treasure, and it was all unloaded and rowed ashore. It took them two days to bury it, and the parrot sat by, thinking: 'Shiver my timbers, but I'd like to get away and live on this island!' But she could not, for one of the pirates had thoughtfully tied her by the ankle to a tree. She sat swearing under her breath and trying to gnaw through the rope, but it was too thick.

Luck, however, was with her. The second day after they had left the island, a great storm sprang up, and the pirates' ship was wrecked.

'Brimstone and botheration and mercy me!' chorused the pirates, clinging frantically to the rigging. They had little time for more, because with a frightful roar the ship went to the bottom, leaving Jake bobbing about on the waves like a cork.

'Swelp me,' she remarked, rose up and flew with the wind, which took her straight back to the island.

'Well blow me down,' she said when she got there. 'This is a bit better than living on biscuit among all those unrefined characters. Bananas and mangoes, bless my old soul! This is the life for me.'

She lived on the island for some time, and became very friendly with a handsome grey gentleman parrot already there, called Bill. Bill seemed to know as much about pirates as she did, but he was always rather silent about his past life, so she gathered that he did not want it mentioned. They got on extremely well, however, and lived on the island for about twenty years, which did not change them in the least, as parrots are notoriously long-lived.

Then one day, as they were sharing a bunch of bananas, a frightful hurricane suddenly arose, and blew them, still clutching the bananas, out to sea.

'Hold on tight!' shrieked Bill in her ear.

'I am holding on,' she squawked back. 'Lumme, Bill, you do look a sight. Just like a pincushion!'

The wretched Bill was being fluffed out by the wind until his tail-feathers stood straight up. 'Well you're not so pretty yourself,' he said indignantly, screwing his head round to look at her. 'Don't half look silly, going along backwards like that.'

'Can't you see, you perishing son of a sea-cook,' squawked Jake, 'it stops the wind blowing your feathers out – have a try.'

'It makes me feel funny,' complained Bill, and he went back to his former position, still keeping a tight hold on the bananas.

'Mountains ahead – look out!' he howled, a moment or two later. They were being swept down at a terrific speed towards a range of hills.

'Is it the mainland?' asked Jake, swivelling round to get a glimpse. 'Doesn't the wind make you giddy?'

'Yes. It's the mainland I reckon,' said Bill. 'There's houses down there. Oh, splice my mainbrace, we're going to crash into them. Keep behind the bananas.' Using the great bunch as a screen they hurtled downwards.

'Mind last week's washing,' screamed Jake, as they went through a low belt of grey cloud. 'I never in all my life saw anything to beat this. Talk about seeing the world.' They were only twenty feet above ground now, still skimming along, getting lower all the time.

'Strikes me we'd better *sit* on the bananas if we don't want our tail feathers rubbed off,' said Jake. 'Oh my, look where we're going.'

Before Bill had time to answer, they went smack through an immense glass window, shot across a room, breaking three vases on the way, and came to rest on a mantelpiece, still mixed up with the bananas, which were rather squashed and full of broken glass.

'Journey's end,' said Jake. 'How are you, Bill?'

'Not so bad,' said Bill, wriggling free of the bananas and beginning to put his feathers to rights.

Then they were both suddenly aware of the fairy Grisel, sitting in one corner of the room, where she had been knocked by a vase, and glaring at them. She picked herself up and came and looked at them closely.

'It's you again is it?' she said. 'I might have known it.'

'Pleased to meet you,' said Jake, who had no recollection of her. 'I'm Jake, and this is my husband Bill.'

'I know you, don't you worry,' said Grisel. Then Jake suddenly remembered where she had seen Grisel before.

'Oh lor – don't you go changing me into a princess again,' she cried in alarm, but hardly were the words out of her beak, when, bang, she was back in her father's palace, in the throne-room. She looked down at herself, and saw that she was human once more.

'Well! Here's a rum go,' she said aloud. 'Who'd have thought it?' She glanced round the room and saw, through a french window, the King and Queen, a good deal older, having tea on the terrace. There was also a girl, not unlike herself. She went forward to them with a very nautical gait, and hitching up her trousers – only it was a long and flowing cloth-of-gold skirt.

'Hello Pa! Pleased to meet you!' she cried, slapping the King on the back. 'Shiver my timbers, Ma, it's a long time since we met. Not since I was no longer than a marline spike. Who's this?'

They were all too dumbfounded to speak. 'Hasn't anyone got a tongue in their head?' she asked. 'Here comes the prodigal daughter, and all they can do is sit and gawp?'

'Are you – are you that baby?' the Queen asked faintly. 'The one that got taken away?'

'That's me!' Jake told her cheerfully. 'Twenty years a parrot, and just when I'm beginning to enjoy life, back I comes to the bosom of my family. Shunt my backstay, it's a funny life.'

She sighed.

The King and Queen looked at one another in growing horror.

'And this'll be my little sissy, if I'm not mistaken,' said Jake

70

meditatively. 'Quite a big girl, aren't you, ducks? If you'll excuse me, folks, I'm a bit thirsty. Haven't had a drink for forty-eight hours.'

She rolled indoors again.

'Well I suppose it might be worse,' said the Queen doubtfully, in the horrified silence. 'We can *train* her, can't we? I suppose she'll have to be the heir?'

'I'm afraid so,' said the King. 'I hope she'll take her position seriously.'

'And what happens to *me*?' demanded the younger sister shrilly.

The King sighed.

During the next two months the royal family had an uncomfortable time. Jake obviously meant well, and was kindly disposed to everyone, but she did make a bad crown princess. Her language was dreadful, and she never seemed to remember not to say 'Stap my vitals' or something equally unsuitable, when she trod on her skirt. She said that trains were a nuisance.

'You don't want to traipse round with the drawing-room curtains *and* the dining-room tablecloth pinned to your tail. I'm used to flying. Splice my mainbrace!' she would cry.

She rushed about and was apt to clap important court officials and ambassadors on the back and cry 'Hallo! How's the missus, you old son of a gun?' Or if they annoyed her, she loosed such a flood of epithets on them ('You lily-livered, cross-eyed, flop-eared son of a sea-cook') that the whole Court fled in horror, stopping their ears. She distressed the King and Queen by climbing trees, or sitting rocking backwards and forwards for hours at a time, murmuring 'Pretty Poll. Pretty Jake. Pieces of eight, pieces of eight, pieces of eight.'

'Will she *ever* turn into a presentable queen?' said the King despairingly, and the Queen stared hopelessly out of the window.

'Perhaps she'll marry and settle down,' she suggested, and so they advertised for princes in the *Monarchy's Marriage Mart*, a very respectable paper.

'We'll have to think of Miranda too,' the King said. 'After all she was brought up to expect to be queen. It's only fair that she should marry some eligible young prince and come into a kingdom that way. She's a good girl.'

Eventually a Prince arrived. He came quite quietly, riding on a fiery black horse, and stayed at an inn near the palace. He sent the King a note, saying that he would be only too grateful for a sight of the Princess, whenever it was convenient.

'Now we must really try and make her behave presentably for once,' said the Queen, but there was not much hope in her voice.

A grand ball was arranged, and the court dress-makers spent an entire week fitting Jake to a white satin dress, and Miranda obligingly spent a whole evening picking roses in the garden to put in Jake's suspiciously scarlet hair.

Finally the evening came. The throne-room was a blaze of candle-light. The King and Queen sat on the two thrones, and below them on the steps, uncomfortably but gracefully posed, were the two princesses. A trumpet blew, and the prince entered. The crowd stood back, and he walked forward and bowed very low before the thrones. Then he kissed Miranda's hand and said:

'Will you dance with me, Princess?'

'Hey, young man,' interrupted the King, 'you've made a mistake. It's the other one who's the Crown Princess.'

Jake roared with laughter, but the Prince had gone very pale, and Miranda was scarlet.

'I didn't know *you* were the Prince of Sitania,' she said.

'*Aren't* you the Princess, then?' he said.

'Have you two met before?' the King demanded.

'Last night in the Palace gardens,' said Miranda. 'The Prince promised he'd dance the first dance with me. But I didn't know, truly I didn't, that he was *that* Prince.'

'And I thought you were the Crown Princess,' he said. There was an uncomfortable silence. Jake turned away and began humming 'Yo ho ho and a bottle of rum'.

'Your Majesty, I am sorry to be so inconvenient,' said the Prince desperately, 'but may I marry *this* princess?'

'How large is your kingdom?' asked the King sharply.

'Well, er, actually I am the youngest of five sons, so I have no kingdom,' the Prince told him, 'but my income is pretty large.'

The King shook his head. 'Won't do. Miranda must have a kingdom. I'm afraid, young man, that it's impossible. If you wanted to marry the other princess and help reign over this kingdom, that would be different.'

The Prince hung his head, and Miranda bit her lip. Jake tried to put her hands in her white satin pockets, and whistled. The crowd began to shuffle, and to quiet them, the Royal Band struck up. And then Jake gave a shriek of delight, and fairly skated across the marble floor.

'*Bill*, my old hero! I'd know you anywhere!' A burly pirate with a hooked nose and scarlet hair was standing in the doorway.

'Well, well, well!' he roared. 'Looks like I've bumped into a party. You and I, ducks, will show them how the hornpipe ought to be danced.' And solemnly before the frozen Court they broke into a hornpipe, slow at first, and then faster and faster. Finally they stopped, panting.

'I'm all of a lather. Haven't got a wipe, have you Jake?' Bill asked.

'Here, have half the tablecloth.' She tore a generous half from her twelve-foot train and gave it to him. They both mopped their brows vigorously. Then Jake took Bill across to where the King and Queen were standing with horrorstruck faces.

'Here's my husband,' said Jake. The Court turned as one man and fled, leaving the vast room empty but for the King and Queen, Jake and Bill, and Miranda and the Prince.

'Your husband? But you never said anything about him. And here we were, searching for Princes,' the Queen began.

'I don't think you ever asked me for *my* news,' said Jake. 'And now, if you'll excuse us, we'll be going. I've waited these two months for Bill, and a dratted long time he took to get here. Told him my address when we were parrots together, before all this happened, and a nasty time I've had, wondering

73

if he'd forgotten it. But I needn't have worried. Slow but sure is old Bill,' she patted his shoulder, 'aren't you, ducks?'

'But –' said the Queen.

'Think I really stayed here all this time learning how to be a lady?' Jake said contemptuously. 'I was waiting for Bill. Now we'll be off.'

'But –' began the King.

'Don't be crazy,' said Jake irritably. 'You don't think I could stop and be queen *now* – when all the Court have seen me and Bill dancing like a couple of young grasshoppers? You can have those brats –' she nodded towards Miranda and the Prince, who were suddenly looking hopeful. 'Well, so long, folks.' She took Bill's hand and they went out.

And now, if you want to know where they are, all you have to do is go to the island where they lived before, and directly over the spot where the treasure was hidden, you will see a neat little pub with a large signboard: 'The Pirate's Rest', and underneath: 'By Appointment to Their Majesties.'

They broke into a hornpipe

John Sculpin and the Witches

ONE day John Sculpin's mother said to him: 'I *must* wash my hair. Run down to the wishing well and fetch me a bucket of water.'

'All right, Ma,' said John, and he put on his beautiful cap, because it was raining and pouring torrents.

'And whatever you do,' she said, 'don't let a witch get that new cap of yours, because it's just the thing one of the old scarecrows would like and I can't afford another one, let me tell you.'

'How am I to stop her taking it, Ma?' asked John.

'If I've told you once how to get rid of a witch, I've told you twenty times,' said his mother. 'Don't let me hear another word from you. Off with you.'

So John went off, but whether it was from stupidity, or whether he just hadn't been listening, he couldn't for the life of him remember anything his mother had ever said to him about dealing with witches. And that was a pity, because, as it happened, the country round about there was just infested with them.

John went along the road, thinking and thinking, and after a while he met an old woman.

'Afternoon, John,' she said, 'you look fretted about something.'

'So would you be,' said John, 'my Ma's told me the way to get rid of a witch, and I've clean forgotten it.'

'If I tell you, will you give me that fine new cap you're wearing?' she said. John didn't like parting with his fine new cap, but the information seemed worth it, so he handed it over.

'If I tell you, will you give me that fine new cap?'

'Well,' said the old woman, 'all you have to do is give her a nice bunch of parsley.'

'Of course that was it!' said John. 'I'll forget my own name next.'

He thanked the old woman and went on down the road. The next house he came to was his uncle Sam's, so he went into the garden and picked a nice big bunch of parsley. Then he walked down to the wishing well.

When he came up to the well, there was an old woman sitting beside it in the rain and muttering to herself. John went straight up to her and handed her the parsley, and she took it with a bit of a grunt and vanished; she'd gone to hang it up in her scullery.

John filled his bucket and went home. He put it down with a clank inside the back door and his mother called out to him from the kitchen:

'Did you see a witch?'

'Yes,' said John, 'there was one sitting beside the well, but I gave her a bunch of parsley and she took herself off.'

'That's a good boy,' said his mother, 'there's nothing like that wishing well water for washing your hair in, I do say. Bring it in here, will you, with the big kettle.'

When John went in, the first thing she said to him was:

'Where's your cap?'

'Oh, I gave it to an old woman,' said John, 'she told me the right way to get rid of a witch.'

'You little misery!' screamed his mother. 'What's the use of telling you anything? You've given your cap to a witch, and not another one do you get till Christmas.'

About a week later John's mother said to him:

'We've finished all the potatoes. You'll have to go over to Malden's Farm and get a sackful. And *this* time, if you meet a witch, maybe you'll have the sense to give her a bunch of parsley right away.'

So John fetched out his bicycle and pumped up the tyres and found an old potato sack. And before he started he picked nearly a whole sackful of parsley and took it with him over his shoulder. It was about five miles to Malden's Farm and the whole way, whenever John saw an old woman on the road, he got off and gave her one of his bunches of parsley. He wasn't taking any chances. Plenty of them looked a bit surprised at being given some parsley in the middle of the road, but that made no difference to John. By the time he had reached Malden's he had been so generous with his parsley that he had none left, and when he got to the farm gate and saw another old woman sitting outside he didn't quite know what to do.

'Haven't you anything for me, dearie?' the old woman asked.

John was a bit embarrassed, so finally he gave her the bicycle pump as that seemed to be the smallest thing he could part with. Then he got his potatoes and went home.

When he came up the garden path his mother called from her bedroom window:

'Got the potatoes, John?'

'Yes, Ma,' John shouted back, 'a whole sackful.'

'But are they good ones?' she said, and came down to see. The first thing she said, when she came into the shed where John had put them was:

'Where's the bicycle pump?'

'Well, you see, Ma,' John explained, 'I'd finished all the parsley, giving it away to old women, by the time I got to Malden's. So I had to give the pump to the last one. Very pleased with it, she was. You should have seen her.'

'You little good-for-nothing,' screamed his mother. 'What do you think we're going to do without the bicycle pump? Not another penny do you get to buy sweets till you've paid for a new one.'

After that, all the witches in the neighbourhood got to know about John, and they plagued him so much that he never dared stir out of doors without about half a cartload of parsley. So one day his mother said to him:

'I've thought of a plan to get rid of the witches, and for goodness' sake listen to what I'm saying, instead of mooning out of the window.'

Next day she went all round the village saying:

'My John's going to town. Have you any messages you want done?'

By the time she got home she had a list of messages as long as her arm, and all the witches knew that John was catching the 9.18 train into Tabchester the next day.

The porter always used to say that he'd never seen such a sight as there was that day. The station wasn't very big, and it was crowded from one end to the other with witches, all waiting for the 9.18 to come in. Some of them bought tickets and some didn't. John came a bit late with his shopping basket and list. He went and had a private talk with the porter, who was also the station master, and the guard, and the engine driver. Presently the porter (whose name was Mr Sims) went off and brought along the train. It wasn't a very big one, for it only went as far as Tabchester. There was no one else in it but John and the witches.

When the train began to move, John got up and made a little speech.

'Ladies,' he said, 'I didn't think I could bring enough parsley for all of you, so I've arranged a little treat for you, and you'll find it in the dining-car at the end of the train.'

So he went along the corridor to show them the way, and all the witches came pushing along behind him, rubbing their hands.

At the end of the train the corridor bent round, and there was a door to join on to another coach, if one should ever be needed. So John stood at the corner, and as each witch came round, he pushed her through the door and off the end of the train. And that was the end of her. All except the last. For the last but one, when he pushed her through the door, gave a kind of squeak, and that warned the one after her. So, quick as a wink, she changed herself into a bluebottle, and when John looked round, he thought he must have finished them all.

He went into the town and did all his errands, and when he got home he and his mother had a good laugh, thinking about all the witches.

But the last witch went home in a frightful temper, thinking how she could be revenged on John.

One day she put on a tweed cap and a false moustache and got on her bicycle and went off with a box on her back. And when she came to John's mother's cottage, she knocked at the front door and asked if they wanted to buy any toothbrushes. John's mother didn't recognize her and she bought a new toothbrush for John. But the witch had poisoned this toothbrush, so that when John brushed his teeth with it, he would drop down dead on the spot.

But you know what boys are, even if the witch didn't. John never brushed his teeth in a month of Sundays. The first night he gave the brush a bit of a rub along the scullery draining-board, to make it look used, and then he stuck it up on the shelf, and that was that.

Next morning his mother called:

'John! Whatever have you been doing on the draining-board? It's all black.'

John came and looked, and sure enough, the board looked as if something like a black stain had been rubbed along it.

'I'm sure I don't know,' he said, 'unless it was my new toothbrush?'

He took it down and looked at it. Just then a fly came and settled on it, and the next minute it fell off on to the floor, as dead as a doornail. John and his mother looked at each other.

'A witch did that,' said his mother. 'You must have left one of them out, and she's got a spite against you. I'll be on the lookout for her the next time she comes selling things to me, the artful old besom.'

A few days later the witch saw John coming down the road as well as ever. So she ground her teeth and began to think out a new way of getting rid of him.

Next morning she came riding up to the cottage in the uniform of a district nurse.

'Morning, Nurse,' said John's mother, 'there's no one ill here, I'm thankful to say.'

'Oh, I heard your little boy was ill,' said the witch.

'It's more than *I* heard,' said his mother, 'but you can see for yourself.'

For John came round the corner with a bundle of faggots.

'Oh dear yes, he's terribly ill,' said the witch. 'I can see it by the way he walks. You must put him to bed at once. I'll give you some medicine for him.'

John's mother was a bit worried at that, and she hustled him into bed. That afternoon the witch came back with a little red bottle of medicine.

'You give him that,' she said, 'and we'll have no more trouble with him.'

John's mother poured it into a glass, but you know what boys are. The minute her back was turned he poured the whole glassful into a jam-jar full of honeysuckle on the wash-stand.

Ten minutes later she came back.

'Good gracious, John!' she said, 'whatever's happened to that honeysuckle? It's all black and shrivelled.'

'It must have been the medicine,' said John, 'I poured it into the jar.'

'That's that witch again,' cried his mother. 'I'll lay for her the next time she comes pretending to be the district nurse. But the next time I catch *you* pouring your medicine down the sink or anywhere else, there'll be trouble.'

A week later the witch saw John cycling through the village, and she nearly burst with rage. She thought and thought, but she simply could not think of anything nasty enough to do to him. While she was thinking, however, she nearly plagued the lives out of John and his mother in small ways. For they'd wake up in the morning to find nothing but giant vegetable marrows growing in the garden, or the fried potatoes would turn to lumps of coal in their mouths, or the tap would start running in the middle of the night, and they would come down to find the kitchen flooded.

'It *is* so distressing,' said John's mother to a friend of hers. 'You never know whether you are on your head or your heels.'

'There's only one thing to do when a witch starts plaguing you like that,' said her friend, 'you ought to pour a bucket of water over her, that's been taken from a running stream less than seven minutes before. Then she turns into a black cat.'

Well, in the next three days John was fairly exhausted. He

spent the whole of his time running backwards and forwards to the stream with buckets. And, of course, the witch never turned up.

But on the fourth day a smart young man came up the garden path, selling fine new dishmops. He had a whole bunch of them in one hand.

'Aha,' said John to himself, 'I've got you now.' He stood behind the door with his bucket and waited for the young fellow to knock.

But as a matter of fact the young man was a real salesman, and if John had looked out again he would have seen the witch herself, sneaking up behind him, with a carrier bag full of scorpions, which she meant to put in the copper to surprise them. John never looked, though, and when a knock came at the door he popped out and flung the whole of the bucket over the young man, and then ran for his life. It was lucky he did, too, for the man was in a terrible temper when he picked himself up.

The first person he saw was the witch, who was laughing enough to split her sides. Of course he thought she had thrown the bucket, and he gave her such a clout with his dishmops that he knocked her spinning into a clump of nettles. Then he took himself off, muttering such things under his breath that John's mother's black spaniel turned quite white to hear them.

But John and his mother were looking out of the side window to see what happened, and when they saw the man go off, and that he hadn't turned into a black cat, they thought that something must have gone wrong, and the spell hadn't worked. So without waiting to see more they packed up all their belongings in the tablecloth and cleared out as fast as they could go.

The witch went home, grumbling and cursing, and after that, she wasn't nearly so lively about making herself a nuisance to people.

John and his mother settled down in a different part of the country where there weren't so many witches; which they might as well have done at first.

The Magic Iron

As John Sculpin was cycling into Tollerton, he saw an old woman by the roadside with a bicycle; it had a very flat tyre and she was looking at it and muttering gloomily.

'Can I help you, ma'am?' asked John, dismounting.

'It's a puncture,' she snapped.

'Just a minute till I borrow a bucket of water from that house,' said John, 'and then it won't take any time.'

Sure enough, when he came back with the pail of water, he was able to find the puncture and mend it quite quickly. The old woman cheered up and became quite friendly as they rode on together (she was going in the same direction).

'And where are you off to this fine afternoon?' she asked.

'I've got some shopping to do for my Ma, and I want to get her a birthday present.'

'And what are you going to get her?'

'I haven't quite made up my mind,' said John. 'I've only got a shilling. I thought I might get some cakes, but a new dishmop would last longer.'

'You seem to be a nice obliging boy,' said the old woman, 'so I'll give you a bit of advice. When you get to town you'll find they are selling raffle tickets in aid of the hospital. The tickets are a shilling each. You take number ninety-nine, and you'll be glad you did, mark my words.'

'What are they raffling?' asked John.

'It's an electric iron, and no common iron either.'

John turned his head to ask another question, but found that the old woman had vanished, bicycle and all, leaving a clear stretch of road. This surprised him very much, for if she could could vanish away so easily, why had she bothered about a mere puncture in her tyre? He rode on his way, scratching his head. When he arrived in Tollerton, however, he found that it was just as she had said. They were selling raffle tickets in the big market hall.

All excited, he padlocked his bicycle, left it at the stand, and rushed off to buy ticket number ninety-nine. Then he went and got the dusters, darning needles, chicken-food, paraffin, and light bulbs which his mother needed.

When he had finished his shopping he still had an hour and a half, for the result of the raffle would not be announced till half-past four. All at once a horrid qualm struck him. Supposing he won nothing, then he would have spent his shilling and have nothing to show for it. This made him feel so miserable that he leant against a wall and wondered what to do.

All at once the front door of the house opposite flew open and a red-faced woman came out.

'Here, you, boy!' she exclaimed. 'You seem to have nothing to do. Just keep an eye on the baby while I pop down the road for some more currants. I'm all behind with my baking.'

She shoved him inside, adding:

'If I'm not back in ten minutes, take the buns out of the oven and put in the next lot.'

John found himself in a very clean, hot kitchen, which seemed to be full of pans of buns, some baked, some put to rise in front of the oven. A large, fierce baby sat in a crib and stared at John. As soon as it was certain that its mother was not coming back it set up a piercing shriek, like a steam-engine but much worse.

'Here, don't do that,' said John anxiously. The baby took no notice and was beginning to go black in the face, so John did his imitation of a man trying to catch a mosquito. He buzzed and flapped, and presently the baby began to watch, and then to laugh, until it was quite breathless. Ten minutes had gone by now, and John began to smell burning, so he opened the oven door and whisked out the buns, just in time. The baby began to shriek again, so he hastily put in a fresh lot of buns and started his imitation once more. By the time the mother came back a third lot of buns was in the oven, John was quite exhausted, but the baby was smiling broadly.

'Well, I had to go half over town to buy some currants,'

the woman exclaimed, 'I can see you've kept things going nicely.'

'No trouble,' said John politely. However, she made him eat a hot buttered bun, and gave him four beautiful little cakes with red and blue icing. John was delighted, for now he had something to give his mother even if he didn't win the raffle. He said goodbye to the mother and baby, and as it was by now nearly half-past four, made his way to the market hall.

They were just pulling the tickets out of the hat when he arrived. What was his joy when he heard the Mayor read out:

'Number ninety-nine wins this handsome electric iron.'

He went up to the platform, presented his ticket, and received his prize. It *was* a beautiful iron. It shone like silver, the handle was red with a little cushion for the ironer's thumb to rest on, and a red light showed when the iron was switched on.

'Congratulations, John,' said a voice in his ear, and he looked up and saw Mr Lightbody, the chimney sweep. John did not much like Mr Lightbody, but he thanked him politely.

'I suppose you don't want to sell that iron? I'll give you three shillings for it,' said Mr Lightbody.

'Oh, no thank you. You see, it's for my mother's birthday.'

'Are you cycling home? Then I'll come with you.'

So John put all his parcels in his bicycle basket, with the precious iron carefully at the bottom, and they set off together, though John would really just as soon have been by himself.

When they had gone a little way they saw a sign saying: 'Penny Ices Sold Here.'

'Here,' said Mr Lightbody, stopping. 'Here's twopence. You pop in and buy us each an ice. I could do with one after all this riding round.'

So John popped in and stood in the queue, and came out in four or five minutes with two cornets. When they had finished they went on, much refreshed. Nothing else happened on the journey.

As soon as John arrived home his mother came bustling out.

'Did you remember the dusters? And the darning needles? And the light bulbs?'

'Yes, yes,' said John, unpacking them from the basket as fast as he could. Then suddenly his jaw dropped and he gave a cry of despair. For where was the iron? It had gone! He had taken everything out of the basket and the iron was not there. John burst into tears.

'Why, good gracious!' cried his mother, 'whatever's the matter?'

John explained to her as well as he could through his sobs.

'Well, never mind,' she soothed him, 'I dare say it was one of those nasty trick things that vanish away when you look at them.'

Luckily the cakes were still there, so John dried his tears and gave them to her.

But what, in the meantime, had happened to the iron? I am afraid it is useless to deny that Mr Lightbody had stolen it. He waited until John was in the ice-cream shop and then slipped it neatly out of the bicycle basket and put it in his own. Directly he reached his home he went down to Mr Miggs, the electrician, to ask if he would come and put a power plug in his kitchen, for up till now Mr Lightbody had not done any ironing. Mr Miggs said he would be along right away, and appeared in ten minutes with his box of tools.

'You want her in here?' he said, tapping the kitchen wall. 'I'll have to put a liddle bit of cable round the skirting board. This here's a stone wall – can't go chipping into that.'

Hardly had Mr Miggs started hammering when my gracious! he must have hammered a nail through a water pipe, for an absolute fountain of water shot out of the wall.

'Turn her off! Turn her off at the stopcock!' he shouted to Mr Lightbody.

'I don't know where it is,' said Mr Lightbody, running about distractedly. By the time they had found the stopcock and turned off the water, the whole kitchen was ankle deep. When it was mopped up, Mr Lightbody went off to Mr Fowler the plumber, who came up with his oxyacetylene blowlamp to mend the broken pipe.

Mr Fowler had hardly started work, when, my gracious!

his hand must have slipped sideways, for he waggled his torch and set the whole skirting board on fire.

'Quick, give us a bucket of water,' he shouted to Mr Lightbody. But of course the water was turned off at the main, and only a trickle came out of the tap. Mr Lightbody pelted off down the road for the fire brigade, who soon arrived, with bells clanging. They quickly had the fire under control, and only broke two windows, flooded the kitchen again, and fused the electric light. Mr Lightbody looked round to ask Mr Miggs to mend the fuse, but Mr Miggs had gone off to his supper. When he came back afterwards, he looked round at the scene of ruin in the kitchen, and said:

'Cor! All this to put in a plug for an electric iron. Reckon you wish you'd stuck to a flat-iron now, don't you?' He selected another nail, to carry on his half-finished job, and put it straight through the pipe again.

Mr Lightbody did not wait for more. He picked up the iron, and, leaving the water spouting out of the wall, ran down the road to John's mother's cottage.

John and his mother were very surprised to see Mr Lightbody, but not half so surprised as they were when he produced the iron and told his shocking story.

'Well there, we'll say no more about it,' said John's mother. 'There's more in this iron than meets the eye, seemingly.'

'Let's see you do a bit of ironing with it, Ma,' said John.

So she plugged it in, fished out some ironing, and switched on the little red light. But what was their astonishment to see, when she began to iron John's handkerchiefs, that they all turned to silk.

'Well, I don't know, I'm sure,' said Mrs Sculpin, and she went on to John's Sunday jacket. As soon as the iron touched it, it became the finest velvet.

'Did you ever,' said Mrs Sculpin, and she picked up her silk Sunday dress. But when she began to iron that, it turned to dazzling cloth of gold, embroidered with pearls!

The neighbours soon heard of this wonderful iron, and wanted to borrow it, but it would only work for John's mother. Soon every stitch of material in the house had turned

first to silk or velvet – dusters, dishcloths and all – and the second time they were ironed they also became cloth of gold. John went to school in a golden shirt and even the potatoes were kept in golden sacks.

'It's very grand, I don't deny,' said Mrs Sculpin sometimes, 'but on washday the wringing doesn't half make your back ache.'

Cooks and Prophecies

'THIS time we'll have an *entirely* private christening,' said the King to the Queen. 'You remember what a time we had with fairies when Florizel was christened – all of them cancelling out each others' gifts till in the end the poor boy had nothing at all.'

'Very well, dear,' said the Queen sadly. But she loved parties, and in spite of the warning she could not resist inviting just one or two old friends. She did not invite the wicked fairy Gorgonzola.

On the day after the christening she received by post a little note written in red ink on black paper. 'Dear Queen,' it read 'I was charmed to read about your christening party in yesterday's evening papers. I quite understand that you would not wish to be bothered with an old *fogey* like myself, so I shall not trouble you by calling, but have sent my christening present to the princess by registered post. Yours affectionately, Gorgonzola.'

Filled with alarm the Queen rushed off to the nursery in order to prevent, if possible, the wicked fairy's parcel from being opened. Too late! The head nurse had already undone the paper and string, and was just then opening a dear little gold casket before the baby's wondering eyes.

The horror-stricken Queen saw a small cloud of black smoke rise from the casket and envelop the princess's head. When it cleared away she had become the ugliest baby born in that kingdom for a hundred years.

At that moment, however, a passing bird dropped a prophecy down the Palace chimney. This said:

> Seek not Griselda's fortune in her looks
> Remember better things are found in books.

This comforted the King, who would otherwise have been inclined to say, 'I told you so,' and he therefore occupied himself by laying out a grand scheme for Griselda's education, for he presumed that this was what the rhyme meant. Though as the piece of paper on which it was written was very sooty, and the writing on it bad, there were some people who insisted that the last word should be read as 'cooks'.

'Ridiculous,' said the King. 'What is found in cooks, pray? Nothing at all. There can be no connection between cooks and my daughter.' And he went on with his neat timetables ruled in red ink, with spaces for Latin, Trigonometry, and Political Economy.

From the age of five poor Griselda was stuffed with these subjects and she hated them all equally. In Latin she could only remember such phrases as 'Give the boy the bread' and 'Each of the soldiers carried his own food'. In mathematics she could only work out the sort of problems in which two men have to pick a given quantity of apples, working at different speeds.

When she was twelve she could stand it no longer, and she went to her father and begged him to let her give up her education and learn cooking.

'Learn cooking?' said the King, horrified. 'Remember you will have to earn your living when we are gone. You won't come into a kingdom like your brother. Do you propose to be a cook, may I ask?'

'Yes,' said Griselda.

'Don't you think it will look rather odd in the advertisements? H.R.H. Griselda. Good plain cooking. Omelettes a speciality. I must say, I should have thought that a daughter of mine could select a better career.'

However, Griselda had made up her mind, and finally she was allowed to learn cooking in the Palace kitchen.

Presently the King and Queen became old and died, and her brother Florizel came to the throne. He was very fond of Griselda and begged her to stay with him, but she decided that the time had come for her to seek her fortune, so she set off one night, secretly and in disguise, in order to avoid any

further persuasions and bother. She asked an obliging
fisherman to take her across the sea in his boat, and he left her
next morning, alone, but not in the least downhearted, on a
foreign shore.

Some lobster-gatherers met her there and asked her who
she was.

'I'm a Princess,' she said absently.

'Go on,' they cried, laughing, though not unkindly, at her
black boot-button eyes and shiny red cheeks.

'I mean I'm a cook,' she amended.

'That's a bit more like it. Over here for the competition,
are you? You'll find the Palace, third turning on the right
down the road.'

Griselda had no idea what they were talking about, but she
followed their directions and soon came to a handsome
Palace. There was a notice on the gate which read:

COOKS!

GRAND COMPETITION

The winner of this Competition will receive the post
of Chief Cook to the Palace together with half the
kingdom (if male) or His Majesty's hand and heart in
marriage (if female). Further particulars within.

Griselda went inside and found that the competition was
just about to begin. Hundreds of cooks were already lined
up in the vast, spotless Palace kitchen, where all the cooking
utensils were of silver, and the dishes of gold.

A pale, anxious-looking young man was running around
dealing out numbers to the competitors. He gave Griselda a
number on a piece of paper and pushed her into line. She
could hear him saying:

'Oh mercy me, whatever shall I do about supper if none
of them come up to standard?'

'Is that the King?' Griselda asked in surprise.

'Hush, they're going to begin. Yes, it is.'

The first event was an apple-peeling competition, which
Griselda won easily by peeling twenty-point-four apples in

three minutes. Next she won the obstacle race, in which competitors had to go over a complicated course, carrying two eggs in one hand and a frying pan in the other, and finish by making an omelette. She then won two more events in quick succession – the Good Housewife Test (which entailed making a nourishing stew out of an old boot and a cabbage leaf), and the Discrimination Test (distinguishing between butter and marge with her eyes shut).

There began to be some muttering among the other competitors, which increased as she went on with a string of successes. She made a delicious meal from two left-over sardines and some cold porridge. Her sponge cake was so light that when the King opened his mouth to taste it, he blew it out of the window. Her bread rose till it burst the oven. She tossed her pancake three times as high as any of the others, and sprinkled it with sugar and lemon as it fell. In fact there was no doubt at all that she was the Queen of the Cooks, and the King was quite exhausted and pale with excitement by the end of the competition, at having found such a treasure.

'I think we all agree,' he announced, 'that Miss – er, that Number 555 has won this contest, and I have much pleasure –'

However, his voice at this point was drowned by the hoarse outcry from the other angry and disappointed competitors, and it looked as if there was going to be a riot. One of the rejected sponge cakes was flung at Griselda, but it was so heavy that it only got half way across the room.

The disturbance did not last long, for the King, knowing that cooks generally have hot tempers, had ordered the Palace Militia to be on guard outside, and all the unsuccessful candidates were soon bundled out of doors.

'In short,' said the King, finishing, 'I have pleasure in offering you the job of Palace Cook.'

'And I have pleasure in accepting it,' said Griselda, curtseying.

'As well as my hand and heart in marriage,' he pursued.

'No, thank you.'

'I beg your pardon?'

'It's very kind of you,' said Griselda, 'but I wouldn't feel inclined to marry someone just because he liked my cooking.'

'But it was a clause of the competition,' said the King, outraged.

'Never mind.'

'And then there was a prophecy about it.'

'Oh dear, another prophecy?' said Griselda, who felt that one in her life had been enough nuisance.

'It said:

> The girl who weds our king so gay and gallant
> Will be a cook of most uncommon talent.

And you can't deny that you are one, can you?'

Griselda couldn't but she did feel that 'gay and gallant' hardly described the pale anxious young creature who stood before her.

'And if you don't marry me you might leave at any time, and then what should I do about my meals?' he said miserably. 'The last cook used to make the cream sauce with *cornflour.*'

'Well, if you don't stop bothering me I certainly shall leave, right away,' said Griselda briskly, 'so run along now, out of my kitchen, or I shall never have dinner ready.' And she shooed him out.

She found that he was a terrible fusser, and always popping into the kitchen to ask if she was sure she had put enough salt in the pastry, or if the oven was hot enough. She found that she was able to manage him, however, for the threat of leaving always quietened him down at once, and things soon settled very comfortably.

But enemies were at work.

The unsuccessful candidates had banded themselves together in order to get Griselda out of favour. They lurked about the Palace in disguise, and took every opportunity of laying obstacles in the way of her work. They sprinkled weed-killer over the parsley in the gardens when they heard the King ask for parsley sauce, bought up all the rice in the kingdom if he wanted rice pudding, and substituted salt for sugar and cement for flour when Griselda's back was turned.

Griselda, however, was never at a loss. She had with her Mrs Beeton's *Palace Cookery*, and in the chapter on Cookery During Wars and Revolutions she found recipes for rice puddings without using rice, and many other equally convenient hints and suggestions which helped her to defeat the conspirators.

They soon found that their tactics were useless, and resolved upon bolder measures. They went to the witch in the nearby wood and asked her to get rid of Griselda for them – expense no object.

'Griselda,' said the witch thoughtfully, 'I wonder if that would be the baby I had to uglify about twenty years ago? What would you like me to do with her?'

'We thought you might send her to the dragon in the desert.'

'Yes, that would do very well. I seem to remember that there's some prophecy:

> When the dragon feels saddish,
> Feed him on radish

but I doubt if there's much chance of her knowing that, and it doesn't say what would happen if she did. Very well, you may take it as settled. That will be ten and six, please.'

At that very instant a black, magic cloud swept down on Griselda as she stood making a salad, and carried her into the middle of the desert where the dragon lived. She was rather annoyed, but put a good face on it, and at once began looking for an oasis.

After a couple of hours of walking through sand she came within sight of some palm trees, but was depressed to see the dragon there too, lying in the shade – a vast, green and gold monster.

'Still,' she thought, 'there's room for us both. If I don't annoy him, perhaps he won't annoy me.'

They grew most attached to each other

And walking up, she nodded to him politely, said 'Excuse me,' and took a drink at the spring. The dragon took no notice at all.

During the next three or four days, Griselda, who was a sociable creature, found that the dragon enjoyed being read aloud to. He stretched himself out comfortably with his nose on his claws, and seemed to take a lively interest in *Palace Cookery*, which was the only book she had with her. During their simple meals of dates he often looked hopefully at the book, and sometimes pushed it towards her with the tip of his tail, as if asking for more. In fact they grew most attached to each other, and Griselda often thought how she would miss him if she were rescued.

One afternoon she had been reading the chapter on 'Magic Foods, and how to deal with Culinary Spells' when she looked up to see that the dragon was crying bitterly.

'Why, dragon?' she exclaimed, 'don't take on so. Whatever is the matter?'

Feeling in her apron pocket for a knob of sugar or something to comfort him, she found a radish, left over from her last salad.

'Here,' she said, holding it out, 'chew this up – it'll make you feel better.'

Meanwhile at home the young King was having a horrible time. When Griselda vanished he hired first one, then others of the wicked conspirators, but they were such bad cooks that he discharged them all, and was finally reduced to living on eggs, which he boiled himself. His health was shattered, and the affairs of the kingdom were in frightful disorder.

He was sitting down to his egg one day, in gloom, when in walked Griselda, looking very brown.

'My goodness!' he exclaimed, jumping up. 'I *am* glad to see you. They told me you had been eaten by a dragon. Now we can have some decent meals again.'

'Well, I must say, I think you might have sent a rescue force or something,' said Griselda with spirit. 'However, as it happens it all turned out for the best. Look who's with me.'

Behind her there was a handsome young man, who came forward and said cheerfully:

'I don't expect you remember me, but I'm your elder brother.'

'Not the one that was stolen by the wicked enchanter?'

'That's right. He turned me into a dragon, and Griselda rescued me with a radish.'

'Well, that is a relief,' said the King happily. 'I was so tired of being King, you can't think. Now you can do all that, and I can live with you in the Palace and eat Griselda's wonderful food.'

'Do you mind his living with us?' asked the new King, turning to Griselda. 'By the way,' he added, 'Griselda and I are married.'

'Of course I don't mind,' said Griselda. 'I'll go and start making supper right away, and you can both come and peel the potatoes.'

So they all lived happily ever after. Griselda stayed very plain, but nobody minded.

The King Who Stood All Night

It was the evening before the Coronation. Although the November day had been cold and blowy, and an icy dust was drifting about the streets of Cuckoo City, people were everywhere. The Mayor and Corporation were clambering up and down grey walls with yards of bunting, and little boys were swinging across streets on ropes of flags. Men had set up stalls of rattles and streamers, hot meat pies were being sold by the dozen, and street sweepers had abandoned their usual job and were scattering sand across the broad square between the Palace and the Cathedral.

Cuckoo Land was not very large, and the whole population had come down to the capital for the celebrations. All day they had been streaming down from the mountains, on foot, on horseback, and in carriages, and now the lucky ones were getting ready to go to bed in inns or friends' houses, while the unlucky stood or sat patiently in the streets and parks. The leaves drifted down from the chestnut trees where cuckoos perched in May, and little boys played conkers and were chased about in the dusk by their anxious parents.

All the population? No, not quite. Far off in the mountains a tearful little boy and his father were loading up their donkey with straw hats. They were very poor, and had waited to finish the last few hats before starting, in order to sell them in Cuckoo City while they were there. But the boy was young, and though both had worked hard, the hats had taken longer than they expected; they were very late in setting out, and it was almost dark as they went down the steep hill towards the plain.

'Up on the donkey with you, Paul,' said his father. 'You must get some sleep tonight, or you'll never stay awake for the fireworks and shows tomorrow evening. I'll lead the donkey – I don't need so much sleep nowadays.'

But Paul's eyes refused to stay shut – he was too excited and too worried in case they missed their way in the dark and arrived late. So he walked on the other side of the donkey and held on to the pannier.

'Hurry, Father,' he kept saying, 'the Coronation begins at eight in the morning, remember.'

'I can't go any faster than this,' grumbled his father, 'and nor can Matilda with that great load of hats.'

Meanwhile in the Cathedral, charwomen were still scrubbing and polishing the great tiled floor, huge silk and satin draperies were being hung from galleries, and officials ran about with bits of paper and pencils, still working out where everyone was to stand, who was to come in first, and how the Dukes and Duchesses were to be given cups of hot tea if they felt faint.

In the Palace the cooks had prepared a wonderful banquet and were still icing the cake, while the Grooms of the Chamber were putting the last touches to the King's robes – flicking minute grains of dust off the ermine, blowing on the crown and polishing it, tweaking the white silk stockings to make sure they would not ladder. Fussily presiding over them was the Lord Chancellor. Every few minutes he hurried away to give the young King some last words of advice on etiquette, and then the Grooms heaved sighs of relief and stopped work for a few minutes, mopping their brows.

The new King had been brought up in the country. He was not used to Court life, and was being worn out by the Lord Chancellor's tiresome advice. When he heard the door open for the fifteenth time he sighed deeply and strolled over to the window. Pushing back the curtains, which had been drawn at least an hour before it was necessary, he looked out into the windy square.

'Just look at all those people!' he exclaimed in surprise. 'What can they be doing in the square at this time of day? There won't be anything to see till tomorrow morning.'

'Oh, they are the people who haven't been able to get

rooms,' replied the Lord Chancellor. 'They'll spend the night in the square. But what I was going to say to Your Majesty was that when you greet the ambassadors –'

'But, goodness gracious,' interrupted the King, 'you don't mean to say that they are going to stand all night in the square? Why, it's freezing!'

'They don't mind,' said the Lord Chancellor, smiling his toothy smile. 'They think it's well worth it to have a good view of the royal procession. Now, as I was saying –'

But the young King was deeply troubled.

'If they are going to stand all night in the cold just for the chance of seeing me, I think it would be only right if everyone inside the Palace stood all night too. Please send out a message to the Court.'

'Your Majesty, that would never do!' exclaimed the Lord Chancellor in horror. 'Have the whole Court stay awake all night! Think of the effect on foreign royalties and ambassadors. Why, they would be terribly offended. No, no, that would never do.'

'Perhaps you are right,' replied the King with a sigh. But when the Chancellor had given his advice and gone away, he gave orders that no one else was to be admitted to the royal presence that evening.

'At least I can do something myself,' he thought, and he dressed quickly in some plain dark clothes, and went out by an inconspicuous side entrance into the square.

At this time little Paul and his father were making good progress down the mountain path, when suddenly there was a clink of iron on stone, and the donkey began to hobble.

'Oh, father,' cried Paul in despair. 'Matilda has cast a shoe. What shall we do?'

'Don't worry,' said his father. 'We aren't far from Matthew the smith's forge. I expect he'll be gone by now, but he won't mind if we borrow his tools. Pick up any firewood you see as we go along, and we'll soon have a fire to shoe Matilda again.'

Grooms of the Chamber were putting the last touches to the King's robes

Soon they reached the forge, and little Paul ran about gathering wood while his father heated the cast shoe in the fire, and Matilda stood patiently waiting. It was not long before the shoe was nailed in position. They loaded the donkey again, and were just about to leave the shed, when they heard a loud and terrible roaring on the mountain side. Even Paul's father turned pale.

'We shall have to stay inside,' he said. 'That is a mountain lion.'

The King strolled across the dusky square to the Park railings and leaned against them, shivering a little. There was an old man selling roast chestnuts and hot pies which smelt very tempting. He put his hand in his pocket for money, and then realized that he had come without any – he was so unused to buying things for himself.

The old man saw his wistful look and chuckled.

'Have one on the house, son,' he said. 'We don't have a coronation every day.' And he gave the King a succulent pie and a generous handful of hot chestnuts.

Paul and his father huddled together in terror as the mountain lion ranged around the little forge. Only the glow of the fire prevented it from breaking down the flimsy door, and soon their stock of wood would be exhausted.

'We shall never get there in time for the procession now,' said little Paul miserably, and his father's thoughts were more gloomy still.

But just at that moment there came the trampling of many horses outside, and the lion slunk off, disappointed.

'Who's in there?' cried a voice, and there came a thunderous knock at the door.

Paul and his father stared at one another. It must be a band of robbers!

Meanwhile the King and the old pieman had fallen into conversation. It was quite dark now, and the pieman had covered up his wares with a tarpaulin, thrown a corner of it over his shoulders to keep out the frost, and lit his pipe.

'They say he's a fine young King,' he said. 'I remember his Dad's coronation, and his Grandad's before him. He was a fine old man, too. Easy and pleasant as you please, but he never let anyone bamboozle him or disobey him. They say he had all the lords and dukes and princes, too, running round as scared as a lot of schoolboys.'

The young King sighed, thinking of the Lord Chancellor. 'I wish I was like that,' he said, half to himself.

'Ah, you're young yet,' said the old man. 'But you'll learn. I don't know what trade you're in, but you'll find people anywhere are like sheep. When I was a young lad I was a shepherd, and the first time I was out with the sheep I could have sat down and cried. However many times I ran round and round the flock, I couldn't fetch them through the gate into the fold. I was getting flustered and fidgety, so I sat down and scratched my head. "Paul," I said to myself, "you're a fool", and I picked up the old bell-wether, the head of the flock, and dumped her through the gate. All the rest of them followed through, easy as pie. People are just the same – once the most important one's through the gate, you've got 'em all. You just have to know your mind.' He sniffed the air. 'Bitter tonight. Reminds me of the old days on the mountain. You'd better have a corner of this over you, lad.' And he threw another corner of waterproof sheet over the King's shoulders. Midnight was striking.

When Paul's father opened the smithy door he found that the men were not robbers after all, but a band of guards patrolling the kingdom to make sure that all was well while people were away from their homes.

'We'll give you a convoy down to the plain,' said the leader. 'You men, take them on your horses, and George, lead the donkey.'

So they went clattering down the gorge with laughter and shouting, under the paling dawn sky.

'We part here,' said the leader. 'Think of us at the celebrations. Here's something for your breakfast.' He gave them a great sausage.

Matilda was loosed, and they set off again, turning now and then to wave to the kindly soldiers.

'How far is it to the city?' asked Paul.

'Twenty miles,' said his father sighing. 'I'm afraid we won't be there till midday now. Your grandfather will be worrying about us.'

Little Paul said nothing, but as he walked manfully forward, two large tears rolled down his dusty cheeks.

As day became brighter over the Palace square, the crowd began to yawn and stretch. People brought out food and had breakfast. The old pieman, who had been telling stories about his mountain days, unpacked his wares once more, and re-lit his brazier, helped by the King. He looked keenly about the square.

'I'm expecting my son and grandson,' he said. 'They were coming down from the mountains last night. They should be here by now.' He began to tell the King about the straw hat business, and how they varied the shapes to suit the customers.

As the hands of the clock moved towards eight the crowd began to crane and peer expectantly towards the Palace gates. The King, too, gazed in the direction towards which all heads were turned.

'What are they looking for?' he asked.

The old man burst into a shout of laughter.

'Have you forgotten it's Coronation day?' he said. 'Any minute now the King will be coming out in his golden coach. Why, what's the matter, lad?' For the young man had turned towards him a face of blank dismay.

'Why, that's me! I'd forgotten all about it,' he exclaimed, and without another word he began running towards the Palace, dodging and twisting through the crowd, and leaving the old man open-mouthed.

There was a scene of terrible confusion in the Palace, as courtiers searched here and there for the King. When he arrived, puffing and panting, the Lord Chancellor turned on him reproachfully.

'Your Majesty! The Grooms have been waiting for three hours to dress you. The whole ceremony will have to be postponed till twelve. We shall never get you robed before then.'

The King looked at him miserably. All those poor people in

the square would now have to wait nearly four hours more, and it was beginning to rain. And this was all his fault.

A sudden idea came to him. 'Very well,' he said. 'If it will take another three hours to dress me – though it seems ridiculous – we must invite all the poor people to come in and have a nap in the Palace.'

The Chancellor looked as if he would burst. 'All those *common* people? Impossible!'

'I mean it,' said the King, coldly. 'Hurry up and have it proclaimed. They can sleep on the carpets, as there won't be enough beds. And tea will be served.'

The Chancellor looked at the King and suddenly collapsed. 'Very well, Your Majesty,' he said meekly, and left to give the order. Soon people began streaming into the Palace and settling gratefully to sleep in the great warm rooms, on thick, soft carpets.

The Grooms of the Chamber began to work on the King, slowly and carefully. But as they put on the silk stockings, his head nodded, and by the time he had been draped in the great velvet cloak, he was fast asleep.

When little Paul and his father arrived in the Palace square, there was not a soul in sight. The great space lay perfectly silent. Paul, who had kept up very bravely till then, began to cry.

'It's all over,' he sobbed. 'Oh, I did hope there'd be some of the carriages and flags still about. Now I'll never know what it was like.'

'We'd better go to Grandfather's house,' said his father sadly. 'He'll be wondering what's happened to us.'

But as they spoke, and were about to turn away, the old pie-seller came hurrying across the square from the Palace.

'I've been watching for you,' he said cheerfully. 'Coronation's been put off because the King's fast asleep, poor young lad, and no one could wake him. We're all having a bit of a lie-down in the Palace, and what do you think – the King's invited you and me and little Paul here to have supper with him tonight.'

All afternoon the tired-out people slept on the soft Palace carpets. Little Paul and his father slept among them, and in the evening they had supper with the King in his private apartments.

Next day the Coronation took place – and what a day that was!

The Rocking Donkey

THERE was once a little girl called Esmeralda who lived with her wicked stepmother. Her father was dead. The stepmother, who was called Mrs Mitching, was very rich, and lived in a large but hideous house in a suburb with a dusty, laurelly garden, an area, and a lot of ornamental iron fencing.

Mrs Mitching was fond of opening things, and getting things up. The things she opened were mostly hospitals, or public libraries, or new by-passes, or civic centres, and the things she got up were sales of work, and bazaars, and flag days. She was in fact a public figure, and was very little at home. When she was, she spent her time receiving callers in her fringy, ornamented drawing-room.

'How is your little girl?' they would sometimes ask. 'Is she still at home, or has she gone to boarding school?'

'Oh, she's at home,' Mrs Mitching would reply, 'but she has her own play-room you know, so that we needn't disturb one another. I don't believe in grown-ups bothering children all the time, do you?'

Mrs Mitching could not afford school for Esmeralda, as she needed all her wealth for opening and getting up. She always took Esmeralda along to the openings, in a white muslin dress, painfully starched at the neck and wrists, because people liked to see a child on the platform. But for the rest of the time Esmeralda had to manage in her old brown dress, much too short now, and a torn pair of gym shoes. She had her meals in the kitchen, and they were horrible – bread and margarine, boiled fish and prunes.

But the most melancholy part of Esmeralda's life was that she had nothing to do. The play-room which Mrs Mitching spoke of was a large dark basement room, shadowed by the laurels which overhung the area. There was nothing in it at all, not even a chair. No one ever came into it, and it would have been thick with dust had not Esmeralda, who was a tidy creature, once a week borrowed a broom from the housemaid's cupboard and swept it. She had no toys. Once Mr Snye, the man who came to cut the laurels, had given her a length of garden twine, and she used this as a skipping rope, to keep herself warm. She became a very good skipper, and could polka, double-through, swing the rope, and other fancy variations, while if she felt inclined to do plain skipping she could go on almost all day without a fault.

There were no books to read in the house, and she was not encouraged to go into Mrs Mitching's rooms or outside, because of her shabby clothes, though she sometimes took a stroll at dusk.

One day Mrs Mitching was to open a jumble sale. She was being driven to it by the Mayor in his Rolls Royce, so she told Hooper, the housemaid, to bring Esmeralda by bus, dressed in her white muslin, and meet her at the Hall. Then she went off to keep an appointment.

'Drat,' said Hooper. 'Now what am I to do? Your muslin's still at the laundry from last week.'

'I'll have to go as I am,' said Esmeralda, who quite liked openings. At least they made a change from wandering about in the basement.

'I don't know what Madam'll say,' said Hooper doubtfully, 'but I should catch it if I didn't take you, sure enough.' So they went as they were, Esmeralda in her old brown dress and shoes.

When Mrs Mitching saw them she gave a cry of dismay.

'I can't let you be seen like that! You must go home at once,' and she hurriedly left them, before anyone should connect her with the shabby child.

Hooper had set her heart on a violet satin pincushion she noticed on one of the stalls, so she pushed Esmeralda into a corner, and said, 'You wait there, I shan't be a moment. It won't matter, no one will know who you are.'

Esmeralda stood looking quietly about her. An elderly gentleman, Lord Mauling, making his way to the platform, noticed what seemed to him a forlorn-looking little creature, and stopping by her he took a coin from his pocket and said: 'Here, my dear. Buy yourself a pretty toy.'

Esmeralda gave him a startled look as he went on his way, and then stared at the coin she held in her hand. It was a shilling. She had never had any money before and was quite puzzled to know what she should buy with it. Almost without realizing what she was doing she began to wander along the stalls, looking at the different things offered for sale. There were books, clothes, bottles of scent, flowers – all the things she saw seemed beautiful, but she could not imagine buying any of them. Then she came to the toy counter. Toys! She had never had one. The only time she ever touched a toy was sometimes when Mrs Mitching opened a children's ward at a hospital, and she would present a ceremonial teddy-bear to a little patient. She gazed at dolls, puzzles, engines, without noticing that most of them were shabby and second-hand. Then at the end of the counter she saw what she wanted; there was no hesitation in her mind, she knew at once.

It was a rocking donkey – grey, battered, weather-beaten, with draggling ears and tangled tail. On the side of his rockers his name was painted – 'Prince' – it hardly seemed the name for someone so ancient and worn. And the price ticket pinned to his tail said '1/-'.

'I'd like the donkey, please,' said Esmeralda timidly to the lady at the stall, holding out her coin. The lady glanced from the coin to the ticket and said, 'Good gracious. Can this really be going for only a shilling? Surely they mean ten? Mr Prothero,' she called to a gentleman further down the room, but he was busy and did not hear.

'Oh well,' she said to Esmeralda. 'You take it. You won't often get a bargain like that, I can tell you.' She took the coin, and lifted the donkey down on to the floor.

'How will you get him home?' she asked.

'I don't know,' said Esmeralda. She was lucky though. As she stood hesitating with her hand on Prince's bridle, someone familiar stopped beside her. It was Mr Snye, the man who cut the hedges.

'You bought that donkey?' he said. 'Well I'm blest. That'll be a bit of fun for you, I reckon. Like me to take it home for you in the van? I've got it outside – been bringing some flowers along for the platform.'

'Oh, thank you,' Esmeralda said. So he shouldered Prince, nodded to her and said, 'I'll be home before you are, like as not. I'll just leave him in the shrubbery for you.'

Esmeralda went to find Hooper, who had bought her pin-cushion, and they caught their bus home.

As soon as dusk fell, and no one was about, she slipped up the back steps and half dragged, half carried Prince from his hiding-place down through the basement passage to her play-room. She put him in the middle of the floor, and sat down beside him.

It was a strange moment. For as long as she could remember she had had no company at all, nothing to play with, and now here, all of a sudden, was a friend. She felt sure of that. She put an arm over his cold smooth neck, and he rocked down and gently touched the top of her head with his nose.

'Prince,' she said quietly, and almost wondered if he would reply, but he was silent. She combed out his tangled mane and tail, and sat with him until the room was quite dark and it was time to put herself to bed.

As she went to her tiny room upstairs it occurred to her that he might be cold, alone in that dark basement. She took one of the two blankets off her bed, slipped down again in her nightdress, and tucked it over him. Back in bed she tried to settle, but could not; it was a chilly night and one blanket was not enough to keep her warm. Also she could not help wondering if Prince felt lonely and perhaps homesick for wherever he had come from? So presently she was tiptoeing back to the play-room with the other blanket. She made a sort of nest for the two of them, and slept all night on the floor, curled up between his front rockers, so that if she wanted company, all she had to do was reach up and pull on a rein, to bring down his cold friendly nose against her cheek.

She was never lonely again. She never rode on Prince – she felt that would be almost an impertinence with someone who was so much a friend, and who moreoever looked so weary and battered. But she would set him off rocking while she skipped, so that they seemed to be keeping each other company, and she talked to him all the time, while he nodded intelligently in reply. And every night she crept down with her two blankets and slept curled up between his feet.

One day Mrs Mitching decided to give a whist-drive in her house for the wives of chimney sweeps, and it occurred to her that the basement play-room would be just the right size for the purpose. She went along to inspect it, and found Esmeralda having her weekly clean-out with brush and dustpan.

'That's right, that's right,' she said absently, glancing about. 'But what is this? A rocking horse?' Esmeralda stood mute.

'Do you not think you are a little old for such toys? Yes, yes, I think it had better be given away to some poor child. It is the duty of children who live in rich houses, such as you, Esmeralda, to give away your old toys to the little slum children who have nothing. It can be taken away when the van for the Bombed Families calls here tomorrow morning. But you must certainly clean it up a little first. You should be quite ashamed to pass on such a shabby old toy without doing your best to improve its appearance. After all, you know, it may gladden some poor little life in Stepney or Bethnal Green. So give it a good scrub this evening. Now what was I doing? Ah yes, seventeen feet by sixteen, ten tables – let me see – '

Esmeralda passed the rest of the day in a sort of numbness. After tea she took some sugar-soap and a scrubbing brush from the housemaid's cupboard and started to scrub Prince.

'Well,' she thought, 'perhaps I didn't *deserve* to be so happy. I never thought of scrubbing him. Perhaps someone else will take better care of him. But oh, what shall I do, what shall I do?'

She scrubbed and scrubbed, and as the shabby grey peeled away, a silvery gleam began to show along Prince's back and sides, and his mane and tail shone like floss. By the time she had finished it was quite dark, and a long ray of moonlight, striking across the floor, caught his head and for a moment dazzled her eyes.

For the last time she went up, fetched her blankets, and settled herself beside him. Just before she fell asleep it seemed to her that his nose came down and lightly touched her wet cheek.

Next day Esmeralda hid herself. She did not want to see Prince taken away. Mrs Mitching superintended his removal.

'Good gracious,' she said, when she saw him shining in the sun. 'That is far too valuable to be taken to Stepney. I shall give it to the museum.' So the Bombed Families van dropped Prince off at the museum before going on to Stepney.

All day Esmeralda avoided the basement play-room. She felt that she could not bear to look at the empty patch in the middle of the floor.

In the evening Hooper felt sorry for her, she seemed so restless and moping, and took her out for a stroll. They went to the museum, where Hooper liked to look at the models of fashions through the ages. While she was studying crinolines and bustles Esmeralda wandered off, and soon, round a corner she came on Prince, railed off from the public with a red cord, and a notice beside him which read: 'Donated by the Hon. Mrs Mitching, November 19 –.'

Esmeralda stretched out her hand, but she could not quite touch him over the cord.

'Now, Miss,' said an attendant. 'No touching the exhibits, please.' So she looked and looked at him until Hooper said it was time to go home.

Every day after that she went to the museum and looked at Prince, and Hooper said to Cook, 'That child doesn't look well.' Mrs Mitching was away from home a good deal, organizing the grand opening of a new welfare centre and clinic, so she did not notice Esmeralda's paleness, or her constant visits to the museum.

One night something woke Esmeralda. It was a long finger of moonlight which lay lightly across her closed eyes. She got up quietly and put on her old brown dress and thin shoes. It was easy to steal out of that large house without anyone hearing, and once outside she slipped along the empty streets like a shadow. When she reached the museum she went at once, as if someone had called her, to a little door at one side. Someone had left it unlocked, and she opened it softly and went into the thick dark.

The museum was a familiar place by now, and she went confidently forward along a passage, and presently came out into the main hall. It did not take her long to find Prince, for there he was, shining like silver in the moonlight. She walked forward, stepped over the rope, and put her hand on his neck.

'Esmeralda,' he said. His voice was like a faint, silvery wind.

'You never spoke to me before.'

'How could I? I was choked with grey paint.'

'Oh,' she cried, 'I'm so terribly lonely without you. What shall I do?'

'You never rode on me,' he said.

'I didn't like to. You were so old and tired, it would have seemed like taking a liberty.'

'Ride on me now.'

Timidly she put her foot into the stirrup and swung herself on to his back.

'Settle yourself in the saddle and hold tight. Are you all right?'

'Yes,' she said.

Like a feather in the wind they went rocking up the ray of moonlight and passed through the high window as if it had been mist. Neither of them was ever seen again.

The Lobster's Birthday

EARLY one fine summer morning, two persons might have been seen making their way somewhat furtively across the fields from the village of Tillingham to Slugdale Halt. Every now and then they glanced cautiously behind them as if they almost expected to be pursued and taken back. Their names were Gloria and Harold. Gloria was a lobster. It was her birthday, and she had persuaded Harold, who was a horse and an acquaintance of hers, to take her into Brighton for the day. The difficulty was that their employer did not approve of days off; he never took one himself, and did not see why other people had to go gadding away, spending money, when they might just as well have stayed quietly at home and behaved themselves. Consequently Gloria and Harold had to leave very early, as they had gone without permission, and were still afraid that Mr Higgs might see them from some window as he stood drinking his early morning tea.

When they reached the station, which was in a cutting, Harold heaved a sigh of relief.

'Thank goodness we can have a bit of a breather,' he said. 'Mr Higgs can't see us here.' He sat down on the station seat, which sagged under his weight. Gloria seated herself primly beside him. She carried a large wicker basket, and wore a festive spotted scarf.

'Dear me, I'm ever so warm. The weather is quite oppressive, isn't it,' she said. Then she looked reprovingly at her companion and exclaimed 'Harold! Put your shoes back on. What will people think of you! I declare I'm quite ashamed of you.'

'All very well to talk,' mumbled Harold. 'You made me wear these confounded shoes. Knew they'd be too tight in this weather.'

However, Gloria insisted that he must put them on again, and he finally did so with many protests, and hobbled off to buy two cheap day returns to Brighton.

At length the little train came in sight, and Gloria immediately began to fuss, running up and down the platform, retieing her veil, rearranging everything in her basket and clamouring that she had lost her gloves, while Harold stood expressionlessly in one spot and tried to look as if she had nothing to do with him. When the train stopped she cried: 'Oh, Harold, we must find a non-smoker. You know I can't stand cigarette smoke.' Without saying a word, Harold opened the nearest door and pushed her in. She subsided in a heap on the seat with her things all round her. Harold slumped down in the opposite seat and at once pulled a paper from under his arm and became absorbed in the racing news.

When Gloria had collected herself a little she began to chatter. 'Harold, do you think we could have the window down a little? This smoke gets in my eyes terribly. Do you think these people would mind?'

There were two other people in the compartment, a man and a woman, who both had their eyes shut. However, the man murmured 'Not a bit, go ahead', without opening his eyes, so Harold opened the window a few inches.

'Now I think when we get there, I'll go right away and buy my new hat,' Gloria went on. 'What sort of a hat would you like me to have, Harold?'

'Don't mind a bit,' said Harold, his nose in the paper.

'I like a nice *fancy* hat,' said Gloria happily. 'Not too big, you know, but striking. What they call flair, a hat's got to have, if it's going to suit me. Mrs Ellis was telling me about a place right on the front, called *Natty Hats*, it is. I thought I might go there first.'

'All right,' said Harold, 'but I'm not going in one of those places. I should feel a fool. I'll go and have my hair cut while you get yourself suited.'

The woman asleep at the other end of the compartment, who had stirred a little at the mention of hats, now opened her eyes and let out a shriek.

'Percival!' she exclaimed. 'Pull the communication cord at once. There's a horse in the carriage!' Then she saw Gloria and screamed again.

'Pray calm yourself, Madam,' said the horse patiently. 'I am quite harmless, I assure you.'

But the woman kept exclaiming, and would have pulled the cord herself if her husband had not stopped her.

'Don't make a fool of yourself, Minnie,' he said crossly. 'Bad enough to have to travel with horses and riff-raff without becoming a laughing-stock. Sit down, do, for heaven's sake.'

'I shall write to *The Times*,' his wife kept protesting. 'They ought at least to have No Horses carriages. As for lobsters, there ought to be a law against their travelling in trains. Pushing in where they're not wanted. What business have lobsters in trains?'

Gloria gave her a spiteful look. 'Some people seem to think they own the whole railway,' she said to Harold. 'They might like to know that other people, who have quite as much right to travel, only want to keep themselves to themselves, and wouldn't demean themselves by intruding.'

Harold looked anxiously at the woman. 'Madam,' he began.

'Don't speak to me,' said the woman vigorously. '*Don't* speak to me or I shall scream, I know I shall.'

'But madam,' Harold began again.

'Percival, *will* you tell this person not to molest me. If you utter a single word more to me I shall have you given in charge the moment we get to Brighton.'

The horse shrugged his shoulders and settled back to his paper. Gloria drew herself up coldly, and looked out of the window. The woman gave them a baleful glare, while her husband tried to dissociate himself from the whole affair.

Twenty minutes later the train arrived in Brighton. During the whole of this time the woman had kept Harold and Gloria under constant observation, as if she expected one of them to throw a bomb the minute her back was turned.

When she stood up to collect her things together she let out a cry of horror. 'Percival! My knitting! The wool has fallen out of the window.'

'That is what I have been trying to tell you, madam,' said Harold calmly. 'It fell out at Bishopsvalley Halt, fifteen minutes ago.'

As Harold and Gloria left the platform they looked back and saw her standing at the very furthest extremity, furiously winding, while ten miles of wool came slowly towards her.

They took a bus down to the front, and Gloria went at once into *Natty Hats*.

'And hurry up,' Harold called after her. 'I want a cuppa. I didn't have my tea this morning on account of you and your blessed treat.' Gloria ignored him and walked haughtily through the door. Madame Arlene at once glided forward to serve her.

'Mademoiselle required a hat?'

'Something nice and fancy,' said Gloria, her eye roaming greedily round the display stands.

'But Mademoiselle is rather short and has – ahem – rather a *bright* complexion. Would not something more simple – we have here a black velvet beret with diamond clip, price fifteen guineas?'

'Now, now,' said Gloria, 'none of your taste for me, thanks. I want something nice and bright, with feathers.' Madame Arlene brought out several other hats, but none of them seemed quite what she wanted, and she was presently aware of Harold, looking very cross, strolling up and down outside. He had had his hair cut and looked very military.

'Oh well, I'll leave it, thanks ever so,' said Gloria, and scuttled out. 'No need to make me conspicuous,' she scolded Harold. 'You could have waited a bit further along, couldn't you?'

When they had had a cup of tea, however, sitting in deck-chairs, good humour was restored, and Harold suggested that they should go on the pier before Gloria looked at any more hats. So they paid their money and clicked through the turn-stile.

Gloria had her fortune told by the Seer from the East – Put One Penny in and Learn the Secrets of the Stars. She put in a penny and pulled out a piece of paper which said, 'You will be your own fate today'. Stupid things they tell you, don't they,' she said, tossing it into the sea. Then she suddenly squealed 'Oo! Look, Harold! Over there!'

She was pointing to the display stand of a shooting gallery. Among the prizes offered were some feather dusters, with red handles and gay red-and-purple feathers.

'Just what I want for my hat! They might have been made for me. Oh, do have a go and win one of them, Harold,' she urged him. Harold rather unwillingly went over to the booth.

'Eight shots for half a crown,' said the man, looking at him suspiciously. 'Never heard of a horse shooting before.'

'I don't suppose you often see horses on the pier at all,' Harold replied coldly. 'I'll have eight shots please. How many bullseyes to win a prize?'

Three, the man told him. Gloria was teetering about behind him in such a state of excitement that he made her go away – he said the sound of her claws on the iron treads made him nervous. So she went and stood round the corner clutching her basket feverishly. As a matter of fact, Harold had never shot before, but he often took part in a game of darts, and he was very anxious not to let Gloria down, so he aimed with great care.

'Eight bulls,' said the proprietor. 'Blimey! On the halls, are yer? What'll you have for your prizes?'

'I'd like two of those dusters, please.'

'Better make it three for luck,' said the man cordially. 'Any time you want to give a display, just let me know and I'll fix it up for you.'

Harold took Gloria the trophies and she squeaked with pleasure. 'Three! Harold, you are a dear!' She was about to embrace him, but he backed cautiously away. She stuck the feathers on her head and rushed off to find a mirror and admire herself.

After this they began to feel hungry and found a sheltered seat where they could eat their sandwiches – grass for Harold and mayonnaise for Gloria. Then Harold wanted to sleep,

Gloria sat bolt upright, giving little cries of pleasure

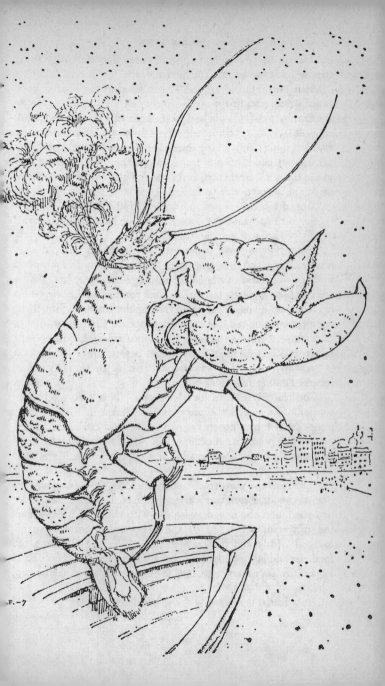

F.-7

but Gloria began to fidget and suggested they should go for a trip in the *Skylark* to see the Seven Sisters.

'All right,' Harold agreed. 'I can sleep in the boat as well as anywhere else, I suppose.'

Off they went. Gloria had never been in a boat before, and sat bolt upright, giving little cries of pleasure and excitement at everything, and taking care that everyone could see and admire her beautiful plumes. Alas! As they went further out to sea the wind freshened, and a sudden gust whisked all three off her head and overboard.

'Stop the boat!' shrieked Gloria. 'My hat!'

'Sorry, miss,' said the owner. 'Should have fastened it on better. No hope of getting it now.'

'Harold!' she cried in despair. 'My hat!' But Harold was nearly asleep, and only grumbled 'Expect me to dive after it? Did you ever hear of a horse swimming?'

Poor Gloria took a last frantic look round and then dived in herself. She managed to seize two of the feathers, and then the propeller of the *Skylark* struck her on the head and she knew no more. Harold had fallen into a blissful doze, and never noticed that she was no longer beside him.

Presently a girl who was swimming near the shore espied a lobster floating near her.

'Coo! Here's a bit of luck,' she said. 'This'll do nicely for supper.' She towed the unconscious Gloria in to land and popped her into a beach bag with some sun-tan lotion, dark glasses and peppermint creams. 'I'll just get my things on and pop into Arlene's, and then I'll be stepping home. Mum will be pleased.'

As soon as she was dressed, she went into *Natty Hats*, where one of the assistants was a friend of hers. Business was slack just then, and she began gossiping with this girl. Meanwhile the powerful fragrance of the peppermint creams partly revived Gloria and she crawled out of the bag in search of fresh air and lay weakly down on a large straw cartwheel hat. By and by a woman came into the shop and began trying on hats.

'How much is the straw?' she inquired.

'Five guineas, madam,' said the assistant, without turning round.

'Very well, I'll take it. You needn't bother to wrap it, I'll wear it. Rather attractive and original, don't you think, Percival?' she said, turning to her husband. He merely shuddered, but she took no notice and put down five guineas on the cash desk. Then she and her husband left the shop and began strolling along the front.

Meanwhile the *Skylark* had put back to shore, and its owner woke up Harold, who stumbled up the beach in a dazed condition, without noticing that his companion was not there. He walked along the front, and soon noticed a commotion ahead of him. The warm sunshine was reviving Gloria, and she began waving her claws about and putting herself to rights before she became aware that she was on a moving platform. People gazed admiringly at this remarkable hat ornamented with a live lobster, and soon a small crowd was following, while the woman who had bought it still walked underneath quite unconscious of what was happening.

Harold saw them coming towards him, and his eyes bulged. 'Gloria!' he said. 'What are you doing up there?'

'Oh!' shrieked the woman. 'It's that horse again. Take it away. Everywhere I go today it's nothing but horses, horses.'

'But, madam,' said Harold, always polite, 'you have my partner on your hat. If you will excuse me one moment, I will assist her to alight.'

'Harold, where am I?' said Gloria faintly.

'Do you mean there is a real lobster on this hat?' cried the woman underneath. 'This is a gross swindle. I paid five guineas for it. I shall take it back to the shop and complain.'

At this moment the representative of the *Brighton Guardian* arrived.

'Please stand still for a moment while I take some pictures,' he begged them. 'This will be quite a sensation. Dashing Dowager Displays Live Lobster on Hat. May I congratulate you, madam. You are the fortunate winner of our Original Headgear Competition. Your prize is a Rolls Royce and a free pass to the Magnificent Cinema every night for the next five years. May I ask where you obtained this novel creation?'

Much mollified by this news, the woman told him that she had bought it at *Natty Hats*.

'This will mean a boom for Arlene,' said the reporter. 'Why, here she comes now.' In fact Arlene, her assistant, and the assistant's friend were hastening along the front, having just discovered that the lobster had been stolen.

'Good afternoon,' the reporter greeted them. 'You will be pleased to learn that your creation here has just won the Original Headgear Prize. Can you tell me if you have any other ideas in the same line – a salad hat, perhaps, or a calves' foot toque?'

While the explanations were going on, Gloria beckoned to Harold.

'Do you think you could lift me down,' she whispered weakly. 'I feel a little faint.'

He did so quietly, without anyone noticing. 'Let's get out of here while they're all talking,' he muttered. 'It's nearly time for our train, and Mr Higgs won't like it at all if we get our names in the papers.' Gloria nodded, and he cantered off up a side street, carrying her on his back. By the time their absence was noticed they were well away. Madame Arlene offered to replace the bare straw hat by another, and everyone parted happily, except the girl who had hoped to have lobster for supper.

Gloria and Harold stopped to have a refreshing cup of tea on their way to the station, and after all only just caught their train. They flung themselves into the last carriage, and only realized after the train had started that they were again in the same compartment with Percival and his wife. She was now wearing a very gorgeous hat, covered with red bouncing cherries.

She gave Gloria and Harold a haughty look and then decided to ignore them. Harold was feeling tired and longing to be back at home and to go quietly to bed. Gloria was still a little faint after her experiences, and insisted on leaning out of the window, in spite of the notice warning her not to.

'You know I can't stand the cigarette smoke,' she said reproachfully.

When they were nearing Slugdale Halt she took out her pocket mirror to adjust her red feathers.

'Oh! They've gone!' she cried in dismay. 'Where are my beautiful feathers?'

'They fell off at Bishopsvalley Halt fifteen minutes ago,' said Percival's wife acidly. Gloria shed a few tears, and then cheered up.

'Oh well, I suppose I was fated not to have them,' she said philosophically. 'It looks that way. And anyway, who ever heard of a lobster wearing a hat?'

She gave Percival and his wife a dazzling smile, and let Harold help her out of the train. They strolled off across the fields towards Tillingham Village and the Horse and Lobster Inn.

The Wolves and the Mermaids

THERE was once an old Doctor, who lived alone with his cat Jupiter in the village of Ware-on-the-Cliff. There were only a few cottages, set in a gap overhanging the sea, and the Doctor's house was on the very cliff-edge. It was old and square, very large, and behind it lay a walled garden, protected from the furious sea-winds. In the garden there were long walks and borders, yew-hedges, a trellis covered with roses, and many fruit trees, but the curious thing was that all the trees were bare, the shrubs were leafless, and winter and summer alike not a plant or a flower grew out of the ground.

It had not always been so. When the Doctor was younger, his son Paul lived with him in the house. The son had learned to be a doctor, too, but as there was no need for a pair of them in so wild a part, he earned his living by driving the bus which ran twice a day, morning and night, to the village of Ware-in-the-Woods. It was a long winding road between the two villages, more than a day's walk, and Paul was greatly blessed when he began driving his bus, for besides this the way was very dangerous. Before the bus began to run, many a man had started out to walk it, and had never been seen or heard of again. This was on account of the wolves and the mermaids.

At first the road curved out along the coast, to avoid the great bare hill which rose behind Ware-on-the-Cliff, and all the way beside this coastal road were the waters where the mermaids sang and combed their hair and enticed travellers down into the sucking waves. Then the road turned inland and ran through a great forest which reached in all directions beyond anyone's knowledge. The forest was inhabited by myriads of wolves, so swift and fierce that if they scented a man he was doomed. But swift as they were, they could not overtake the bus, and loud though the mermaids sang, the roar of its engine was louder still, and so the people were able to travel from one village to the other in safety, and to go shopping and visit their relatives – a thing only the bravest had attempted before. As for Paul, he was indifferent to both the wolves and the mermaids, for he carried a charm, a magic silver watch-chain which would protect him from either beasts or men. Indeed, if the bus happened to be empty, he would often stop in the middle of the forest, and climb down from his cab, and go off hunting for rare plants and flowers among the trees. The wolves took no notice of him, and nobody minded if the bus was an hour late, for they knew that the plants he found were given to his father, who used them in the compounding of many healing ointments and drugs. Besides these he brought home beautiful wild plants which he set in the garden, for he was a skilled gardener and when he was not driving he spent much of the time there, digging, raking and pruning. The flowers and fruits he grew were larger and more beautiful than any others in the two villages.

They were very happy living together, the father and son. They needed little, for the people whom the Doctor cured mostly paid him in kind, a cake, a platterful of mackerel, or a dozen eggs, and this, with the vegetables that Paul grew in his garden, was enough for their wants. Old Jupiter would sometimes sit on the end of the pier which sheltered the fishermen's boats and scoop up a fine lobster or a crab, or bring them in a fat rabbit from the down. In the mornings when the Doctor was off on his rounds, Paul would come back from his first trip of the day and tidy up the house and make their midday meal. Then in the evenings, after the surgery which the Doctor held in their kitchen, he went off for his evening trip, and his father would lean from the front door to shout:

'Don't be late now. Sausages for supper!' and Paul, high in his cab, would wave and nod his head reassuringly.

But one evening, as the Doctor looked out to wave good-bye, he noticed that the end of Paul's chain was loose. He called out 'Mind your chain!' but his voice was drowned by the roar of the engine starting, and Paul did not hear him. It was winter, and dusk was falling. The lights of the bus were on, but there were no passengers inside, and the Doctor could see the rows of empty seats as the bus swung away up the cliff road. It was the last time he saw his son. Whether the wolves caught him or the mermaids enticed him into the sea, nobody knew, for the bus did not come back. And from that day the garden, which had been Paul's pride, began to wither and die away, the plants faded and then rotted into the earth, and the trees dropped their leaves and grew no more.

The people in the village were very kind to the Doctor, bringing him gifts and trying to stop him grieving. He went on working even harder than before, and became more and more skilful at healing people's illnesses and wounds until he was spoken of with wonder in both villages. A sum of money was collected and a new bus was bought. The Doctor drove it himself, for he felt so old and sad that he did not greatly care if the wolves or the mermaids caught him. If they ran or swam beside the bus he noticed them little more than flies.

But one evening when he was washing his hands after his surgery, before taking the bus out on the late journey, he felt a nudging and a pushing against his leg, and turning round was surprised to see a large grey wolf, who caught the Doctor's sleeve in his teeth and began to drag him towards the door. The Doctor was more puzzled than afraid, and he called to old Jupiter, the black cat. Since Paul's disappearance, the Doctor and Jupiter had grown very close together and could understand each other very well.

He said now: 'Ask him what he wants, Jupiter.'

The wolf began to explain something in a pleading whine, scratching impatiently on the ground with his paw. At the end he again caught hold of the Doctor's sleeve and tried to pull him out of the house.

'What does he mean?'

Jupiter explained to the Doctor, by means of the sign language which they used, that the wolf wanted him to come to the aid of a friend who lay sick or wounded somewhere in the forest.

'Very well, tell him I'll come, but he must wait a moment while I get my bag.'

When he was ready he went out and climbed into the cab of the bus, indicating to the wolf that he should travel inside. This the wolf was not very anxious to do, and only went in with many nervous starts. When the bus began to move he growled fiercely, but luckily there were no other passengers. The Doctor took Jupiter with him as well, in case he needed an interpreter.

When they reached the middle of the forest the wolf tapped on the glass panel which separated him from the Doctor, and made signs to him to stop. They got out, the Doctor carrying Jupiter and his black bag, and the wolf plunged off the road and led them a long way until they reached a dense thicket of thorn and hazel. Here they found another wolf lying, desperately hurt, with more than a dozen wounds on his head, back and sides.

'You've been fighting,' the Doctor said severely, just as he did when Jupiter came in with a torn ear. The wolf, which was very weak, raised its head a little and then let it drop again; then the Doctor quickly went to work, stitching some of the worst wounds, bandaging others, and applying his healing ointment.

'There,' he said at length. 'He'll be all right now. Make him understand that he's not to move for three days, and I'll come back then and have another look at him.' Jupiter explained this with many lashing of his tail and whiskers. The guide wolf, which had meanwhile been sitting and watching attentively, now rose and licked the Doctor's hand. Then he led them back to the bus, waited till it had started, and trotted back into the undergrowth again.

From this time on the Doctor was quite often called in by the wolves. He learned that if two wolves fight, it is customary, if one becomes exhausted, for him to lie down on the ground and expose his defenceless throat to the conqueror. When he has thus acknowledged defeat he is spared by the winning wolf, and is allowed to get up and run away. It became usual in these cases, if the defeated wolf was badly wounded, for the victor to gallop off and fetch the Doctor, who soon began to have a large practice among the wolves. As they had nothing to pay him with, he taught them to know the herbs and wild flowers he used, and then they found the places where these grew and took him there.

One moonlit night the Doctor was driving slowly back through the forest from Ware-in-the-Woods, when there appeared on the road in front of the bus a wolf larger than any he had seen before. He pulled up, and as usual was led into the trees by the wolf, which every now and then glanced over its shoulder to make sure he was following. Each time this happened, he thought he saw a sort of gleam on its throat as if there was a white patch there, but he was not near enough to see it clearly, in that uncertain light. He found his patient, when they reached the hiding place, surrounded by a ring of wolves. They all stood up and bowed their heads when the Doctor and his guide approached, making him realize that the large wolf must be the king of them all, who had nobly deigned to bring the Doctor to a rival vanquished in combat.

The beaten wolf was very severely wounded, and it took the Doctor a long time to make him comfortable. When he raised his head at last all the other wolves were gone; only the King remained to lead him back to the bus. The Doctor was able to look at him closely for the first time, and then saw what he had mistaken for a gleam of white fur on the wolf's neck. It was Paul's silver chain.

For a moment he was struck dumb, and then pointing at it he stammered:

'Where did you get that?'

The wolf did not understand, but Jupiter, who had accompanied the Doctor, as he was now in the habit of doing, interpreted. The wolf made some explanation, which involved much waving of his tail and gesturing with his paw, and Jupiter explained that he had found it on the seashore, many months before, twined about a great shell.

'Since it is yours, you must have it back,' the King-wolf said, and lowered his stately head so that the Doctor could remove the chain. He held it for a long time in his hands, looking at it as if he thought it could tell him where his son was. It seemed to him that this story must mean that Paul had been ensnared by the mermaids, and perhaps was not dead, but at this moment captive in some fastness under the sea.

From this time he began to feel a little spark of hope. He did not know how Paul might be saved, but he felt that somehow, perhaps it could yet be done. And the day after the king of the wolves had restored the chain, when he went into the garden, he found that on one rose tree a tiny bud had sprouted.

Some weeks later there had been fewer patients than usual at his evening surgery, and he had a little time before it was necessary to start the bus for the late trip. He went down and walked on the beach looking out to sea through the spring dusk.

Something moving on the breakwater caught his eye as he strolled, and he turned and climbed the stone steps to see what it was. He found an albatross which had hurt its wing, and lay weak from lack of food, sheltered by the low wall. He took it back to his house to set the broken bones, and fed it with some of the fish which Jupiter had caught for his supper. Then, locking it in his bedroom for fear of the cat, he set out on his evening journey.

The albatross stayed with him for several days, until he judged that the wing was fully recovered. On the fifth day it was as strong as ever, and he took it to the end of the pier and let it loose. It circled round him once and then flew straight out to sea.

That night, as he sat at his lonely supper, he heard a tap at the window. It was a gentle tap, but it turned him cold with fear, though he had thought he was no longer afraid of anything. He slowly crossed the room, raised the casement, and looked out, into the greenest and clearest eyes he had ever seen. They were set slanting in a white face, which rested on two long-fingered white hands.

His heart beat quickly and softly. 'What do you want?' he said.

'You must help me.' Her voice was like the soft, mournful

whisper of the tide when the sea is far out, almost out of sight across the sand.

'If I can.'

'You healed my albatross,' she said, 'so perhaps you can heal me.'

He turned automatically across the dark room to find his black bag, and saw Jupiter in a corner, stiff with fear, every hair on end. Picking up the bag, he came back to face her again.

'What is your trouble?' he asked.

'A broken heart.'

'Ah,' said the Doctor sadly, 'if I could mend that, I should have mended my own. Nothing can cure a broken heart, my friend, except the person who broke it.'

'But he never will,' she answered, 'for he hates me. Day after day I sing to him, I bring him the rarest treasures of the sea, but he sits grieving for his father and his lost garden, and never listens to me or looks at me.'

The Doctor's heart gave a great throb at this, but he only answered gently:

'There is no cure for you my friend. I cannot help you.'

She sighed – a long sigh like the breaking of a wave on a windless day.

'Yet you healed my albatross,' she said presently, 'and I must repay you for that. What reward do you ask?'

'May I ask for anything?'

She bent her head in reply.

'Then give me back my son.'

For the last time her sad green eyes looked into his, and then she turned and beckoned him to follow her. They went down the winding cliff steps to the shore, and there the Doctor untied and dragged down his little boat, beached for many months. She waited for him by the water's edge, and then turned and swam straight out to sea, while he rowed slowly after her into the dark.

It seemed to him that they went on for hours, until his arms

And in the cab, imprisoned, tied with a rope of seaweed –

and back were so tired that he could no longer feel them. But presently as he glanced from time to time over his shoulder, he thought that he could see a shadowy light glimmering through the water, and this became brighter and closer, until at length he could look down and see the whole ocean floor illuminated below him. There, fathoms down, was the bus, encrusted now with pearl, covered with waving plants and coralline growths of every colour. And in the cab, imprisoned, tied with a rope of seaweed – was it?

'Paul!' he called, and the sound of his voice set off the ripples, shimmering away from the boat in every direction. His guide had dived down and now with a stroke of her shell-knife set Paul free from his bonds. The Doctor leaned over the side of the boat and stretched down his hand to take his son's.

'Paul!'

'Father!'

The Doctor turned the boat towards the shore.

'Let me row,' said Paul, 'you're tired.' They moved slowly away into the darkness again, heading for the coast. All the way they were accompanied by the sweetest, most sorrowful singing that the Doctor had ever heard, until it gradually died away out to sea, and the lights of the village began to show on the cliff.

'Nearly home, my son,' said the Doctor. 'And it's sausages for supper.'

For
Storm, the Head Hen, dear Blackie,
and all animals and friends
in Suffolk

More Than You Bargained For

ONCE there was a little girl called Ermine Miggs, who lived with her mother in a flat in Southampton Row. Her real name was Erminetrude, but that was too long for anyone to pronounce. Her mother went out to work ever day except Sundays, but Ermine was not strong, so she did not go to school. In the winter she sat in the big front room by the warm, popping gas fire and read and read and read. In the summer she used to wander along Theobalds Road, Lambs Conduit Street, Great Ormond Street and the Gray's Inn Road, or sit in Russell Square or Lincoln's Inn Fields.

They were very poor – the furniture in the flat consisted of a tin box, a home-made table, a stool and a bed, and they had painted the floor green to do for a carpet, but they were happy; they had enough to eat, the gas fire to sit by, hot water for baths, and the sun shone into their window; moreover there was a fig tree across the street in a bit of garden behind a wall, and in the summer Ermine used to drag the bed up to the window and lie there looking at it. Their greatest treasure was an old gramophone and half a dozen records which they played again and again; Mrs Miggs when she was ironing or mending and Ermine when she was by herself in the flat and feeling lonely. The only thing she did long for was a cat to keep her company, but Mrs Miggs said that it was unkind to keep a cat where there was no grass for it, so Ermine had to do without. She always stopped to stroke the black cat in the ABC, the tortoise-shell in the grocery, the kitten in the laundry and the putty-coloured cat in the bicycle shop.

It was a hot, dusty May. Everything seemed very grimy. Layers of soot settled more quickly on the window ledges because of the lack of wind, and the pavements looked dirty because it had not rained for weeks. People went about saying how they longed to get away from London into the country. Ermine and her mother did not wish it. They liked London in the summer, and Ermine, in any case, had never been in the country and did not know what it was like at all.

They kept the flat cool and clean with the floor scrubbed and the curtains drawn, and a bunch of radishes soaking in a blue bowl of water, ready for anyone who came in to take a cool peppery bite. Ermine used to take an apple and some cheese, and twopence to buy ice-cream, and go out for the whole day into one or another of the squares or the cool galleries of the British Museum.

One evening as she was coming home under the dusty blue dome of sky she found a dirty-looking shilling lying on a path in Bloomsbury Square. She took it home and left it to soak in the radish-bowl (when they had eaten all the radishes).

'You'd better keep it,' said her mother. 'It's your birthday in a few days and I'm afraid you won't be getting any present except a new shirt, and that you need anyway.'

Ermine polished the shilling with the dishcloth, wondering what she should do with it – there were so many different possibilities. A shilling would buy quite a few books off a twopenny or threepenny stall in the Charing Cross Road – but in a way it was wasteful to buy books when she could get them at the Public Library for nothing. Or she could go on a river trip or a long bus ride, or wander round Woolworth's and find half a dozen pretty trifles.

On her birthday she put on the new blue shirt, polished her sandals, took her apple and the special birthday cream cheese which her mother had left for her and went out into the hot May day. She ate her lunch in Russell Square and then strolled down to the little streets south of the British Museum where there are all sorts of odd small shops selling secondhand books and antiques. She spent an hour or so browsing through dirty old books and looking at twisted Persian slippers, little brass figures from Burma, Italian powder horns, Egyptian wall hangings and many other things, without finding anything that she wanted.

She was delving in a box of articles marked 'Ninepence'

outside a shop in Museum Street when she felt a pain in her finger as if something had jabbed it. She withdrew her hand hurriedly – it must have been pricked by an old brooch or pin – and stood sucking it. Then she noticed something covered with bright beads underneath the heap of bric-a-brac. She pulled it out. It was a little snake, about a foot long, worked all over with tiny glass beads – red, blue and black. On its stomach the black beads were formed into letters which read: 'Turkish Prisoners, 1917.'

'What a queer creature,' thought Ermine, dangling it between her hands. She did not quite like it, but somehow it interested her.

'Do you want the snake, dear?' said a brisk little sandy-haired woman, coming to the door of the shop.

'I don't think so, thank you,' Ermine answered.

'It's a real bargain – you won't often find a thing like that for ninepence.'

'No, I think I won't, just the same, thank you.'

'Well put it back in the box then,' the woman snapped angrily, and went inside. Ermine could see her looking through the window, and hurriedly moved on to the next shop which sold secondhand gramophone records.

'Of course,' she thought, 'I'll get a record – something we've never heard before. Then it will be a surprise for mother as well.'

She stooped over the box marked 1/- and started looking slowly through the records, twisting her head about to read the titles which always seemed to be upside down. Most of the records looked rather battered, and some were bent or cracked, but one seemed to be brand-new – it was clean and glossy and its paper case was uncrumpled. Ermine studied the title. It was a concerto grosso for oboe and orchestra by Mr Handel. The name was unfamiliar to her, but she preferred that – it would be more of a surprise, and it would take them longer to learn it. She was standing half-decided, holding her shilling, when a man came out from inside the shop with a huge stack of records in his arms. All of a sudden they began to slip different ways, and the whole pile would have crashed on to the pavement had not Ermine jumped forward and steadied them with both hands.

'Thank you duck,' said the man. 'That wouldn't have done, would it? They're a lot of junk but still, no one wants broken records all over the street. Just help me tip them into the two-and-sixpenny box would you? That's the stuff.'

'May I have this one, please?' Ermine said, going back to the shilling box and pulling out her concerto grosso.

'Ah, you've found yourself something nice there,' said the man cheerfully. 'I guess that one slipped in out of the five bob box by mistake – however, that's my lookout. But you can reckon you've got quite a bargain.'

'I'm glad of that,' said Ermine, following him in to the shop. 'It's my birthday present.'

'Is it then? Well, you treat it carefully and it'll last you for plenty of birthdays. I'll tell you what – seeing you've saved me the trouble of sweeping fifty records off the pavement, I'll give you some fibre needles. And a sharpener, as it's your birthday.'

'Oh, thank you *very* much,' said Ermine, overwhelmed, as he handed her the two parcels.

'Now don't run home with it – walk.'

'I shouldn't dream of playing it until Mother gets home anyway,' she replied with dignity. He laughed. 'Goodbye, and thank you – it *was* kind of you to give me these.'

Towards tea-time she walked slowly and happily home, hugging her presents. The sun was still very hot, and it was pleasant to go into the cool, curtained flat and wash her dusty hands and feet. She cut some bread and butter, made lemonade in a jug, and then carefully undid the record and put it on the turntable, wound the gramophone and put in one of the new needles, all ready for her mother's arrival.

Soon she heard a quick footstep on the stairs, and Mrs Miggs came in saying: 'Ouf, isn't it hot. Had a nice birthday, lovey? What did you get yourself?'

'A new record – and the man gave me some needles and a sharpener because it's my birthday; wasn't it nice of him?

And it was really a five-shilling one anyway, got into the shilling box. It's all ready to play while we're having tea.'

'Shan't be a second then – I must just wash and I'll be with you. Oh, lovely, you've made cress sandwiches.'

She was back in a moment with a tiny birthday cake decorated with pink candles and silver balls.

'There you are, dearie – I made it last night when you were asleep.'

'Oh, *Mother* –'

'Come on, goose – let's hear this record.'

As soon as Ermine put the needle down and the disc began to revolve, a strange thing happened.

Ermine found herself walking down a steep, narrow lane, in between two high walls. At the bottom of the lane she crossed a cobbled road and came to another wall in which there was a door. She opened the door, and passing through found herself in a garden. There were tall trees close at hand, interspersed with holly bushes. A little path led among them, and following it she came to a wide lawn, with a stone terrace at one end and a pool at the other. Beyond the pool was a hedge and an arched gateway with a glimpse of bright flowers through it. Ermine went this way and found a little formal garden with brick paths and all sorts of sweet-smelling flowers whose names she did not know, besides roses and wallflowers and others which she remembered seeing in flower shops. Another archway led from the paved garden to a smaller lawn, in the centre of which grew a huge tree, all covered with blossom. Ermine thought that it was an apple tree, but she had never seen one so large. She started to cross the grass to it, but at that moment the music slowed down and came to an end.

Ermine rubbed her eyes in bewilderment, and looked at the record, lying quietly on its turntable.

'Goodness,' said her mother. 'That music made me think of all sorts of things I haven't remembered for years. I was in such a dream I never even noticed you turn over.'

'I didn't turn over.' But when Ermine looked at the record the uppermost side was numbered ' 2 '. 'It must have turned itself – we certainly started it on the right side.'

'What a curious record,' said her mother. 'And only a shilling – there's a bargain for you. Come on now – cut your cake.'

Ermine wondered if her mother had seen the garden too, but did not quite like to ask her.

Later on in the evening when Mrs Miggs was having a bath Ermine played the record again, and exactly the same thing happened. She walked down the alley between the walls, went across the road and through the door, under the trees, and then wandered about in the garden. She went a different way this time, past a lily pond and a little brick-paved stream with forget-me-nots trailing on its banks, but as before, finally came to the lawn with the great apple tree on it, and as before, was just starting to cross the grass when the music ceased. She looked at the record. It was on its second side.

Next day she went back to the shop and told the man how much they had enjoyed it.

'Glad you liked it,' he said. 'Come in and have a look round any time you like, and a chat. Always pleased to see friends in the shop.'

As Ermine left, her eye was caught again by the little bead-covered snake in the box next door. She glanced down at it, and then looked up to see the woman staring at her in an unfriendly manner through the window. She went hastily on.

That evening she told her mother about the woman and the snake.

'Funny to be so cross just because you didn't buy it,' commented Mrs Miggs. 'Ninepence wouldn't make much difference to her, you'd think. But I expect the people who keep those curio shops do get rather odd – it's only natural when you think that they spend their lives among stuffed crocodiles and the like. Let's play your record again – I've taken a great fancy to it.'

Goodness knows how many times Ermine played her record over during the next month or two. She never tired of it, and

– exactly the same thing happened

every time she played it, it performed its trick of turning over in the middle without any help – only Ermine never saw this happen because by that time she was in the garden, finding some new path to walk down, or some new flower to examine. On the hottest days she had only to wind the gramophone, place the needle on the disc, and at once be transported to the shade of those trees and the spreading green of the great lawn. The apple tree gradually shed its blossom in a pale carpet on the grass and small green apples formed. More roses came out, and the narcissi withered.

In London it grew hotter. Ermine became disinclined to go out, and spent more and more time indoors listening to the record. One afternoon she had only been as far as the bottom of Southampton Row to buy a lettuce, but when she came home her head ached and she could hardly drag herself up the stairs.

'You look feverish, dearie,' said her mother. 'Better go to bed. Goodness, your head is as hot as fire.'

Ermine gratefully climbed in between the cool sheets, but she could not get comfortable. She seemed to ache all over, and the bed soon became hot and tangled. She moved about miserably, listening to the lorries rattling past outside; it seemed to become dark all of a sudden, though of course the street lamps were shining on the ceiling.

'Try to keep still,' her mother's voice said. 'Would you like some music? Do you think that would help you to sleep?'

'Oh yes,' Ermine answered eagerly. Now she was going down the walled lane. It was dark, and a single lamp threw leaf-shadows across the road at the bottom.

When she reached the garden she saw bright moonlight falling across the lawns. She wandered for some time in and out of the shadows and at length came to the apple tree. She could dimly distinguish green apples the size of plums hanging among the leaves. Below them something glittered. She crossed the grass (which she had never been able to do before) and then stood drenched with icy fear. A great serpent was twined round the trunk of the tree, gazing at her with ruby-coloured eyes. The moonlight struck on it here and there, and she could see that it was striped and barred, red, black and blue. She opened her mouth to shriek but no sound came out; it was like a nightmare. And then, thank heaven, the music stopped and she was back in her hot bed, tossing and turning.

'The snake, the snake!' she said desperately, but her mouth seemed to be clogged with fur, and her tongue was as large as a football.

'What snake, lovey?' she heard her mother say, and then she was swept off into red-hot darkness. People came and went, her mother and a doctor; drinks and medicine were trickled between her lips, darkness alternated with light. Sometimes she was tormented by a glimpse of apples, hanging in cool clusters among leaves, sometimes she saw a huge snake spiralling round and round like a catherine wheel on the gramophone and playing a jangling tinny tune. Sometimes everything vanished altogether and she was only conscious of her aching self.

One day she began to get better and sat propped up on pillows sipping chicken broth.

'Well, you gave us a fright,' said her mother, who looked pale and thin, but cheerful.

'I had a fright too,' Ermine answered slowly, thinking of the snake. Speech was tiring, and she lay silent, staring about the room at the dusty golden sunlight. Presently her eyes dropped to the little home-made table by her bed and she gave a faint cry.

'What is it, ducky?' said Mrs Miggs coming anxiously.

'That snake. How did it get here?'

'Well, when you were feverish – you know you've been ill for three weeks, darling – you kept calling out, "The snake, the snake!" and I thought perhaps you were thinking of the one in the shop that you'd told me about. So I went along and bought it in case you were fretting for it.'

Fretting for it! Ermine eyed the snake with revulsion. She wanted to cry Take it away! but that would have seemed rude and heartless.

Suddenly a thought struck her.

'Mother!'

'Yes, ducky?'

'You've been here all day?'

'Yes, what about it?'

'But what about your job?'

'Oh, I had to give that up,' said Mrs Miggs lightly. 'Never mind, I'll soon get another one when you're better. Don't you fret your head about that.'

'But how have you been managing?' Ermine asked mistily, and then another thing about the room struck her. 'The gramophone?'

'Yes, I had to sell it. I'd much rather have you than a gramophone, after all. We'll get another one by and by. Now come along – drink up the last of that soup and off to sleep with you.'

It took Ermine a long time to recover. She sat about the flat, thin and weak, looking wearily at her books. Sometimes she took the record out of its paper case and rubbed her finger round it curiously, wondering if she could hear a faint sound of the wind in those trees. She could not help longing to hear it again, though at the same time she dreaded it. Was the snake still twined in the apple tree? Had it been there all the time?

She always put the record back hurriedly if she heard her mother coming.

One day she announced that she was perfectly able to look after herself and was going out to sit in the square.

Mrs Miggs looked at her searchingly, gave her a quick pat, and said:

'Take care of yourself then. I'll go off and do a bit of job-hunting if you're sure you're all right.'

'Quite sure.'

The leaves were beginning to hang heavily on the trees, and the grass was yellow and parched. Ermine walked very slowly to a seat in Bloomsbury Square and sank on to it. Her legs felt like skeins of wool.

Everything round her was dead and quiet. People were away on holiday, she supposed, and London was empty. It smelt of tar and dust. She thought of early morning in her garden, the dew thick on uncut grass and apples hanging among the leaves.

Suddenly behind her she heard a faint mew, a tiny note of distress. Turning her head she saw a strange little animal with a head like a cat, but a long thin body and a rusty-coloured coat. When she put out her hand he ran up eagerly and rubbed against it, purring.

'Well, you funny puss,' she said, stroking it. 'Where do you come from?'

Her finger found a collar, and running it round she came to a little engraved nameplate which said 'Adamson' and gave a number in Museum Street.

'I'd better take you home,' she said, and picked it up. It seemed quite willing to be carried and sat with its forepaws dangling over her arm, looking alertly round as she walked along Great Russell Street and turned into Museum Street.

When she came to the number on the collar she found to her surprise that it was the record shop.

'Mr Adamson?' she said.

'Hullo, it's the birthday girl. What's happened to you, though? You've grown, or got thinner or something. And you've brought back Ticky for me – I was beginning to worry about him. You're a fine one, you are,' he scolded the cat. 'Giving me heart failure like that. I suppose you want some milk. Now *you* sit down *there* – ' he moved an armful of sheet music off a backless chair and pushed Ermine gently on to it – 'while I give Ticky his milk. Where did you find him?'

'Only in Bloomsbury Square, but he seemed very miserable.'

'He's partly mongoose, you see – his granny was one. He's not used to city life and he goes out and gets scared. He's taken a fancy to you, though, I can see. Now, what shall I give you for bringing him back? Like another record? You're fond of Handel, I seem to remember.'

'It wouldn't be much use to me now, I'm afraid,' she said, laughing a little. 'I got ill, and Mother lost her job and had to sell our gramophone.'

'A lady selling a gramophone, eh? Rather thin, youngish, dark hair? An old model in a walnut box with a detachable handle?'

He went to the back of the shop and pulled it out from under a typing desk.

'Haven't got rid of it yet, you see. To tell you the truth, never thought I would. People won't go for this sort of thing now, all for these automatic pickups with short and long-playing, though mark you, this has a beautiful tone, one of the best I've heard for a long time. But I could see she wanted to sell it pretty badly, so I thought, Well, why not let it lodge here for a bit. So you've been ill, eh? And your ma's out of a job? That won't do. Well now, I'll tell you what. I'll put on my jacket and shut up, because it's closing time anyway, and we'll take this gramophone, which is your reward for bringing back Ticky, and we'll go and call on your ma and have a chat with her.'

He began putting up the shutters, slamming them into their grooves.

'Oh, you are kind,' said Ermine, her eyes full of tears.

'Nonsense, nonsense. One good turn deserves another. Are we ready now?'

'Yes, you take Ticky, he won't be left behind. Southampton Row? Blimey, did your ma come all that way with this?'

It only took them five minutes, though. It was dusk by now, and Ermine saw a crack of light under the flat door which showed that her mother was back. Her footsteps sounded discouraged, though she put on a cheerful smile for Ermine as she said:

'No luck yet, ducky –' Then she saw Mr Adamson behind, and her expression became inquiring.

'I expect you remember me, Ma'am,' he said. 'Your daughter did me a good turn this afternoon – brought back my cat that had been missing for two days. So I'm just carrying home her reward, a gramophone I happened to have by me.'

Mrs Miggs's jaw dropped.

'I – I don't know what to say,' she began. 'You must let me –'

'No, I certainly will not let you.'

Ermine noticed that Ticky, whom she still held in her arms, was beginning to get very restless and anxious. She let him jump down, and he raced across to the little bedside table and pounced upon something that lay on it.

'What's he got there?' asked Mr Adamson anxiously, turning from Mrs Miggs. 'You don't keep pet mice, do you?'

'No, it's the snake,' said Ermine, fascinated. 'He's tearing it to bits.' Tiny beads and bits of stuffing were flying about as Ticky, growling tremendously, worried and gnawed at it.

'Oh, I say, what a shame. I *am* sorry. Here, Ticky, you bad –'

'No, no, don't stop him. It doesn't matter.'

The elders fell into talk again. Ermine heard Mr Adamson say:

'I'm opening another branch in St Martin's Lane – think you could look after this one for me?' and her mother answered:

'Well it's very kind of you and I'd jump at the chance –'

'Kind? Nonsense. Then that's settled. Here, you, bright-eyes, put that Handel record on the gramophone and let's make sure it's still working.'

Ermine was half afraid as she put on the record and wound the handle, but she could not have disobeyed. With the first notes she forgot her fear, for she was walking down the alley and a few red leaves were drifting ahead of her. Smoke from a bonfire hung cloudily among the trees in front. She went through the door in the wall, down the path among the hollies, along beside the lawn and through the paved garden. Then she came to the apple-tree lawn. The tree was weighed down by its heavy golden fruit, but today there was no serpent – not so much as a blue or red glass bead in the grass.

She ran to the tree, and reaching up, felt one of the apples come away, heavy and round, into her hand. Then the music stopped and she came back to herself, blinking, in the familiar room.

'That child's been asleep, I do believe,' remarked her mother. 'Look how pink her cheeks are.'

'If I was asleep,' said Ermine, 'where did I find this?'

She held out her hand. In it, heavy and round, lay a golden apple.

Rocket Full of Pie

'In heaven's name what is that?' said Mr Armitage, coming in and finding his wife with a length of scarlet muffler apparently intended for an ostrich dangling from her knitting needles.

'Comforts for the Lifeboatmen,' she told him. 'My Women's Union members are making mufflers for the Shambles Lifeboat crew.'

Mr Armitage carefully picked his way through the tangle and sat down in front of the fire, moving a large model yacht to make room for his feet, and eliciting a cry of protest from Mark, who was sitting by the wireless.

'Careful, Father! The paint's not nearly dry yet.'

'Christmas holidays,' grumbled Mr Armitage. 'How thankful I shall be when they're over. Mark, turn off that awful voice, will you?'

'But it's interesting,' complained Mark, turning it off. 'It was an appeal for more weather ships and I wanted to find out about them.'

'You'll have to find out some other way. I want peace and quiet,' said his father unsympathetically. 'Lifeboats – weather ships – my family seems to have gone marine crazy.'

'Mummy's going for a sail on Monday,' Harriet told him.

'A sail? In December? For mercy's sake, why?'

'It's the Women's Union Christmas Outing,' Mrs Armitage explained patiently. 'We're having the presentation of the mufflers to the lifeboat crew, and then the club members are being taken for a trip out to the Shambles Lighthouse, where we shall have tea. The lighthouse keepers are providing the tea and we are providing the food. I'm one of the hostesses this month, so I shall have to get busy.'

'Make some of your mince-pies,' said Mr Armitage. 'That'll

fetch 'em. But isn't Monday rather an unwise day for your excursion?'

Monday, in the Armitage family, was a day on which unexpected things were likely to happen – a live Cockatrice had once settled in the garden and eaten up all the vegetables, breathing out fire as he did so, and on another Monday the Fairy Queen had held an At Home on the front lawn, completely preventing any tradesmen from calling for twenty-four hours. The Armitage parents were always relieved when Monday was over, and tried not to embark on any risky venture upon that day if they could help it.

'Can't be avoided this time, I'm afraid,' Mrs Armitage said sighing. 'It was the only day when all the members could come.'

All that week Mrs Armitage and Harriet were busy making mince-pies. Mark, for once, was not helpful.

'He's making another of his model yachts, I suppose,' Harriet said. 'That's why he always comes to meals late, with gluey hands.'

'You can come on the trip, as you've been such a help, Harriet,' said her mother. 'But I shan't ask Mark. That'll teach him to co-operate a bit more next time I'm busy.'

Mark did grumble when he heard that he had not been invited. 'I've always wanted to see inside the lighthouse,' he said. But as his protests were unavailing he soon retired to his den and began sawing away.

'Who is the other hostess and what is she providing?' said Mr Armitage on Saturday, eyeing the growing mountain of mince-pies.

'It's Mrs Slabb,' his wife said gloomily.

'Oh dear.'

'She's making some rock cakes. I tried to persuade her that sandwiches would be nice, but she didn't take the hint. She said she reckoned her cakes would fill up the boys' stomachs better.'

'Fill them up? They'll *cement* them up, more likely,' said Mr Armitage. 'Remember the cake she made for the Guess the Weight Competition at last year's Christmas Bazaar – the only person who guessed within a stone was the Strong Man from the Bumstead Circus.'

'Never mind, she's a kind old thing and we can't hurt her feelings,' Mrs Armitage said firmly.

Monday dawned grey and bleak without a breath of wind.

'Looks like snow,' said Mr Armitage, but the barometer stood at 'Set Fair'.

The Women's Union members assembled on the launching ramp punctually at two o'clock for the presentation amid cries of, 'Did you remember to lock the back door?' and 'Are the hens shut up?' from the crew, who were mostly their husbands and relatives.

Mrs Armitage made a short speech before unveiling the huge cardboard carton which contained the gift mufflers.

'Thank you kindly one and all,' said the coxswain (his name was Alf Putnam) 'I hereby have pleasure in handing them out to the men who I'm sure will thoroughly appreciate them – specially as they've seen them being knitted for the last six months. Bert Althorpe!'

Bert stepped forward to receive his muffler and Alf pulled a generous blue length out of the box, which Bert wound round his neck before stepping back again.

'Hey, you've left one end behind – you haven't got it all yet, chum,' someone called out. As Bert pulled, more and more muffler unreeled from the carton. The blue length was followed by a red one and that by an orange one.

'Oh dear,' exclaimed Mrs Armitage in dismay, 'can someone have joined them all together? There's been some bad co-ordination somewhere.'

This, it seemed, was the case. Rods, poles, perches, chains and furlongs of endless muffler, every colour of the rainbow, were drawn out and lay about the beach and ramp in gorgeous festoons.

'Looks like Christmas all right, don't it,' muttered Bert to Lofty Wainright.

'Alf, you better stop pulling it out. If you once get lost in that lot we shan't see you again alive.'

'Maybe we should cut it,' said Alf, mopping his brow.

'You can't do that,' cried a dozen ladies, 'it would all unravel. The ends will have to be stitched up.'

'Well let's put it out of the way for now,' said Alf rather desperately, 'and get on with the next part of the programme.'

Several people clapped at this.

'Ladies, please take your places in the lifeboat, as indicated to you by Bert, William and Nobby,' said Alf. 'Fred, you give me a hand with the grub.'

The mince-pies had been brought down in two large laundry baskets covered with clean cloths, and Mrs Slabb had put her cakes in a couple of canvas kitbags which had once belonged to Mr Slabb. When Fred seized one of these he turned pale.

'Blimey!' he said. 'What's in them? Lead piping?' He and Alf tottered with difficulty to the boat and heaved the sack over the side. When they had put in the second with equal difficulty, Alf muttered to Fred:

'We'd better leave the two baskets behind, accidentally like. Another two of these would sink us. As it is we'll have to move the passengers forrard or we'll be down by the stern.'

So the laundry baskets were lef tbehind on the beach, and the Women's Union were packed farther along, amid cries of 'What do you think we are? Sardines? Mind my toe you big lump! Oo!' Harriet, in between Mrs Slabb and Mrs Lightbody, was nearly crushed to death.

The rest of the crew piled in, all except Fred who was the spare, and in any case had said he had more sense than to go joy-riding with a passel of females. Alf leaned over the gunwale and pulled the lever and the lifeboat slid majestically down the ramp and into the sea.

Fred, left alone on the beach, dragged the two baskets of mince-pies into the shed, noticing as he did so that they were not nearly so heavy as the sacks of cakes, and then began methodically coiling up the length of muffler. There seemed to be roughly a thousand yards of it – nearly a hundred yards for each man. 'Them women,' he muttered to himself, 'not a stitch of arithmetic in any of 'em.'

When he finished he straightened his back and glanced up at the sky.

'Lumme,' he exclaimed. 'They're going to cop it if they don't look out.'

The clouds were becoming almost as black as ink, and the wind, which had been rising, was now whipping the tops of the waves in a very ugly way. A more unpleasant day for an outing could not have been imagined.

Mark, who had just arrived on his bicycle, too late for the launching, gazed in dismay at the lifeboat, which was bouncing uneasily through the sea about half-way between the shore and the lighthouse rock.

'Blowing up for a proper gale,' Fred said to him gloomily.

The passengers in the boat were not at all happy. There were several green faces, and shrieks of dismay were heard as waves occasionally slopped over and soused some of them.

'Never mind, Mum, soon be there and you can cheer yourself up with a nice cuppa,' said Alf to Mrs Lightbody, but Harriet, who had sharp ears, heard him mutter to Nobby: 'Look here, we're getting lower in the water all the time. D'you think we could throw some of these perishing granite buns overboard without anyone seeing?'

He dug an experimental hand into one of the kitbags, pulled out a cake, and tossed it to starboard. A passing gull swooped and deftly caught the cake, staggered in its flight and fell like a stone beneath the waves. Harriet opened her mouth to gasp with horror, but was relieved to see the gull pop up again in a moment, without the cake, but with an expression of extreme astonishment on its face.

'Strewth,' said Nobby, awestruck.

'See what I mean? If we don't jettison those cakes we're going to founder.'

The waves, as large as houses now, towered over the heavily burdened lifeboat, which was settling deeper and deeper between them. Harriet thought they looked like huge black

The passengers . . . were not at all happy

Christmas trees. She watched Alf pick up one of the sacks and stagger towards the side, and then Nobby shouted:

'No, hold it, here we are!'

Another of the large waves, rolling to one side, had revealed the lighthouse just ahead. The three members of its crew were dancing about on a little spur of rock at the foot, anxiously waiting to catch a rope.

'Come on,' they called encouragingly. 'You made it! That's the stuff!' They spoke too soon, however.

As Bert leaned over with the painter a gigantic wave tipped the lifeboat sideways, and crew, passengers and cargo were all flung into the sea together as neatly as peas flipped out of a pod. Fortunately they were within a few feet of the rock and all managed to clamber ashore, but they heard the boat slam grindingly on a rock behind them, and turned to see it drift away and then submerge.

'That's that,' said Alf. 'Now how are we going to get back?'

'Oh, Fred will have seen her go down. He'll phone along to Slimehaven and get their boat to come and take us off.'

'Not in this weather they won't. We haven't had a gale like this since '38.'

'Well don't stand here gossiping,' said Mrs Lightbody tartly. 'Let's get inside and have a warm up, for goodness' sake, and where's that cup of tea? If we don't get some dry clothes on soon they needn't bother to send a boat – they can just float over some coffins.'

The shipwrecked party trooped into the lighthouse, and soon clouds of steam began coming out of its windows, as, in turn, members of the Women's Union and lifeboat crew wrapped themselves in blankets and dried themselves in front of the twenty thousand candle-power light. Cups of tea were provided by their kind hosts, but, alas, there was nothing to eat, for Mrs Slabb's cakes had gone down with the boat.

'Better get ready for a hungry Christmas, ladies,' said the head lighthouse keeper. 'This time of year we're often cut off for two or three weeks if the weather turns nasty.'

Cries of 'Oo-er' and 'Love a duck' greeted this, but he

continued: 'We've got supplies of bully beef and biscuits, but they won't go far among ten lifeboatmen and twenty Ladies' Union. It'll be one biscuit and one slice of bully per day till further notice.'

Some of the ladies began to cry, thinking of the turkeys hanging in their larders, and the Christmas puddings all ready for boiling. Mrs Armitage tried to cheer them, but even Harriet felt glum, and her lunch seemed to have been a long time ago. She would have welcomed one of Mrs Slabb's buns.

Just then Alf came in looking puzzled.

'Old Fred's got the rocket apparatus out on the beach,' he said. 'Can't rightly see what he's doing, it's come over so dark, but there's a boy helping him and it looks as if they're trying to send something over.'

Most of the party crowded out on to the rock platform to see what was going on. Over the raging water they could dimly see two figures active on the shore, and presently they saw a flash, though it was impossible to hear the report of the rocket through the gale. But they could soon see a missile hurtling towards them, and amid cries of excitement a large rocket landed a few feet away from where they were standing. Alf went over to it.

'What's in it?' inquired the lighthouse keeper when he staggered back with it in his arms. They all gathered round as he unscrewed the canister.

A large heap of little round golden objects rolled out, from which came a delicious spicy smell, most inviting to the hungry castaways.

'Mince-pies! It's Mother's mince-pies!' shouted Harriet. 'Three cheers for Fred!'

There were enough mince-pies for everyone, and a few minutes later another rocket landed with a second cargo, which was eagerly gathered up and taken inside. Then Fred apparently decided that the light was too bad to risk sending any more, for he and his helper took the firing apparatus back into the shed.

It was not such a miserable party after all which sat munching the mince-pies and toasting Fred in mugs of tea, and presently they all went to sleep, wrapped in blankets and packed together on the floor like sardines.

The awakening next morning was not so cheerful, as they were stiff and uncomfortable, and worse still, the storm was raging more fiercely if anything than the day before. After breakfast (one biscuit, washed down with tea) Fred managed to send over two more rocket-loads of pies, but then the gale worsened until it was impossible to see the shore, and the lifeboat crew shook their heads over the chances of any rescue that day.

Mrs Armitage, seeing the Women's Union members looking very glum, organized them into giving the lighthouse a spring cleaning, which it badly needed.

'We'll each scrub twenty steps of the stairs and polish three windows,' she said. 'At least there's one thing we're not short of, and that's water. And there seems to be plenty of soap too – they're not extravagant with it out here, it's plain.'

The male inhabitants retired outside while this was going on, and waited patiently in the storm, rather than be bumped continually with brushes and buckets.

On Wednesday Fred managed to send over the last of the mince-pies but it was too rough for a rescue. On Thursday, however, which was Christmas Eve, the Slimehaven lifeboat came along the coast, but could not get near the lighthouse because of dangerous lumps of rock which were being flung about by the waves. Several of these pierced the sides of the boat, which were only just patched in time. It was discovered that these lumps were in fact Mrs Slabb's cakes, which the action of salt water and cold air had rendered hard as bullets.

The Slimehaven crew tried several times to get a line to the shore which would pass by the lighthouse, so that provisions could run along it. At first they were unsuccessful, as no ordinary rope could stand the strain of the wind and waves, but finally the marooned group saw them put in to the shore and come battling out again trailing a cable which, even through the storm, could be seen to consist of sections in different vivid colours.

'Well I'm blest! They're using our muffler. What a sauce!' exclaimed Mrs Slabb.

'At least it's holding,' said Alf rather sourly.

The Slimehaven boat put out beyond the lighthouse, keeping well clear of it, and then hove to. The crew could be seen feverishly winding away at a winch, and bit by bit the multicoloured line twitched and jerked itself tight, until it was a foot above the waves.

'Look! Look!' cried Harriet. 'Someone's walking out along the rope.'

They all gazed at the point where the line ran up the beach and saw a tiny figure coming slowly but steadily out along the rope. Some of the women could not stand it and went inside, but most of the party watched in fascination, expecting every minute that some extra large wave would knock him from his position.

Harriet saw that it was Mark when he had come about half way, but she could not make out what he was carrying. It seemed like a model ship, but of no design that she recognized. He was holding it with both hands in front of him and using it to keep his balance.

'I didn't know Mark could tight-rope walk,' murmured Mrs Armitage distractedly, without taking her eyes off him.

'Oh yes, we both learned last year from the trapeze artiste at the Bumstead Circus,' Harriet answered absently. 'What's he doing now?'

Mark had come level with them, though he was about twenty yards away to port. He deliberately dropped his little boat on to the water, staggered, nearly missed his balance, recovered it again, and made his way on to the Slimehaven boat, where he was received with clapping and cheers.

'But what's the use of that?' said Mrs Lightbody, puzzled. 'One little toy boat isn't going to help us. It's not worth all that trouble.'

But even as she spoke they saw that all round the little ship the waves were dying down. Presently the sea near the lighthouse was as calm as a mill-pond, and in scenes of the wildest rejoicing the members of the Women's Union and Shambles crew were rescued from their watery jail, and a Christmas dinner was handed over to their hosts.

'But what was the little ship?' demanded Harriet, and everyone was asking the same question.

'It was a weather ship,' Mark replied. 'You know, there was a radio appeal for more of them, so I thought I'd make one. For calming down the weather, you see.'

'But weather ships are for recording the weather, not for calming it down.'

'Are they? Oh, well, there you are. Father would turn the radio off, so I never did hear about them and I had to guess how to make it. Anyway I think my sort's more useful,' said Mark. 'I'm going to make some more, but I suppose I'd better make a new lifeboat first.'

Armitage, Armitage, Fly Away Home

'WHAT's all this?' said Mr Armitage. The dining-room was littered with collecting boxes and trays full of blue paper cornflowers.

'Cornflower day,' said Mrs Armitage.

'So I had inferred,' replied her husband patiently. 'But what's it in aid of?' He peered at some posters lying half-unrolled on the floor which showed a sweet, pathetic old face under a steeple-crowned hat.

'It's to raise money for a bazaar.'

'Yes?'

'And the bazaar is to raise money for a progressive whist drive which is to raise money for a garden fête.'

'So far so good,' said Mr Armitage, stepping over Harriet who was counting cornflowers, and helping himself to porridge. 'And what's the garden fête in aid of?'

'The S.A.D.O.F.L. of course.'

'And that is?'

'Society for the Aid of Distressed Old Fairy Ladies.'

'Do you expect to raise much for them?'

'Oh yes,' said Mrs Armitage confidently. 'Last year we made a terrible lot for the N.S.P.C.M. – enough to provide a warm swimming bath for rheumatic mermaids *and* a beach canteen serving them with hot soup and fish rolls throughout the winter months.'

'Most praiseworthy.'

Mr Armitage shuddered a little at the thought of the fish rolls and hurriedly took some bacon.

'So we expect to be able to do something of the sort this year. There's a slight difference of opinion on the committee unfortunately; some people want a free dispensary for magical ingredients – eye of newt and toe of frog, you know, and belladonna and so forth; but some committee members think that ought to come under the National Health Service anyway, and that we should write to our M.P. about it.'

'So what do they want?'

'A mobile library of magical reference books and free replacements of worn-out wands.'

'Well it all sounds very fine,' said Mr Armitage gulping down the last of his coffee and preparing to rush off, for this was his office day; 'provided you think these people *deserve* to be helped.'

'Oh yes, darling, poor old things. Have you finished counting those out, Harriet? Here come the other helpers and we must be off.'

The flag-sellers were beginning to crowd the front hall and Mrs Armitage gave each her set of tray, collection box and poster and then took the last set and, with Harriet, started off along her own beat, which was the section of the village in between the post office and the green.

At first all went excellently. Heads were shaken and sighs heaved over the plight of the poor resourceless old fairy ladies in want of comforts, money flowed in, and the tin box became heavier and heavier, until by eleven o'clock it was nearly full. They were approaching a small cottage, set back from the road among apple trees. It was called The Bat's Nest, and in it lived old Mr Grogan, with his housekeeper, old Miss Hooting. Mr Grogan made dolls' furniture. He was stone deaf and hardly talked to anyone except Miss Hooting, who had a very shrill voice which he could just hear. If anyone wanted dolls' furniture they came and told Miss Hooting their requirements; the size, period, design and materials wanted. She would pass the information on to Mr Grogan, and in due course the article would arrive, very beautifully made. Harriet, had a Queen Anne walnut chest of drawers with brass handles, of his workmanship, and also a rosewood grand piano, its tiny keys made from spillikins, which really played. Miss Hooting, as well as looking after Mr Grogan, kept what was thought to be a hen-battery and sold the eggs. She also made hats and did weaving.

'I do admire Miss Hooting,' people often said.

When Harriet and her mother came up to the cottage they saw Miss Hooting walking down the garden path towards the battery-shed, and as they knew it would be useless to apply to Mr Grogan, they went round to intercept her.

'Good morning,' she said in her creaking voice. 'Would you like to see me feed my birds?'

'Oh yes please,' said Harriet, and Mrs Armitage inquired: 'What do you give them?'

'Pellets,' replied Miss Hooting, opening a bin which contained tiny whitish balls and shovelling some of them into two buckets.

'Now they are tipped into these containers, so, and I pull the rope to raise them to roof-level. Now we can go inside.'

As she opened the door into the battery, which was very dark, pandemonium broke loose.

'Those don't sound like hens,' said Mrs Armitage, puzzled.

'Hens? Who said they were hens?'

There was a squawking and a screeching, a hooting and a snoring, and a noise almost like barking.

'I'll have to switch on the light,' said Miss Hooting, and did so. The birds immediately became quiet in their little cages and sat watching her with great round eyes.

'Goodness,' said Mrs Armitage in surprise. 'They're owls. Do you sell the eggs?'

'Yes, to Health Food Stores. And to the United Sorcerers' Supply Stores. They collect the eggs once every six months or so – owls' eggs don't have to be fresh, in fact the less so the better from many points of view.'

She pulled the two pellet containers through the hatches and the visitors saw that they ran on wheels along two little overhead railways. When they were pushed they trundled the whole length of the battery, tipping off a portion of food into each owl's cage. The owls bounced up and down with excitement, but kept quiet. Water followed the food in the same manner.

'Now,' said Miss Hooting, dusting her hands. 'You are collecting, are you not? For some worthy cause, no doubt, but

I haven't got my spectacles or my purse, so we must go indoors, and I will show you the bit of weaving I am engaged on at present.'

They followed her back to the house and into a front room which smelt strongly of raffia, wool, artificial flowers and basket-canes, all of which were lying about in large quantities. A loom also occupied a good deal of space.

'Oh,' said Harriet in admiration. 'What lovely stuff.' The piece of cloth on the loom was not at all the sort of hand-woven stuff she had expected to see. It was a thick, rich-looking red velvet with a black-and-gold design woven through it.

'It's for a cloak,' explained Miss Hooting carelessly, coming back with her bag and glasses. 'There's the hat to match.' She nodded at a black steeple-crowned one lying beside the bunch of red ribbons which was to trim it. 'I'm making them to order – for old Mrs Lomax. Now what is it you are collecting in aid of?'

'The S.A.D.O.F.L.' said Mrs Armitage. 'For helping poor old fairy ladies of various kinds. When they're old they often get a bit past their work, you know, not up to much, poor old things, and we ought to do a bit for them. This is going to a fund for replacing worn-out wands and things of that sort. Gracious, is something the matter?'

Miss Hooting had gone perfectly pale with rage and was pointing a trembling finger at them.

'The impertinence!' she exclaimed. 'The bare-faced, unparalleled effrontery of coming here and saying that to *me*! I suppose you did it as a deliberate insult.'

'No indeed,' said Mrs Armitage, much bewildered. 'I certainly had no such intention.'

'Fiddlestick! I suppose you'll say next you didn't *know* I was a retired enchantress (fairy lady, indeed). I am not in the least distressed, I'll have you know. I have my pension, my salary from Mr Grogan, besides what I make from my owls and handcrafts. I am hard-working and self-respecting, and there are plenty more like me who won't say thank you for your charity. The door is behind you. *Good* morning.'

Unfortunately at that moment Mr Grogan came downstairs,

having heard Miss Hooting's voice upraised in rage. He rather liked Mrs Armitage and Harriet, so he said good morning to them and asked Miss Hooting what they had come for.

'Impertinence,' she screeched.

'Furniture? Yes, I daresay, but what sort of furniture?'

'*Not* furniture. They are collecting for a most offensive cause.'

'Chest of drawers? Yes, I can do a chest of drawers, but what period?'

'Not a chest of drawers, an appeal.'

'Made of deal? Never touch the stuff.'

Harriet and Mrs Armitage felt that if they did not leave Miss Hooting might do something drastic – she was casting meaning looks at a tall black stick leaning against the mantelpiece. If it was a wand, they thought it would be prudent not to chance the possibility of its not being worn out, so nodding and smiling at Mr Grogan they made their escape.

When the contents of the various collecting-boxes were added together, the total sum was found to be quite a handsome one, though several of the collectors had had unfortunate experiences, like that of the Armitages, with innocent-and seeming old ladies about the village.

Mr Armitage shook his head when he heard about it.

'I should leave the whole affair alone, if I were you,' he said. 'Buy a grand piano for the Ladies' Social Club, or a machine gun for the Boy Scouts, or something harmless. It's always better to collect for a charity that's a long way off, in Africa or somewhere like that, if you must. These old fairy ladies are devilish touchy and independent, and there's sure to be trouble.'

He was an obliging man, however, and he consented to say a few words to open the bazaar which was due to follow in three weeks, because he said he might not make such a hash of it as the Vicar.

Everyone was working early and late making things for the stalls – cakes, embroidered milk-bottle covers, tea-cosy cases, jam-pot containers, bags to put dusters in and bags to put those bags in, dolls with crinolines to put over the coal-scuttle and crocheted chocolate-bar containers. There was also to be a jumble stall, and all the village flocked to the bazaar in the hope of picking up cheap the clothes of the children next door which they had been despising and condemning as unsuitable for the past year.

Mr Armitage stood on the platform to say his opening words, supported by his wife and the members of the committee.

'Good afternoon ladies and gentlemen,' he remarked, spurred on to rashness by several cups of very strong tea which he had just drunk. 'We are all assembled here to enjoy ourselves (I hope) and to raise money for all the poor old distressed fairy ladies living round about. Well now, let's give the poor old things a big hand and buy everything in sight, however nasty or useless it appears to be – '

Here he paused with his mouth open, for several old ladies near the front of the hall were standing up and looking at him in a very unfriendly way. Old Mrs Lomax was pointing her stick at him.

'Hush, man, hush,' she croaked,

> 'By the magic of this wand,
> Be a tadpole in a pond.'

Nothing happened.

'*You're* no use,' said old Mrs Lockspith acidly. 'You're one of the ones they need to help, evidently.' She pointed a long malacca cane at the speechless Mr Armitage, and exclaimed:

> 'Powers of witchcraft in this cane,
> Turn him to a drop of rain.'

Nothing happened.

'Here, this is ludicrous,' said Miss Hooting furiously. 'It's my turn. You ladies are a disgrace to the profession.' She grabbed her own black staff, levelled it at the platform and recited:

> 'Enough of useless spells and wasted words,
> Turn Armitage and wife to ladybirds.'

There was a hush, as the people in the audience craned over each other's shoulders to see if the spell had worked this time, and then a spontaneous burst of applause. Miss Hooting bowed haughtily, turned on her heel, and left the hall.

On the platform the remaining committee members gazed at each other blankly across a gap. Then the Vicar, peering long-sightedly at the floor, remarked:

'Ah! What a fortunate thing that I have my collecting-box with me.'

He took it from his pocket, tipped out a Hummingbird Hawk Moth and placed in it the two ladybirds who were dazedly crawling about the floor.

'Perhaps I'd better take charge of those,' suggested Harriet coming up. 'They'll want to go home, I expect.' Secretly, she was a little afraid that the Vicar, who was notoriously absent-minded, might forget that there was anything special about the ladybirds and add them to his collection, impaled on pins.

She and Mark left the bazaar (which went on swimmingly after such an eventful start and netted two hundred pounds) and took their parents home. They put the ladybirds in a shoe-box with some biscuit crumbs and drops of hot sweet tea (for shock) and sat down to discuss the situation, feeling very grown up.

'Perhaps it's the sort of spell that will wear off in due course,' said Harriet hopefully.

'Not if I know Miss Hooting, and I somehow feel it wouldn't be much use going to her and begging her to take it off.'

Harriet grinned. 'I've got an idea,' she said. 'But let's wait till tomorrow. After all, it's rather nice and peaceful the way we are.'

After next day's breakfast (at which they felt it necessary to eat twice as much as usual and open a pot of strawberry jam to fortify them in their orphaned state) they went and looked into the shoe-box.

Much to their surprise they were greeted with a stream of shrill and indignant expostulation. Apparently Mr and Mrs Armitage had recovered the use of their voices. They were scolded for the uncomfortable bedding they had provided and for not bringing breakfast sooner. Harriet ran off for toast and bacon crumbs.

'Now, Mark,' said Mr Armitage, 'I have a most important conference at my office today – there's a meeting of the World Organization of Agricultural Producers being held there, and I'm the Chairman. So you'll have to take me. Go and put on some presentable clothes, find a nice dry airy matchbox with some cotton wool in it, and you can catch the 9.18 and bring the file of papers on my dressing table.' Mark went off rather gloomily to, obey. He had had the best intentions of trying to recover his parents from ladybirdhood, but he had agreed with Harriet that a few days' freedom from grown-ups would be a pleasant change, and now it seemed that, on the contrary, they were going to be much more parent-ridden than usual.

'Harriet,' Mrs Armitage was saying. 'You'll have to carry me on my National Savings round, and this afternoon I'm going to have tea with Mrs Mildew, so you'll have to take me there. Just give my back a spot of polish will you – Mansion will do.'

Harriet complied, thinking regretfully of the day she had planned, riding the unicorn and spring-cleaning her dolls' house.

The 9.18 was crowded that morning, but when it was observed that a tiny voice was speaking to Mark from his breast-pocket, his fellow passengers moved well away from him, and at the next stop along the line they all got out and went elsewhere.

When Mark and his father reached the office Miss Choop, the secretary, was sitting on her desk varnishing her nails with stencil eraser.

'Hello, Sonny,' she said condescendingly. 'You're in town early. Your pa's not in yet. Was he at a party last night?'

'Choop!' barked Mr Armitage, so threateningly that she jumped, and the bottle of Correctine rolled across the floor. 'Get off that desk and lay out the agendas for the W.O.A.P meeting.'

'Where is he?' she said fearfully. 'I thought I heard his

voice, but it was sort of shrill and far away. He's – he's not *haunting* me, is he? I swear I never meant to upset the card index.'

'It's all right – he's in here,' said Mark comfortingly. 'He's been turned into a ladybird. You hurry up and get those things laid out in the Board Room – I can hear people coming.'

Members of the World Organization of Agricultural Producers were coming up the stairs, talking in a lot of different languages and stamping the mud off their boots.

'And where is our esteemed Chairman?' an enormously tall Swedish farmer asked Miss Choop.

'He's there,' she replied tremulously, indicating the matchbox. Mr Svendsen raised his eyebrows. They all filed into the Board Room and Mark took his father's place holding the matchbox. Miss Choop supplied him with an amplifier.

'Order, Gentlemen,' said Mr Armitage shrilly from his perch. 'I call upon the Secretary to read the minutes of the last meeting.'

Several of the delegates turned pale and asked each other if it was ventriloquism. A Latin-American, whose nerves were in a bad state because a revolution was in progress in his country fainted dead away.

Mr Armitage was a very efficient chairman and bustled his meeting through several motions without giving the delegates any time for argument, until they were a little more accustomed to his voice coming from the matchbox.

'Item Six,' he said. 'Spraying crops of underdeveloped territories from helicopters. Ah yes, we have received tenders from two different firms manufacturing insecticides, one British, one Russian. Both their prices are about the same, so it remains to be seen which of their products is the more efficient.'

Heated discussion broke out. It seemed that this was a matter on which the delegates felt very strongly. They shouted in their different languages, gesticulated, and jumped up and down. As far as Mark could make out, the opposing groups were about evenly matched.

'There are representatives of the two firms outside with samples of insect-powders which they wish to demonstrate,' said Miss Choop. 'Shall I ask them in?'

'I hope that will not be necessary,' said Mr Armitage hurriedly. 'We'll have a vote.'

The voting was exactly even.

'As Chairman I have a casting vote,' said Mr Armitage. 'Being British I naturally give it to the Br – '

'I demand to have a trial of these powders,' cried the Russian delegate. Mr Armitage was obliged to give in.

Two young men in white came in carrying tins of powder, sprays and little cages of assorted insects. One had mud on his boots, one snow.

'This powder produced by my firm,' said the first of them, 'is guaranteed to destroy any insect life within 500 cubic metres.'

'600 cubic metres,' cried the second, putting down his little cage on the table near Mr Armitage's matchbox. A particularly enormous spider gazed yearningly at Mr Armitage through the bars. His nerve broke.

'I – I've changed my mind,' he declared. 'I think the Osnovskov powder is undoubtedly the better, and it is also a halfpenny a ton cheaper. I am going to give my casting vote in favour of it.'

Both the young men looked greatly disappointed at losing the opportunity of demonstrating their products. The Russian delegate beamed.

'Come out to lunch with me,' he said. 'I shall carry you most carefully, and you shall have a thimbleful of vodka and one grain of caviare.'

'Mark, you wait here till I come back,' his father instructed.

Mr Armitage arrived home in good spirits singing the Volga Boat Song, but his children were most dispirited.

'I've had an awful day,' said Harriet to Mark after supper. 'National Savings all morning, and that tea with Mrs Mildew! Somebody had brought a baby and it kept grabbing Mother and trying to swallow her. And once the cat nearly caught her and she fell into a cream-jug.'

'Who do you think you are, Dior?'

'We must certainly get them changed back somehow. What was that idea of yours?'

Harriet jumped up. 'I thought we'd go and see Mrs Lomax,' she said. 'Come on – we'll shut the parents in their shoe-box and put them in the meat-safe so that they won't come to any harm.'

Mark followed her doubtfully. 'I don't see that she's very likely to help,' he argued. 'She wanted to change father into a tadpole.'

'Yes, but that was before Miss Hooting called her a disgrace to the profession. Think how touchy they are.'

Dusk was falling when they reached Cobweb Corner, Mrs Lomax's bungalow. While they were still at the bottom of the garden they could hear angry voices, and when they came nearer they saw Miss Hooting and Mrs Lomax at opposite sides of the path.

'And if you think I'm going to pay you twenty guineas for that cloak, you're greatly mistaken,' Mrs Lomax was saying furiously. 'Who do you think you are, Dior? The hem is five inches off the ground, I shall look a sight. And the hat is too small. I shan't give you a penny more than fifteen. Disgrace to the profession, indeed. You can hardly talk.'

Miss Hooting turned, her face black as thunder, and swept past the children without noticing them.

Mrs Lomax pointed a walking-stick after her and shouted: 'Be a woodlouse,' but nothing happened, and she went inside and slammed the door.

Harriet firmly rang the bell, and when the door flew open again she looked (with some courage) into Mrs Lomax's furious face.

'Mrs Lomax,' she said. 'I know you're not very fond of my family, but I think we might strike a bargain. We want our parents back again, and I expect you'd like a new wand, wouldn't you? That one doesn't seem to be much good. Unfortunately the Committee has decided that it's not safe to hand out new wands, so they're all being sent back to the United Sorcerers' Supply Stores and there's going to be a free library instead. But I know where they are now, and I expect

I could borrow one – just for half an hour or so – if you'd promise to turn our parents back into human beings for us.'

Mrs Lomax looked much more friendly by the end of this speech.

'I think that might be arranged,' she said. 'One can't be too careful over one's associates and I find I have been quite mistaken in my estimate of Miss Hooting's character. If I can repair any harm she has done to your dear parents I shall be delighted.'

'You stay here and talk to her and see she doesn't change her mind,' hissed Harriet to Mark. So he chatted politely to Mrs Lomax and looked at her collection of lizards while Harriet dashed off to the Vicar and begged for the loan of one of the wands which he had in temporary storage, pending their dispatch back to London.

'Just for half an hour,' she pleaded, 'while we get Mother and Father changed back. You can't think how we miss them.'

'Very well,' he agreed. 'But please take the greatest care. Once these things get into the wrong hands – '

Harriet ran triumphantly back with a heavy ebony stick.

'That should do,' said Mrs Lomax, looking at it professionally, and she recited:

'Oh stick well-seasoned, elegant and sage,
Change ladybird and wife to Armitage.

That should do the trick for you.' Then she went on, rather hastily:

'All fairy ladies, from tonight,
Turn into owls – and serve them right!'

A confused sound of screeching came from the trees in her garden. Several owls brushed past them.

'Oh dear,' Harriet said doubtfully. 'I don't think the Vicar would like – '

A blue flash wriggled up the stick to Mrs Lomax's hand, she shrank, her eyes became enormous, and all of a sudden she flew off into the trees, crying: 'Too whit! Too whoo!'

'She's turned herself into one too,' said Mark. 'She shouldn't have said *all*. Oh well, let's take the wand back to the Vicar.'

When they reached home they found their parents completely restored, but of course still shut inside the meat-safe and very cramped and indignant.

'What were you doing out so very late, anyway?' said Mr Armitage.

The number of owls about the village was found to have greatly increased, and as a good many old ladies had mysteriously vanished, the proceeds of the progressive whist drive and the garden fête were used to buy a cannon to put in the school playground.

Dolls' House To Let, Mod. Con.

THE family were at breakfast when the front door bell rang, and Harriet went to see who it was.

'It's old Mrs Perrow,' she said returning. 'She says can she speak to you, Mother?'

'Oh dear,' said Mrs Armitage sadly. 'What can she want?'

She left her bacon and went into the front hall. The rest of the family watched the bacon sympathetically as it gradually went cold on her plate while they listened to a shrill stream of complaints going on and on, punctuated occasionally by a soothing murmur from Mrs Armitage.

'Wretched woman,' said Mr Armitage crossly. 'She must be telling all her family troubles back to Adam, by the sound of it. Mark, put your mother's plate in the hot-cupboard.'

Mark had just done this when his mother came back looking indignant.

'It really is too bad, poor things,' she said, sitting down. 'That miserable Mr Beezeley has turned them out of Rose Cottage on some flimsy excuse – the real reason is that he wants to do it up and let it to a rich American. So the Perrows have nowhere to live.'

'What an old scoundrel,' exclaimed Mr Armitage. 'All the same, I don't see that there's much we can do about it.'

'I said they could live in our loft till they found somewhere else.'

'You did *what*?'

'Said they could live in the loft. I don't know if they'll be able to climb in, though. Children, you'd better go and see if you can rig up a ladder for them.'

Mark and Harriet ran off, leaving their father to fume and simmer while his wife placidly went on with her breakfast.

The loft was over the kitchen, but it was approached from outside, by a door over the kitchen window. Harriet and Mark used it as a playroom and always climbed up by means of the toolshed roof, but grown-ups used a ladder when they entered it.

'Will the Perrows be able to use the ladder?' said Harriet doubtfully. 'The rungs are rather far apart.'

'No, I've had a better idea – Father's new trellis. We'll take a length of that. It's still all stacked by the back door.'

The trellis was ideal for the job, being made of strong metal criss-crossed in two-inch squares. They leaned a section over the kitchen window, fastened the top securely with staples to the doorsill of the loft, and jammed the bottom firmly with stones.

'That should take their weight,' said Mark. 'After all they're not heavy. Here they come.'

The Perrow family were peculiar in that none of them was more than six inches high. Ernie Perrow and his wife were cousins and lived with his old mother and their nine children. There had always been some Perrows in the village, but no one knew exactly why they were so small. There were various theories about it. Some people thought that a Perrow ancestor had been frightened by Stevenson's Rocket when he was young, and had never grown any more. Others said that it was a curse laid on the family by someone who had suffered from their bad temper, or that the Perrows always gave their children juniper wine instead of milk to keep them small.

Whatever the cause of their small size, they were very proud of it, and seldom married outside the family. They were a hard-working, self-respecting clan, rather dour and surly, earning their living mostly by rat-catching, chimney-sweeping, drain-clearing and other occupations in which their smallness was useful. The women did marvellous embroidery.

They had always owned Rose Cottage, portioning it off, one or two rooms to each family. But Ernie's father, old Mrs Perrow's husband, had been a waster and had been obliged to sell the cottage to Farmer Beezeley's father, who had let him stay on in it and pay rent. The present Beezeley was not so accommodating, and had been trying to get them out for a long time.

Harriet and Mark watched with interest as the Perrows made their way up the path to the loft. Lily and Ernie were each pushing barrows loaded with household belongings, and a trail of minute children followed, some of them only an inch or so high. Harriet began to wonder how the children would manage to climb up the trellis, but they scrambled up like monkeys, while Ernie was rigging a pulley to take the furniture. At the end of the procession came old Mrs Perrow carrying a bluebottle in a cage and keeping up a shrill incessant grumble.

'What I mean to say, fine place to expect us to live, I'm sure. Full of cobwebs, no chimney – where's Lily going to put her oil stove. We shall all be stunk out with paraffin.'

Harriet was enraptured with the oil stove, which the resourceful Ernie had made out of biscuit tins and medicine glasses. She rushed off to call her father to come and see it. Unfortunately he arrived just as the stove, dangling at the end of the rope, swung inward and cracked a pane of the kitchen window. Mr Armitage growled and retired again. He decided to soothe himself by watering his tomatoes, but had only just begun when he was startled by tiny, but piercing shrieks; he found a small Perrow in a pram the size of an eggshell (and in fact made from one) in the shade of one of his tomato plants. He had just copiously sprinkled it with Liquifert. He hurried off in a rage, tripped over a long line of washing which had been strung between two hollyhocks and had to replace twenty nappies the size of postage stamps fastened with clothes pegs made from split matches bound with fuse wire.

He strode indoors to find his wife.

'This arrangement won't do,' he thundered. 'I'll go and see that miserable Beezeley myself. I cannot have my garden used in this manner. I'm sure to tread on one of those children sooner or later.'

Mrs Armitage ruefully looked at a little Perrow sobbing

over the fragments of a doll's tea-set made from corn husks which she had trodden on before she saw it.

'They do seem to spread,' she agreed.

They heard frantic yells from the garden and saw two more children slide down from a cloche and run off, pursued by Ernie with a hairbrush.

'You touch any of these things and I'll tan you,' he shouted.

'It's no use, though,' Mrs Armitage said. 'Ernie and Lily do their best, but they can't be in nine places at once.'

Her husband clapped on his hat and rushed off to Beezeley's farm. He met Mr Beezeley himself, just outside the gate of Rose Cottage.

'Now look here, Beezeley,' he shouted. 'What right have you to turn those Perrows out of Rose Cottage? They paid their rent, didn't they? You can't do things like that.'

'Oh yes, I can, Mr Armitage,' Beezeley replied smoothly. 'Rose Cottage belongs to me, and it's supposed to be an agricultural labourer's cottage intended for men working on my farm. Perrow never did a hand's turn for me, he was all over the village.'

'Indeed,' said Mr Armitage dangerously, 'and who is the agricultural labourer that you have put in, may I ask?'

He turned to look at a huge Packard which stood outside the gate of Rose Cottage.

'Here he comes now,' replied Mr Beezeley agreeably. 'Meet my new farm worker, Mr Dunk R. Spoggin.'

'Well, well!' said that gentleman, strolling towards them. He wore a silk check shirt, diamond tiepin and red and white saddle shoes. 'I sure am pleased to meet another new neighbour. Quaint little rural spot you live in here, Mr Er. I aim to wake it up a little.'

'Mr Spoggin is going to work on my farm for a year,' explained Mr Beezeley. 'He has invented a new all-purpose agricultural machine which he wishes to try out, and my farm is going to be the testing ground. You can see them putting it up over there.'

Indeed a small army of men in blue jeans were putting

together something the size of a factory on the big meadow behind Beezeley's Farm.

'It ploughs, harrows, sows, manures, hoes, applies artificial heat, sprinkles with D.D.T., reaps, threshes and grinds,' Mr Spoggin informed them. 'It raises a crop in three days and has it harvested and out of the way in another three. Three days later the field is ready for a second crop. We should get sixty crops off that field of yours, Mr Beezeley, in the course of the next year.'

Mr Armitage looked incredulous. Dunk R. Spoggin drew himself up.

'You don't believe me, eh? Let me tell you I am *the* Dunk R. Spoggin, maker of the Spoggin Combine, the Spoggin Diesel Dam Dredger, the Spoggin Potato Clamper, the Spoggin Gloucester Old Spot Scratcher and the Spoggin Gilt-Edged Pig Palace. I could buy out Henry Ford any time, *if* I wanted to. Have a cigar.' He held out a two-foot one.

Mr Armitage accepted, and turned to find that Mr Beezeley had strolled away to inspect the new machine.

'Won't you find it rather confined in Rose Cottage? Surely it is smaller than the sort of thing you are used to?' he asked. Mr Spoggin smiled expansively.

'Why no, I just love your quaint little old houses. This one is genuine Tooder, I understand. Mr Beezeley wanted to lease it to me but I said straight out "No, Mr Beezeley, I'm a buying man. I'll give you twenty thousand for it, take it or leave it."'

'Twenty thousand *pounds*?'

'Pounds, yes sir.'

'And did he take it?'

'He did, and a cheaper property I've never bought. I felt downright mean, and nearly clapped another twenty on top of the first.'

Mr Armitage came home to lunch very thoughtful, and told his wife about their new neighbour.

'No hope of getting the Perrows back if he's bought the place,' he said. 'I'm afraid we're fixed with them for life.'

After lunch Mrs Armitage said: 'Children, if you're going

into Bunstable this afternoon, could you get me some embroidery silks? I don't seem to have as many as I thought I had.'

'I know where they are,' thought Harriet, who had seen all the little Perrow girls with beautiful new hair ribbons and sashes.

'And some napkin rings in Woolworths, please. All those seem to have gone too.'

A loud cry outside the window startled them, and Mark got there in time to see the butcher's boy trip on the path and scatter chops all over the pansies. The object that had tripped him appeared to be a napkin ring, which was being bowled by a small Perrow boy.

'Right, napkin rings and embroidery silks,' he said. 'That all? Coming, Harriet?'

Harriet always preferred the right-hand side of Bunstable High Street, because the left side was all taken up with banks, house agents, coal merchants and building societies, none of which have interesting shop windows. Today, however, her eye was caught as she cycled slowly along by a notice in a house agent's window, and giving a shout to Mark, who was in front, she jumped off and went to investigate.

TO LET: DOLLS' HOUSE 4FT. HIGH.   MOD. CON.

DESIRABLE RESIDENCE, NEWLY DECORATED

SEEN BY ARRANGEMENT   INQUIRE WITHIN

Harriet and Mark ran inside and saw a shady, seedy, young man picking his nails behind a deal desk. On a table at the back of the room was an elegant Queen Anne house with steps up to a pillared porch, and bow windows.

'Oh,' breathed Harriet, all eyes. Mark was brisker.

'We wish to inquire about the dolls' house,' he said.

'Yes, sir. A delightful family residence. Two recep., three bed, kitchen, bath, usual offices. Calor gas lighting and heating installed by last tenant, who vacated suddenly. Do you wish to have an order to view?'

'Can't we just *view* it?' asked Harriet, gazing covetously through a bow window at one of the two recep.

'Oh dear, no, madam. It's all locked up. The keys are obtainable from the owner.'

'Where does the owner live?'

'The address is Mrs Maria Nightshade, Cobweb Corner, Dead Man's Lane, Blackwood.'

Harriet and Mark burst in to tea full of enthusiasm.

'We've found a house for the Perrows,' they cried. Their parents looked sceptical.

'Old Mrs Nightshade? I seem to know the name. Isn't she a witch?'

'Very likely,' Harriet said. 'She lives in a dark little den full of pots and jars with a black cat and an owl. But the dolls' house is *lovely*, just think how pleased the Perrows will be.'

They were having their tea in the kitchen, and at that moment an outburst of thuds and angry screeches reminded them that the Perrows were just overhead.

'It will certainly be nice for them to have a separate room for old Mrs Perrow,' Mrs Armitage agreed. 'I always think it's a mistake to live with your mother-in-law.'

She took the lid off the jam-jar and found a small Perrow girl inside, having a peaceful feast and coated from head to foot in raspberry.

'Oh dear. Harriet, put Elsie on this saucer – I should pick her up with the sugar tongs – and take her to her mother. Really it's just like the evacuees all over again.'

Harriet did as she was requested, holding Elsie under the tap on the way in spite of howls.

'*There* she is, the wicked little thing,' exclaimed Lily. 'I'm sorry miss, I'm sure, but really they're that active it's a job to keep up with them all.'

She was putting them to bed, so Harriet postponed telling her about the house and ran back to the tea-table where Mark was explaining that they had paid a quarter's rent in advance.

'And they are bringing the house out tomorrow.'

'Where are they going to put it? Not in my garden I beg.'

'No, no, Miss Rogers said it could go at the end of her field.'

'What's the rent?'

'I should pick her up with the sugar tongs'

Harriet and Mark looked a little guilty.

'It's three packets of birthday candles a week – the pink, white and blue ones.'

'Funny sort of rent,' remarked her father suspiciously.

'Well you see she can't get them herself. People won't sell them to her in case she makes wax images, you know, and sticks pins in them.'

'She'll be able to make plenty now,' Mr Armitage said drily. 'However, far be it from me to interfere in any arrangement which rids us of the Perrows.'

An aniseed ball thudded against the window and cracked it. The Perrow boys were playing hockey with pencil hockey sticks from Woolworths which Mark had generously but thoughtlessly given them.

'That's the eighth window,' said Mrs Armitage resignedly.

Next day the Perrows moved out amidst universal rejoicing. Harriet and Mark went along to Miss Rogers's field to hear cries of delight at the sight of the beautiful house, but the Perrow enthusiasm was very lukewarm.

'Just look at all those big windows to clean,' said Lily gloomily. 'And Calor gas. Where am I going to put my oil stove? These old-fashioned houses are always draughty too.'

'Don't you take any notice of her, miss. She's pining for the cottage and that's the truth,' Ernie apologized.

They seemed to settle in comfortably enough though, old Mrs Perrow taking the best front room, and Harriet and Mark presently strolled away to see how Mr Beezeley's new cultivator was getting on. It now covered the entire hundred-acre field and looked like the Crystal Palace. Through the glass walls nothing could be seen but machinery, with Mr Dunk R. Spoggin darting among the cogs and belts.

They saw Mr Beezeley and said good morning to him rather coldly.

'Morning, morning young people,' he replied. 'Bitter weather for the time of year, isn't it. My rheumaticks are terrible bad.'

Indeed he was walking with great difficulty, almost doubled up.

'You'll be glad to hear that the Perrows have found a suitable house,' Harriet said shortly. 'They've rented Mrs Nightshade's dolls' house.'

'Old Mrs Nightshade over at Blackwood?' said Mr Beezeley, bursting into hearty laughter. 'I sold her a couple of hens that had the henbane once. She's never forgiven me; I bet she'd do me a bad turn if she could. But all's fair in love and farming, *I* say. Ugh, this rheumatism is fairly crippling me.'

The children left him and went home.

'Gosh,' said Harriet, 'do you suppose Mrs Nightshade is giving him rheumatism?'

'Well he jolly well deserves it. I hope she ties him in knots.'

When they arrived home they were dismayed to hear Mrs Perrow's shrill, complaining voice in the kitchen.

'What I mean to say, it's a fine thing, first to turn us out of our house, then have to live in a loft, all cobwebs though kindly meant I daresay, not what we're used to, and then when we move into the new house what do we find?'

'Well, what *do* you find?' said Mrs Armitage patiently.

'Nothing won't stay put!' cried Mrs Perrow. She had climbed on to a chair and was standing on it, quivering with indignation. 'You put down the kettle and it flies across and sticks on the wall. There's all Lily's bottled elderberries fallen down and broken and the daisy wine full of ashes that blew out of the fire by themselves, and young Sid's got a black eye from the mustard, and the bedroom door slammed and knocked baby down the stairs, and the dishes fall off the dresser all the time, it won't do, Mrs Armitage, it really won't do.'

'Oh dear,' Mrs Armitage said sympathetically, 'it sounds as if you have a poltergeist.'

'Can't say about that, mum, but it's not good enough for me and Ernie and Lily, and that's a fact. We'd sooner live in your loft, though it's not what we're used to, but stay in that house we cannot and will not.'

Mrs Armitage gazed at her in despair.

Just at that moment they all heard an extraordinary noise from the direction of Beezeley's farm, a sort of whistling which rose to a roar.

'What can be going on?' exclaimed Harriet. 'Let's go and see. I bet it's the new cultivator.'

They all ran out, leaving Mrs Perrow to continue her complaints to an empty kitchen. A strange sight met their eyes as they reached the new cultivator. It was swaying from side to side, shuddering and groaning as if at any moment it might leave the ground and take off into the air. Mr Spoggin was rushing about in great agitation with an oilcan. Mr Beezeley was there too, but did not seem to be taking much notice; he was standing hunched up looking very miserable and groaning from time to time.

'Look!' said Mark, 'there's corn sprouting through the walls.'

Wheat ears of an enormous size were pushing their way out between the panes of glass, and through the windows they could see that the whole inside was a tangled mass of stalks which continuously writhed and pushed upwards.

'It's cursed,' cried poor Mr Spoggin frantically. 'None of my other machines has done this. Someone's put a hoodoo on it.'

As he spoke there was a shattering explosion. Bits of broken glass and ears of corn the size of vegetable marrows filled the air. Fortunately the spectators were all blown backwards across several fields by the blast, and came to rest, breathless but unhurt, in Miss Rogers's field outside the dolls' house.

'Well that certainly is the end,' said Mr Spoggin, struggling to his feet. 'Never again do I try any experiments in your country. There must be something peculiar about the soil. I'm going straight back to the U.S.A. by the next boat.' He paused, with his mouth open and his eyes bulging.

'That dolls' house! Am I dreaming, or is it real?'

'Oh, it's real right enough,' they assured him gloomily as a saucepan and two little Perrows, inextricably entangled, rolled screaming and kicking down the front steps.

'I must add it to my collection. I have the largest collection of dolls' houses in five continents, including a real Eskimo child's dolls' igloo, made out of genuine snow. I definitely must have that house.'

'That's a fine thing,' shrieked Mrs Perrow, who had come up behind him in time to hear this. 'And where do we live, I should like to know?'

Mr Spoggin was visibly startled but recovered himself quickly and bowed to her.

'I'll make you a present of my place, ma'am,' he said. 'It's a poky little hole, I only paid twenty thousand pounds for it, but such as it is, it's yours. Just up the road, Rose Cottage is the name. Here are the title deeds.' He pulled them out of his pocket.

'We'll take you to see the agent,' Harriet said quickly. 'The dolls' house doesn't belong to the Perrows, and I don't know if the owner will want to sell. I fancy she prefers letting it.'

'She'll sell,' said Mr Spoggin confidently. 'Where's Tin Lizzie?'

He found his Packard roosting in a nearby hawthorn tree and whirled them off to the agent who received them warily. He was evidently used to complaints from tenants.

'If you want your quarter's rent back, I'm afraid it's out of the question,' he said at once. 'It's been used already.'

'I want to buy that dolls' house,' shouted Mr Spoggin. 'Name your figure.'

'I should warn you that it's haunted,' Harriet muttered. 'There's a poltergeist in it.'

'Haunted?' said Mr Spoggin, his eyes like stars. 'A haunted dolls' house! It'll be the gem of the whole collection.' He was in ecstasies.

'I don't know if my client wishes to sell,' said the agent repressively.

'I'll give you forty thousand pounds for it, not a penny more, so it's no use acting cagey in the hope that I'll put my price up, I shan't,' said Mr Spoggin. 'You can take it or leave it.'

The agent took it.

Mr Spoggin took them home and carried off the dolls' house then and there in Tin Lizzie, having telephoned the *Queen Mary* to wait for him. He left the remains of the cultivator.

Mr Beezeley was not seen for some hours after the explosion, but finally turned up in a bed of stinging-nettles, which had cured his rheumatism but left him much chastened. He spent a lot of time wandering round the deep hole which was all that was left of the hundred-acre field, and finally sold his farm and left the neighbourhood.

As the children came down to breakfast next morning they heard the grumbling voice of old Mrs Perrow in the porch:

'It's all very well, Mrs Armitage, but what I mean to say is, Rose Cottage is not what we've been used to. Cooking on that old oil stove of Lily's after Calor gas and a bathroom and all, say what you like, it's not the same thing, and what I mean to say –'

The People in the Castle

THE castle stood on a steep hill above the town. Round the bottom of the hill ran the outer castle wall with a massive gateway, and inside this gate was the doctor's house. People could only approach the castle by going in through his surgery door, out through his garden door, and up a hundred steps; but nobody bothered to do this, because the castle was supposed to be haunted, and in any case who wants to go and see an empty old place falling into ruins? Let the doctor prowl round it himself if he wanted to.

The doctor was thought to be rather odd by the townspeople. He was very young to be so well established, he was always at work writing something, and he was often quite rude to his patients if they took too long about describing their symptoms, and would abruptly tell them to get on and not beat about the bush.

He had arranged his surgery hour in a very businesslike way. The patients sat in rows in the large waiting-room amusing themselves with the illustrated papers or with the view of the castle, which filled up the whole of one window in a quite oppressive manner. Each patient picked up a little numbered card from a box as he arrived and then waited until the doctor rang the bell and flashed his number on the indicator. Then the patient hurried to the surgery, breathlessly recited his symptoms before the doctor grew impatient, received his medicine, dropped his card into another little box, paid for his treatment (or not, after the National Health Service arrived), and hurried out by another door which led straight back to the main castle gateway.

By this means the incoming and outgoing patients were not allowed to become entangled in halls and passageways creating confusion and holding up proceedings. The doctor was not very fond of people, and the sooner he could clear them all out of his house and get back to his writing, the better he was pleased.

One evening there were fewer patients than usual. It was late in October. The wind had been blowing in from the sea all day, but it dropped before sunset, and what leaves remained on the trees were hanging motionless in the clear dusk.

'Is there anyone after you?' the doctor asked old Mrs Daggs, as he gave her some sardine ointment.

'Just one young lady, a stranger I reckon. Never seen her in the town.'

'All right – good night,' said the doctor quickly, and opened the door for the old woman, at the same time pressing the buzzer for the next number. Then he thought of a phrase for the paper he was writing on speech impediments and twiddled round in his revolving chair to put it down in the notebook on his desk. He was automatically listening for the sound of the waiting-room door, but as he heard nothing he impatiently pressed the buzzer again, and turning round shouted:

'Come along there.'

Then he stopped short, for his last patient had already arrived and was sitting in the upright chair with her hands composedly folded in her lap.

'Oh – sorry,' he said. 'You must have come in very quietly. I didn't know you were in here.'

She inclined her head a little, as if acknowledging his apology. She was very white-faced, with the palest gold hair he had ever seen, hanging in a mass to her shoulders. Even in that dusky room it seemed to shine. Her dress was white, and over it she wore a grey plaid-like cloak, flung round her and fastening on her shoulder.

'What's your trouble?' asked the doctor, reaching for his prescription block.

She was silent.

'Come along for goodness' sake – speak up,' he said testily. 'We haven't got all night.' Then he saw, with surprise and some embarrassment, that she was holding out a slate to him. On it was written:

'I am dumb.'

He gazed at her, momentarily as speechless as she, and she gently took the slate back again and wrote on it:

'Please cure me.'

It seemed impolite to answer her in speech, almost like taking an unfair advantage. He felt inclined to write his message on the slate too, but he cleared his throat and said:

'I don't know if I can cure you, but come over to the light and I'll examine you.' He switched on a cluster of bright lights by his desk, and she obediently opened her mouth and stood trustfully while he peered and probed with his instruments.

He gave an exclamation of astonishment, for at the back of her mouth he could see something white sticking up. He cautiously pulled it farther forward with his forceps and discovered that it was the end of a long piece of cotton wool. He pulled again, and about a foot of it came out of her mouth, but that seemed to be nowhere near the end. He glanced at the girl in astonishment, but as she appeared quite calm he went on pulling, and the stuff kept reeling out of her throat until there was a tangle of it all over the floor.

At last the end came out.

'Can you speak now?' he asked, rather anxiously.

She seemed to be clearing her throat, and presently said with some difficulty:

'A little. My throat is sore.'

'Here's something to suck. I'll give you a prescription for that condition – it's a result of pulling out the wool, I'm afraid. This will soon put it right. Get it made up as soon as you can.'

He scribbled on a form and handed it to her. She looked at it in a puzzled manner.

'I do not understand.'

'It's a prescription,' he said impatiently.

'What is that?'

'Good heavens – where *do* you come from?'

She turned and pointed through the window to the castle, outlined on its hill against the green sky.

'From *there*? Who are you?'

'My name is Helen,' she said, still speaking in the same husky, hesitant manner. 'My father is King up there on the hill.' For the first time the doctor noticed that round her pale, shining hair she wore a circlet of gold, hardly brighter than the hair beneath. She was, then, a princess?

'I had a curse laid on me at birth – I expect you know the sort of thing?' He nodded.

'A good fairy who was there said that I would be cured of my dumbness on my eighteenth birthday by a human doctor.'

'Is it your birthday today?'

'Yes. Of course we all knew about you, so I thought I would come to you first.' She coughed, and he jumped up and gave her a drink of a soothing syrup, which she took gratefully.

'Don't try to talk too much at first. There's plenty of time. Most people talk too much anyway. I'll have the prescription made up' – 'and bring it round,' he was going to say, but hesitated. Could one go and call at the castle with a bottle of medicine as if it was Mrs Daggs?

'Will you bring it?' she said, solving his problem. 'My father will be glad to see you.'

'Of course. I'll bring it tomorrow evening.'

Again she gravely inclined her head, and turning, was gone, though whether by the door or window he could not be sure.

He crossed to the window and stood for some time staring up at the black bulk of the castle on the thorn-covered hill, before returning to his desk and the unfinished sentence. He left the curtains open.

Next morning, if it had not been for the prescription lying on his desk, he would have thought that the incident had been a dream. Even as he took the slip along to Boots to have the medicine made up he wondered if the white-coated woman there would suddenly tell him that he was mad.

That evening dusk was falling as the last of his surgery patients departed. He went down and locked the large gates and then, with a beating heart, started the long climb up the steps to the castle. It was lighter up on the side of the knoll.

The thorns and brambles grew so high that he could see nothing but the narrow stairway in front of him. When he reached the top he looked down and saw his own house below, and the town with its crooked roofs running to the foot of the hill, and the river wriggling away to the sea. Then he turned and walked under the arch into the great hall of the castle.

The first thing he noticed was the scent of lime. There was a big lime tree which, in the daytime, grew in the middle of the grass carpeting the great hall. He could not see the tree, but why was a lime tree blossoming in October?

It was dark inside, and he stood hesitating, afraid to step forward into the gloom, when he felt a hand slipped into his. It was a thin hand, very cool; it gave him a gentle tug and he moved forward, straining his eyes to try and make out who was leading him. Then, as if the pattern in a kaleidoscope had cleared, his eyes flickered and he began to see.

There were lights grouped round the walls in pale clusters, and below them, down the length of the hall, sat a large and shadowy assembly; he could see the glint of light here and there on armour, or on a gold buckle or the jewel in a head-dress as somebody moved.

At the top of the hall, on a dais, sat a royal figure, cloaked and stately, but the shadows lay so thick in between that he could see no more. But his guide plucked him forward; he now saw that it was Helen, in her white dress with a gold belt and bracelets. She smiled at him gravely and indicated that he was to go up and salute the King.

With some vague recollection of taking his degree he made his way up to the dais and bowed.

'I have brought the Princess's linctus, Sire,' he said, stammering a little.

'We are pleased to receive you and to welcome you to our court. Henceforth come and go freely in this castle whenever you wish.'

The doctor reflected that he always *had* come and gone very freely in the castle; however, it hardly seemed the same place tonight, for the drifting smoke from the candles made the hall look far larger.

He lifted up his eyes and took a good look at the King, who

had a long white beard and a pair of piercing eyes. Helen had seated herself on a stool at his feet.

'I see you are a seeker after knowledge,' said the King suddenly. 'You will find a rich treasure-house to explore here – only beware that your knowledge does not bring you grief.'

The doctor jumped slightly. He had indeed been thinking that the King looked like some Eastern sage and might have information which the doctor could use in his study on occult medicine.

'I suppose all doctors are seekers after knowledge,' he said cautiously, and handed Helen her bottle of medicine. 'Take a teaspoonful after meals – or – or three times a day.' He was not sure if the people in the castle had meals in the ordinary way, though some kind of feast seemed to be in progress at the moment.

From that time on the doctor often made his way up to the castle after evening had fallen, and sat talking to the King, or to some of the wise and reverend knights who formed his court, or to Helen. During the daytime the castle brooded, solitary and crumbling as always, save for some occasional archaeologist taking pictures for a learned monthly.

On Christmas Eve the doctor climbed up with a box of throat tablets for Helen, who still had to be careful of her voice, and a jar of ointment for the King who had unfortunately developed chilblains as a result of sitting in the chill and draughty hall.

'You really should get him away from here, though I'd miss him,' he told Helen. 'I don't know how old he is – '

'A thousand – ' she interjected.

' – Oh,' he said, momentarily taken aback. 'Well in any case it really is too damp and cold for him here. And you should take care of your throat too; it's important not to strain it these first months. This castle really is no place for either of you.'

She obediently flung a fold of her grey cloak round her neck.

'But we are going away tomorrow,' she said. 'Didn't you know? From Christmas to Midsummer Day my father holds his court at Avignon.'

The doctor felt as if the ground had been cut from under his feet.

'You're going away? You mean you'll none of you be here?'

'No,' she answered, looking at him gravely.

'Helen! Marry me and stay with me here. My house is very warm – I'll take care of you, I swear it – ' He caught hold of her thin, cold hand.

'Of course I'll marry you,' she said at once. 'You earned the right to my hand and heart when you cured me – didn't you know that either?'

She led him to her father and he formally asked for her hand in marriage.

'She's yours,' said the King. 'I can't prevent it, though I don't say I approve of these mixed marriages. But mind you cherish her – the first unkind word, and she'll vanish like a puff of smoke. That's one thing we *don't* have to put up with from mortal man.'

As soon as Helen married the doctor and settled in his house she became a changed creature. The people in the town were surprised and charmed to find what a cheerful, pretty wife their hermit-like doctor had found himself. She left off her magic robes and put on check aprons; she learned to cook and flitted around dusting and tidying; moreover as her newly won voice gathered strength she chattered like a bird and hummed the whole day long over her work.

She abolished the buzzer in the surgery because she said it frightened people. She used to look through the door herself and say:

'The doctor will see you now, Mrs Jones, and will you try not to keep him waiting, please – though I know it's hard for you with your leg. Is it any better, do you think? And how's your husband's chest?'

'She's like a ray of sunshine, bless her,' people said.

The doctor was not sure about all this. What he had chiefly loved in her was the sense of magic and mystery; she had been

A royal figure, cloaked and stately

so silent and moved with such stately grace. Still, it was very pleasant to have this happy creature in his house attending to his comfort – only she did talk so. In the daytime it was not so bad, but in the evenings when he wanted to get on with his writing it *was* trying.

By and by he suggested that she might like to go to the cinema, and took her to a Disney. She was enchanted, and after that he was ensured peace and quiet on at least two evenings a week, for she was quite happy to go off by herself and leave him, only begging him not to work too hard.

One night he had nearly finished the chapter on Magic and its Relation to Homeopathic Medicine, and was wishing that he could go up and discuss it with the King. He heard her come in and go to the kitchen to heat the soup for their late supper.

Soon she appeared with a tray.

'It was a Western,' she said, her eyes sparkling. 'The hero comes riding into this little town, you see, and he pretends he's a horse-dealer but really he's the D.A. in disguise. So he finds that the rustling is being run by the saloon keeper –'

'Oh, for goodness' sake, *must* you talk all the time,' snapped the doctor. Then he stopped short and looked at her aghast.

A dreadful change had come over her. The gay print apron and hair ribbon dropped off her and instead he saw her clad in her white and grey robes and wreathed about with all her magic. Even as she held out her hands to him despairingly she seemed to be drawn away and vanished through the thick curtains.

'Helen!' he cried. There was no answer. He flung open the door and ran frantically up the steps to the castle. It was vacant and dark. The grass in the great hall was stiff with frost and the night sky showed pale above him in the roofless tower.

'Helen, Helen,' he called, until the empty walls re-echoed, but no one replied. He made his way slowly down the steps again and back to his warm study where the steam was still rising from the two bowls of soup.

From that day the townspeople noticed a change in their

doctor. He had been hermit-like before; now he was morose. He kept the castle gates locked except for the surgery hour and disconnected his telephone. No longer was there a pretty wife to tell them that the doctor would see them now; instead they were confronted by a closed door with a little grille, through which they were expected to recite their symptoms. When they had done so, they were told to go round by an outside path to another door, and by the time they reached it they found the necessary pill or powder and written instructions lying outside on the step. So clever was the doctor that even with this unsatisfactory system he still cured all his patients, and indeed it seemed as if he could tell more about a sick person through a closed door than other doctors could face to face; so that although people thought his treatment strange, they went on coming to him.

There were many queer tales about him, and everyone agreed that night after night he was heard wandering in the ruined castle calling 'Helen! Helen!' but that no one ever answered him.

Twenty years went by. The doctor became famous for his books, which had earned him honorary degrees in all the universities of the world. But he steadfastly refused to leave his house, and spoke to no one, communicating with the tradespeople by means of notes.

One day as he sat writing he heard a knock on the outer gate, and something prompted him to go down and open it. Outside stood a curious looking little woman in black academic robes and hood, who nodded to him.

'I am Dr Margaret Spruchsprecher, Rector of the University of Freiherrburg,' she said, walking composedly up the path before him and in at his front door. 'I have come to give you the degree of Master of Philosophy at our University, as you would not come to us or answer our letters.'

He bowed awkwardly and took the illuminated parchment she offered him.

'Would you like a cup of coffee?' he said, finding his voice with difficulty. 'I am most honoured that you should come all this way to call on me.'

'Perhaps now that I have come so far I can help you,' she said. 'You are seeking something, are you not? Something besides knowledge? Something that you think is in the castle, up there on the hill?'

He nodded, without removing his gaze from her. The keen, piercing look in her old eyes reminded him vividly of the King.

'Well! Supposing that all this time, what you seek is not *inside*, but has gone *outside*; supposing that you have been sitting at the mouth of an empty mouse-hole; what then?' There was something brisk, but not unkindly in her laugh as she turned and made off down the path again, clutching the voluminous black robes round herself as the wind blew them about. The gate slammed behind her.

'Wait – ' the doctor called and ran after her, but it was too late. She was lost in the crowded High Street.

He went out into the town and wandered distractedly about the streets staring into face after face, in search of he hardly knew what.

'Why, it's the doctor, isn't it?' a woman said. 'My Teddy's been a different boy since that medicine you gave him, Doctor.'

Someone else came up and told him how thankful they were for his advice on boils.

'My husband's never forgotten how you cured his earache when he thought he'd have to throw himself out of the window, the pain was so bad.'

'I've always wanted to thank you, Doctor, for what you did when I was so ill with the jaundice – '

'You saved my Jennifer that time when she swallowed the poison – '

The doctor felt quite ashamed and bewildered at the chorus of thanks and greeting which seemed to rise on every side. He finally dived into a large doorway which seemed to beckon him, and sank relieved into a dark and sound-proof interior – the cinema.

For a long time he took no notice of the film which was in progress on the screen, but when he finally looked up his attention was attracted by the sight of galloping horses; it was a Western. All of a sudden the memory of Helen came so suddenly and bitterly into his mind that he nearly cried aloud.

'Excuse me, sir, that's the one and nine's you're sitting in. You should be in the two and three's.'

He had no recollection of having bought any ticket, but obediently rose and followed his guide with her darting torch. His eyes were full of tears and he stumbled; she waited until he had caught her up and then gave him a hand.

It was a thin hand, very cool; it gave him a gentle tug. He stood still, put his other hand over it and muttered:

'Helen.'

'Hush, you'll disturb people.'

'Is it you?'

'Yes. Come up to the back and we can talk.'

The cinema was pitch dark and full of people. As he followed her up to the rampart at the back he could feel them all about him.

'Have you been here all these years?'

'All these years?' she whispered, mocking him. 'It was only yesterday.'

'But I'm an old man, Helen. What are you? I can't see you. Your hand feels as young as ever.'

'Don't worry,' she said soothingly. 'We must wait till this film ends – this is the last reel – and then we'll go up to the castle. My father will be glad to see you again. He likes your books very much.'

He was too ashamed to ask her to come back to him, but she went on:

'And you had better come up and live with us in the castle now.'

A feeling of inexpressible happiness came over him as he stood patiently watching the galloping horses and feeling her small, cool hand in his.

Next day the castle gates were found standing ajar, and the wind blew through the open doors and windows of the doctor's house. He was never seen again.

Don't Pay the Postman

YOUNG Miss Wind lived with her father in his cottage on an island north of the Hebrides. It was a lonely life for her, as her mother was dead, and her father, Wind, was out all day, and often all night too, on his work, blowing.

Miss Wind kept the cottage tidy, dusted (which she did very well), knitted warm woolly socks for her father and generally looked after him as far as she was able, cooked the supper and dug in their little patch of garden where nothing would ever grow. Her only possessions were a comb and a gold ring, which had been her mother's. She spent long hours sitting gazing out to sea, wondering what life was like in the south, where she had never been.

The cottage was built of breeze-blocks, with huge windows made from slices of wind, and dark curtains of night-wind for use in the summer when the sun is still shining at midnight in those northern regions. No one ever called there except the postman who visited all the islands in his motor boat. Old Wind did not encourage callers. He could not prevent the postman, who had to bring his licence to blow, certificates of proficiency and other government documents, but he told his daughter never to let the man into the cottage, and that she was not to gossip with him.

Wind was not fond of society. By the time he came home from his work all he wanted to do was fall on his great bed and pass into a sleep so heavy that it took three alarm clocks and Miss Wind with a cup of boiling tea to wake him.

On Sundays he went to be cleaned, for by the end of the week he had collected up so much dust, paper, straws, leaves, bits of wool and general odds and ends, not to mention chimney-pots, masts of ships, trees and waterspouts that he was quite choked up and unable to function. The cleaning took all day, and was done backwards and forwards, many times over.

Miss Wind used to find Sunday her loneliest day until she learned about the Sunday paper, and then it was her happiest. She was very fond of reading, but there were no books or magazines in the cottage, as Wind did not hold with them. He said that paper was flimsy, useless stuff and it stood to reason that anything written on it would be useless too. So Miss Wind had to hide her Sunday paper, and when she had read it right the way through she burned it, though very regretfully.

The postman brought the Sunday paper when he made his weekly visit on Saturday afternoon. Miss Wind did not obey her father's rule. She always asked the postman in and gave him a cup of tea. Moreover, she paid him twopence for the paper and another penny for delivery; he had told her that this was the regular fee. This was not the case, but Miss Wind, who lived very much out of the world, believed him. He also told her that the reason for the arrival of the Sunday paper on a Saturday was that, as they were so far north and the sun rose at midnight, their day began before everybody else's. Miss Wind did not quite understand this, but she believed it too.

She always turned first to the Great Fashion Competition and filled in her entry for it while the postman drank his tea. Then she would give him some money for stamps to stick on the completed form and he would take it away when he went. She had never won anything, and this was not surprising for she knew very little about fashion. When the postman had gone she used to read her horoscope. This was the treat of the week. She took it most seriously, and would often become very excited if it said something like:

'A promising social opening this week will mean a widening of your horizon and many new friendships', or

'After a gay and lively week you will need to relax at the weekend', or

'A new business contact will lead to heavy and important responsibilities.'

Miss Wind faithfully followed their directions as well as she was able.

One Saturday she was feeling low. Her father had been bad-tempered all week because it was the Equinox and he had extra work to do with the gales and spring tides. Moreover, Miss Wind was beginning to think about the spring-cleaning. She wished that she could get a woman in to help her, but unfortunately there was no one available within fifty miles. She was afraid that her father might decide to help, and find one or two cherished horoscopes which she had not been able to resist cutting out and keeping.

When she heard the chug of the postman's motor boat she put the kettle on for tea and decided that she would cheer herself up by turning to her horoscope first instead of doing the fashion competition.

She saw the postman into his chair, with the sugar bowl beside him, and eagerly turned to page three, looking for the square block in the two middle columns. When she had read through it she looked up with an exclamation of dismay.

'What's up?' asked the postman, drinking his tea.

'It says "Don't pay the postman who brings you this paper. He is paid by the Government and requires nothing further from you. You will receive a newspaper bill in due course."'

'Eh? What's that?' said the postman, grabbing the paper from her. When he read it an ugly expression came over his face.

'And I suppose you'll believe a wretched, twopenny paper rather than me, who's been bringing it regularly all these months.'

'I must believe it,' replied Miss Wind with dignity, though she was rather frightened. 'I always believe my horoscope.'

'Anyway it's last week's so it doesn't apply,' snapped the postman.

She looked at the date (which she had never thought to do before) and turned pale.

'So you've been deceiving me when you said it was to-morrow's paper,' she said slowly. 'In that case I certainly shall not continue paying you.'

The postman swore in a nasty way, took hold of her wrist before she realized what he was going to do, and snatched off her gold ring. Then he made off with it, shouting:

'That'll pay you out, you miserly little skinflint.'

She heard the chug-chug of his boat as she reached the door, and knew she could never hope to catch him.

Wind arrived home early that day, and in a bad temper. He had become quite clogged up with blowing on a fire in a sock factory in Glasgow. He wanted his tea and he wanted to go to bed. When he entered the cottage he found his daughter in tears seated before a fire which was nearly out, surrounded by the pages of the *Sunday Illustrated*. There was no kettle on, no hot scones, no girdle cakes, no kippers.

'What's the meaning of this?' asked Wind furiously.

Poor Miss Wind sobbingly let out the whole story – the postman, the papers, the tea, the horoscopes, the payments, the fashion competitions, and worst of all, the loss of the ring.

As Wind listened his face grew darker and darker, and finally at the end of the recital he gave her a stinging slap on the cheek – the sort that you feel when you go out in a north-east gale.

'This is a pretty kettle of fish!' he said. 'I knew how it would be if you let anyone into the house. Here's this fellow been cheating you out of threepence every week – I don't suppose the newsagents saw a penny of it – not to mention the entry money for the competitions – and now he's got away with your mother's ring. Perhaps you'll obey my orders another time. Now leave the house, and don't come back unless you have the ring with you – and take that disgusting trash out of my sight.'

Poor Miss Wind picked up her Sunday paper and wrapped her comb and some oatcakes in it. Then she went down to the anchorage where she kept her little boat, for she guessed that the postman would never come back to the island, and if she wanted the ring she would have to go after him.

Wind raged furiously round the house trying to light the fire. He blew so hard that a great clot of half-burned socks, which had been stopping him up, suddenly flew out and finished off the fire completely. That made him angrier than ever, and he determined to go in search of the postman himself. He set off across the islands, and by pure chance met the postman's motor boat just rounding a promontory. Wind pounced on him, intending to grab the ring, but the man had it in his pocket. The motor boat capsized, the wicked postman was drowned, and the ring was lost.

Then Wind was sorry, and went looking for his daughter to tell her to come home again and cook his supper, but she was nowhere to be seen.

Miss Wind had gone in quite the other direction, and was rowing her boat slowly south. She felt very sad. Her father was angry, she had lost her ring, and she had been following the wrong horoscope every week. She felt that she had nothing left but the fashion competition, so in order to cheer herself a little she turned over the scattered pages of her paper until she found it, and set seriously to work, trying to judge the merits of twelve different hair styles.

Miss Wind had quite a lot of hair herself, of a strange, silvery colour. She never wore it in any particular *style*, merely keeping it combed and wishing that she could cut it short – but she had no scissors. So she gazed with interest at the different pictures of curled hair, waved hair, upswept hair, downswept hair, and sideswept hair. The last picture was one which particularly took her fancy; it was short and comfortable-looking, not too tidy (she had such difficulty in keeping her own hair tidy) and the caption underneath was 'Windswept'. That decided her; she unhesitatingly put a cross under it and wished that she had some stamps, or some money to buy them.

These reflections had taken time, and when she looked over her shoulder she found that she was approaching the mainland. A row of mountains stood up out of the sea, and at the foot of them was a little fishing village.

'Hey there, are you a mermaid?' somebody called, and she saw a young fisherman bobbing in a boat near by.

'No I am not,' she replied with dignity. 'My name is Miss

Wind and I am looking for the postman. Can you assist me?'

'I'm afraid you're unlucky, Miss,' he said. 'The postman was drowned in a gale this afternoon off Point Ness.'

'Oh dear,' exclaimed Miss Wind.

'I shouldn't worry,' the fisherman consoled her. 'He was a bad lot. Been taking money out of the registered envelopes for years. He's no loss.'

'No, but he had my ring in his pocket,' said Miss Wind sadly. 'Now I shall never get it back.'

'Oh I don't know. Rings often turn up inside fish. You stay around in Port Lomas for a while, and it's odds someone finds your ring in a herring.'

'Is this Port Lomas?'

'Yes it is. My dad keeps the fish shop.'

A fat man in a white apron appeared in a door and stuck up a notice which said 'Frying Tonight'. When he saw them he shouted:

'Jock! The fan's gone wrong again.'

'That's bad,' said Jock gloomily. 'I've no more repair parts left. It's the fan we use for cooling the fish,' he explained to Miss Wind.

'Perhaps I could do it instead,' she suggested. 'I'm very good at blowing.'

They agreed to take her on temporarily until the fan was mended, and Mrs Andrews, the fishmonger's wife, let Miss Wind have a room. Her pay was five shillings a week.

Miss Wind liked her work, and the Andrews family took a great fancy to her. Mr Andrews started teaching her to play the bagpipes, and Mrs Andrews helped her fill in and post her fashion competition entry.

Unfortunately the time came when the fan was mended, and then Miss Wind was out of a job. There were only two other shops in Port Lomas, a butcher and a baker. The butcher kept his meat in a huge refrigerator, and the baker heated his oven by means of an electric bellows, so neither of them needed Miss Wind's services; moreover, the baker said

'I'm very good at blowing'

that Miss Wind's presence in the bakehouse was enough to make the dough sink.

Luckily the Provost, who had seen her at work in the fishmonger's, offered her a job as a street cleaner. It was not very well paid, but she did not mind; she tied up her hair in a blue and white cloth to keep out the dust and toffee papers, and much enjoyed seeing all the people go by and saying good morning to them.

One day she was working hard clearing away a lot of confetti left over from a wedding when the sky became black, and looking up she saw her father standing with arms folded and regarding her in a very awful manner.

'So this is where you have got to! What is the meaning of employing yourself in the public streets in this manner?' he said.

'Well,' replied Miss Wind with spirit, for she was no longer the timid little thing she had been when she lived at home, 'you turned me out, so I had to earn my own living.'

'It is quite out of the question for you to do it in *this* way,' said Wind. 'You have no training, no diploma, no certificate, no licence to blow, and you are not a union member. You had better come home right away before the union gets to hear about this.'

'I don't want to come home – it's too dull – besides I haven't found the ring yet. And I like street cleaning, and I do it just as well as anybody else.'

'That is not the point,' pronounced Wind. 'Are you coming home or not?'

'Not.'

Wind flung his plaid round him and stalked off to the post office without another word. His daughter placidly continued removing the bits of confetti and sweet papers from the pavement.

Wind sent telegrams, saying that a non-union cleaner was operating in Port Lomas, to the Amalgamated Union of Trade Winds, the International Transport, Propulsion and Motivation Workers' Union (a somewhat sluggish union generally known as the Doldrums), the Federated Roaring

Forties (a progressive splinter group), the Sirocco, Simoon and Mistral Co-operative Union, and the North-East Trades Council.

As a result of these telegrams the various wind unions met and decided to work to rule. This meant that there was just enough wind to encourage housewives to hang out their washing, but not enough to dry it; enough wind to get yachtsmen out on the water but not enough to move them; enough wind to persuade farmers to cut their grass, but not enough to make hay.

Still Miss Wind went on with her job. She did not see why she should stop for a lot of unions, though she was visited by dozens of shop stewards who tried to persuade her to stop, and picketed by breezes, light airs, gusts, eddies and capfuls of wind who got in her way and tried to hinder her work.

Then a general strike of wind was decided on, and this was more serious.

Poor Miss Wind began to get beseeching letters: from drought-parched farmers in California who saw rain-clouds in the next valley which never moved; from ship-owners; from millers; from the Lord Mayor of London to say that the city was enveloped in a dark cloud of smog and people would soon be dying of it; from gliding clubs; from children who could not fly their kites; from directors of airlines; all imploring her to leave her job and allow the winds of the world to get started again.

In the end she gave in. With tears in her eyes she pounced on her last bit of newspaper and then started slowly back to her digs at the Andrews'. As she came within sight of the door she saw them all there, jumping up and down and waving.

'You've won it, lass!' shrieked Mrs Andrews. 'You've won the hair-style competition.'

A fat agreeable man came forward, said he was from the *Sunday Illustrated*, and presented her with a cheque for £500.

'May I ask how you will use it?' he asked, whipping out his notebook.

'I shall start a hairdressing establishment in Port Lomas,'

replied Miss Wind at once. 'I already have a comb and an interest in hair (not to mention waves) and I can do the drying myself; there is no hairdresser's for two hundred miles so I shall have plenty of custom.'

This plan proved most popular and in no time Miss Wind was doing a roaring trade, creating newer and more elegant windswept styles, larger and more permanent waves.

A week after she was installed young Jock Andrews came into the shop with something in his hand.

'Guess what I found inside a herring?' he said.

'My ring,' answered Miss Wind at once. She took it from him and put it in a registered envelope, addressing it to Wind, Esq. 'I hope the new postman is more reliable than the last one.'

'Aren't you going to go back and live at home?'

'When I'm so happy here? Not likely. I'll visit Father on my half days and do a bit of cleaning for him.'

'How about marrying me?' suggested Jock Andrews, pulling another ring out of his pocket.

So she married him and they lived happily ever after. If custom was ever slack, she went out with her husband in his smack and blew him along, and every August they went for their holiday to stay with Wind in the little house built of breeze-blocks.

The Third Wish

ONCE there was a man who was driving in his car at dusk on a spring evening through part of the forest of Savernake. His name was Mr Peters. The primroses were just beginning but the trees were still bare, and it was cold; the birds had stopped singing an hour ago.

As Mr Peters entered a straight, empty stretch of road he seemed to hear a faint crying, and a struggling and thrashing, as if somebody was in trouble far away in the trees. He left his car and climbed the mossy bank beside the road. Beyond the bank was an open slope of beech trees leading down to thorn bushes through which he saw the gleam of water. He stood a moment waiting to try and discover where the noise was coming from, and presently heard a rustling and some strange cries in a voice which was almost human – and yet there was something too hoarse about it at one time and too clear and sweet at another. Mr Peters ran down the hill and as he neared the bushes he saw something white among them which was trying to extricate itself; coming closer he found that it was a swan that had become entangled in the thorns growing on the bank of the canal.

The bird struggled all the more frantically as he approached, looking at him with hate in its yellow eyes, and when he took hold of it to free it, hissed at him, pecked him, and thrashed dangerously with its wings which were powerful enough to break his arm. Nevertheless he managed to release it from the thorns, and carrying it tightly with one arm, holding the snaky head well away with the other hand (for he did not wish his eyes pecked out), he took it to the verge of the canal and dropped it in.

The swan instantly assumed great dignity and sailed out to the middle of the water, where it put itself to rights with much dabbling and preening, smoothing its feathers with little showers of drops. Mr Peters waited, to make sure that it was all right and had suffered no damage in its struggles. Presently the swan, when it was satisfied with its appearance, floated in to the bank once more, and in a moment, instead of the great white bird, there was a little man all in green with a golden crown and long beard, standing by the water. He had fierce glittering eyes and looked by no means friendly.

'Well, Sir,' he said threateningly, 'I see you are presumptuous enough to know some of the laws of magic. You think that because you have rescued – by pure good fortune – the King of the Forest from a difficulty, you should have some fabulous reward.'

'I expect three wishes, no more and no less,' answered Mr Peters, looking at him steadily and with composure.

'Three wishes, he wants, the clever man! Well, I have yet to hear of the human being who made any good use of his three wishes – they mostly end up worse off than they started. Take your three wishes then – ' he flung three dead leaves in the air ' – don't blame me if you spend the last wish in undoing the work of the other two.'

Mr Peters caught the leaves and put two of them carefully in his notecase. When he looked up the swan was sailing about in the middle of the water again, flicking the drops angrily down its long neck.

Mr Peters stood for some minutes reflecting on how he should use his reward. He knew very well that the gift of three magic wishes was one which brought trouble more often than not, and he had no intention of being like the forester who first wished by mistake for a sausage, and then in a rage wished it on the end of his wife's nose, and then had to use his last wish in getting it off again. Mr Peters had most of the things which he wanted and was very content with his life. The only thing that troubled him was that he was a little lonely, and had no companion for his old age. He decided to use his first wish and to keep the other two in case of an emergency. Taking a thorn he pricked his tongue with it, to remind himself not to utter rash wishes aloud. Then holding the third leaf and gazing round him at the dusky under-growth, the primroses, great beeches and the blue-green water of the canal, he said:

'I wish I had a wife as beautiful as the forest.'

A tremendous quacking and splashing broke out on the surface of the water. He thought that it was the swan laughing at him. Taking no notice he made his way through the darkening woods to his car, wrapped himself up in the rug and went to sleep.

When he awoke it was morning and the birds were beginning to call. Coming along the track towards him was the most beautiful creature he had ever seen, with eyes as blue-green as the canal, hair as dusky as the bushes, and skin as white as the feathers of swans.

'Are you the wife that I wished for?' asked Mr Peters.

'Yes I am,' she replied. 'My name is Leita.'

She stepped into the car beside him and they drove off to the church on the outskirts of the forest, where they were married. Then he took her to his house in a remote and lovely valley and showed her all his treasures – the bees in their white hives, the Jersey cows, the hyacinths, the silver candlesticks, the blue cups and the lustre bowl for putting primroses in. She admired everything, but what pleased her most was the river which ran by the foot of his garden.

'Do swans come up here?' she asked.

'Yes, I have often seen swans there on the river,' he told her, and she smiled.

Leita made him a good wife. She was gentle and friendly, busied herself about the house and garden, polished the bowls, milked the cows and mended his socks. But as time went by Mr Peters began to feel that she was not happy. She seemed restless, wandered much in the garden, and sometimes when he came back from the fields he would find the house empty and she would only return after half an hour or so with no explanation of where she had been. On these occasions she was always especially tender and would put out his slippers to warm and cook his favourite dish – Welsh rarebit with wild strawberries – for supper.

One evening he was returning home along the river path when he saw Leita in front of him, down by the water. A swan had sailed up to the verge and she had her arms round its neck and the swan's head rested against her cheek. She was weeping, and as he came nearer he saw that tears were rolling, too, from the swan's eyes.

'Leita, what is it?' he asked, very troubled.

'This is my sister,' she answered. 'I can't bear being separated from her.'

Now he understood that Leita was really a swan from the forest, and this made him very sad because when a human being marries a bird it always leads to sorrow.

'I could use my second wish to give your sister human shape, so that she could be a companion to you,' he suggested.

'No, no,' she cried. 'I couldn't ask that of her.'

'Is it so very hard to be a human being?' asked Mr Peters sadly.

'Very, very hard,' she answered.

'Don't you love me at all, Leita?'

'Yes, I do, I do love you,' she said, and there were tears in her eyes again. 'But I miss the old life in the forest, the cool grass and the mist rising off the river at sunrise and the feel of the water sliding over my feathers as my sister and I drifted along the stream.'

'Then shall I use my second wish to turn you back into a swan again?' he asked, and his tongue pricked to remind him of the old King's words, and his heart swelled with grief inside him.

'Who would darn your socks and cook your meals and see to the hens?'

'I'd do it myself as I did before I married you,' he said, trying to sound cheerful.

She shook her head. 'No, I could not be as unkind to you as that. I am partly a swan, but I am also partly a human being now. I will stay with you.'

Poor Mr Peters was very distressed on his wife's account and did his best to make her life happier, taking her for drives in the car, finding beautiful music for her to listen to on the

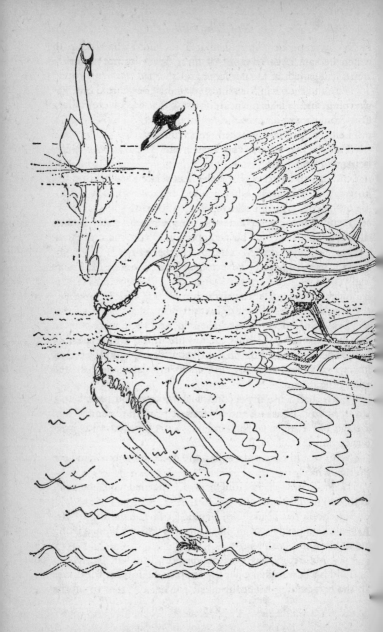

radio, buying clothes for her and even suggesting a trip round the world. But she said no to that; she would prefer to stay in their own house near the river.

He noticed that she spent more and more time baking wonderful cakes – jam puffs, petits fours, éclairs and meringues. One day he saw her take a basketful down to the river and he guessed that she was giving them to her sister.

He built a seat for her by the river, and the two sisters spent hours together there, communicating in some wordless manner. For a time he thought that all would be well, but then he saw how thin and pale she was growing.

One night when he had been late doing the accounts he came up to bed and found her weeping in her sleep and calling:

'Rhea! Rhea! I can't understand what you say! Oh, wait for me, take me with you!'

Then he knew that it was hopeless and she would never be happy as a human. He stooped down and kissed her goodbye, then took another leaf from his notecase, blew it out of the window, and used up his second wish.

Next moment instead of Leita there was a sleeping swan lying across the bed with its head under its wing. He carried it out of the house and down to the brink of the river, and then he said 'Leita! Leita!' to waken her, and gently put her into the water. She gazed round her in astonishment for a moment, and then came up to him and rested her head lightly against his hand; next instant she was flying away over the trees towards the heart of the forest.

He heard a harsh laugh behind him, and turning round saw the old King looking at him with a malicious expression.

'Well, my friend! You don't seem to have managed so wonderfully with your first two wishes, do you? What will you do with the last? Turn yourself into a swan? Or turn Leita back into a girl?'

'I shall do neither,' said Mr Peters calmly. 'Human beings and swans are better in their own shapes.'

Next day he saw the two swans

But for all that he looked sadly over towards the forest where Leita had flown, and walked slowly back to his empty house.

Next day he saw two swans swimming at the bottom of the garden, and one of them wore the gold chain he had given Leita after their marriage; she came up and rubbed her head against his hand.

Mr Peters and his two swans came to be well known in that part of the country; people used to say that he talked to the swans and they understood him as well as his neighbours. Many people were a little frightened of him. There was a story that once when thieves tried to break into his house they were set upon by two huge white birds which carried them off bodily and dropped them in the river.

As Mr Peters grew old everyone wondered at his contentment. Even when he was bent with rheumatism he would not think of moving to a drier spot, but went slowly about his work, milking the cows and collecting the honey and eggs, with the two swans always somewhere close at hand.

Sometimes people who knew his story would say to him:

'Mr Peters, why don't you wish for another wife?'

'Not likely,' he would answer serenely. 'Two wishes were enough for me, I reckon. I've learned that even if your wishes are granted they don't always better you. I'll stay faithful to Leita.'

One autumn night, passers-by along the road heard the mournful sound of two swans singing. All night the song went on, sweet and harsh, sharp and clear. In the morning Mr Peters was found peacefully dead in his bed with a smile of great happiness on his face. In between his hands, which lay clasped on his breast, were a withered leaf and a white feather.

Pigeon Cake for Miss Samphire

A SALESMAN was walking along a lonely coast road in the west of England. He carried a wicker suitcase, which he swung lightly in one hand, and a heavy bag hanging over his shoulder. In his pockets were a toothbrush, a razor, and some nylon webbing. He travelled in eggs, which sounds a risky proceeding, but was really very easy.

When he came to a house he knocked at the door and asked the housewife:

'Any delicious new-laid eggs today, Madam?'

If she said yes, or asked if the eggs really were fresh, he put down the suitcase on the step and opened it. It was empty. While the housewife laughed scornfully, or looked annoyed, he called:

'Pauline, Madeleine, Estelle, Annette, Louise, Sophie, Caroline, Odette, Marguerite, Josephine, Suzanne, Lily!'

At once twelve beautiful white pigeons would come wheeling down and each lay an egg in the suitcase. Then the salesman would hold it out to the astonished housewife and say:

'There you are, Madam. New laid, as you can see for yourself.'

On another occasion it would be Jacqueline, Marianne, Lucille, Antoinette, Seraphine, Diane, Nicolette, Catherine, Charlotte, Adelaide, Stephanie and Claudette that he called. He had about fifty birds who took it in turns to lay eggs for him and followed him everywhere at a discreet distance. In the sack over his shoulder he carried grain for them, and at night, wherever he was staying, whether at an inn or under a haystack, he would clap his hands and the pigeons would come flocking round for their supper. Then, if it was a cold night, they would all sleep huddled together with the salesman underneath a sort of quilt of pigeons.

Housewives were always delighted to get such fresh eggs, even if they were only pigeon-size, and he was hardly ever turned away from a door, so that as his wants were few he made a comfortable living.

On this particular day the salesman had already sold three dozen eggs at a fishing village, and as the wind was rising and it was turning cloudy he decided to finish business and look for somewhere to pass the night. It was midsummer eve, but quite cold; the wind was whipping up the tops of the waves and blowing little eddies of sand or 'travellers' off the beach, which stung the salesman's legs and got into his turnups.

The road ran right beside the beach across a bay between two headlands. Inland was a sandy marsh which stretched for miles. It was an isolated, empty part of the country, and the salesman began to wish that he had stayed in the village or struck inland instead of keeping along this deserted road. His pigeons trailed along dispiritedly after him, spread out across the bay in small groups. A casual eye would have taken them for gulls.

About two miles in front of him at the foot of the opposite headland he thought he could see a house. He wondered if the people in it would put him up for the night or tell him where he could get a lodging. As he walked on he came to a notice which said:

ONLY ANOTHER 1000 YARDS TO THE OYSTER CAFÉ
SHRIMP AND OYSTER TEAS

The salesman was encouraged by this. The notice looked quite new, so he hoped that he could get a meal at the Oyster Café, and possibly a bed too, if the proprietor was friendly.

At a nearer view of the place his hopes sank. It looked very quiet; there were no cars standing near, the garden was full of weeds and the house itself wanted a lick of white paint. He began to wonder if it was empty but as he came round the corner of the garden wall he heard children's voices and saw two boys playing on the grass. He went up a path made of oyster-shells to the front door and knocked. After a longish time it was opened and a pale, timid-looking woman peered at him.

'Did you want something?' she asked, looking nervously over his shoulder along the road.

'Can I get some supper here?' he asked.

'No we never serve suppers,' she said flatly. 'Only teas, and that's finished at six.'

He looked at his watch. It was seven.

'Well, can you tell me where I can get a bite to eat and a bed for the night?'

'There's no other house round here, not till you get to Penbarrow and that's another seven miles. You might be able to stay at the Fisherman's, though they don't mostly take visitors.'

His heart sank, as he thought of walking on through the chilly evening for another seven miles.

A couple of his pigeons, Jacqueline and Louise, fluttered near, hoping that it would soon be supper time, and he impatiently waved them off.

'Those are pretty,' said the woman. 'Are they yours?'

'Yes,' he answered curtly. 'Wouldn't like some eggs in return for a meal, I suppose?'

Her face lit up. 'Oh yes, I *would*! It's my little boy's birthday tomorrow and I haven't an egg in the house to make him a birthday cake. The – the manager forgot to go in for the groceries. Could you spare me a dozen?'

The salesman called up some more pigeons and presented her with a dozen little white eggs.

'Come inside,' she said quickly, glancing round once more. 'There isn't much in the larder but I'll see what I can do for you.' She showed him into a chilly, dreary room full of flimsy little tables; its walls were decorated by lemonade and ginger beer advertisements.

He sat down at one of the tables and studied a menu which read:

> Oyster Tea. Off.
> Whelk Tea. Off.
> Shrimp Tea. Off.

Prawns, Cockles, Mussels. Off.
Scones. Off.
Bread and Butter.
Cakes. Off.
Mustard and Cress. Off.
Salad. Off.
Devonshire Tea. Off.

In contrast to this discouraging list a savoury smell of frying bacon stole into the room. He looked idly out of the french window and saw the two boys playing close by. One of them, the larger, kept poking the other with a stick and teasing him until he was on the point of tears.

'You wouldn't do that if Miss Samphire was here,' the smaller boy blubbered, trying ineffectually to grab the stick.

'Oh, go on. Who cares for you and your old Miss Samphire?' All the same, the salesman noticed that the bigger boy glanced behind him nervously. Then as if ashamed of himself, he leaned forward and viciously tugged at the other boy's nose, at the same time hitting him on the side of the head with the stick. The salesman opened the window and stepped through.

'Stop that, you bully,' he said angrily to the bigger boy, who gaped at him in astonishment, and then ran off round the house.

The younger boy was almost as startled and gazed at the salesman as if he were a ghost.

'Who's Miss Samphire?' asked the salesman. 'Your teacher?'

'Hush!' said the little boy hurriedly. 'I'm not allowed to tell people about her.'

Just at that moment the woman appeared at the french window to say that supper was ready.

'I must just feed my pigeons,' said the salesman. He clapped his hands three times and the whole fifty dropped down round him like bullets for the grain he scattered. The woman and boy watched wide-eyed.

He found quite a good supper of fried ham, bread and butter and coffee waiting for him in the dining-room, and started eating ravenously. Presently he heard a car draw up outside and heavy footsteps clumped into the house. Then there was a silence, and looking up he saw a man staring at him through the dining-room door – a tall man with black hair and a pair of very cold eyes. The man turned on his heel and went on into the kitchen without saying a word. Then the salesman heard a deep growling voice in the next room:

'What's *he* doing here?'

There was a low, apologetic murmur from the woman.

'Eggs be blowed. You get him out, d'you understand? I've told you before that I won't have people here after six. I'm going now to fetch Skid and Duke, and when I come back, he's got to be gone. Maybe this will help you to remember.'

He heard a cry from the woman as if she had been hit.

'And put that snivelling brat of yours to bed.'

Then there were running footsteps and the bigger boy went past the dining-room door. There was a confused mumble of complaint from him:

'– wasn't doing anything to Rob and he said he'd hit me –'

'Said he'd *what*?'

The black-haired man swung into the dining-room and leaned over the salesman's table.

'You leave my boy alone or I'll knock your block off.'

'I didn't touch him. I told him not to hit his brother.'

'Brother be hanged. That's the housekeeper's brat, and what Les does to him is none of your business. Now get out of here.'

'I haven't paid my bill yet,' the salesman said calmly. He got up and went into the kitchen to find the housekeeper, who was just putting a cake into the oven.

'That'll be two and six, please,' she said. He noticed a red mark on her cheek. As he gave her the money he heard a car start, and looking out through the kitchen window saw the black-haired man and his boy drive off.

'A nasty type,' he said. 'What's his name?'

The woman looked terrified. 'Mr Abel,' she answered.

'What's going on here?' the salesman asked curiously.

'Everyone seems to be frightened of something. What happens here in the evenings? And who's Miss Samphire?'

'Miss Samphire?' She looked bewildered. 'Oh, that's just some nonsense of Robbie's – nothing to do with Mr Abel.'

'The other boy seemed to know about her.'

'No, it's just children's games.'

'What does Abel do, then?'

'I can't tell you about that – you must go. If he found you when he came back with Skid and Duke he'd probably kill you. This is a dreadful place – oh, why did I ever answer the advertisement for a housekeeper and come here?'

'Why don't you leave?'

'They'd murder me if I tried to – I know too much about what they do.'

'Dear me,' said the salesman. 'This is all very shocking.'

He was a good citizen, and did not at all approve of these sinister goings-on. Moreover, he was very curious to know what Abel and his associates *did* do in the evenings – could they be smugglers? Or wreckers?

Not wanting to get the woman into further trouble he said a polite goodbye, picked up his case and went out of the garden gate, but then he doubled back behind the wall and made his way round to some outbuildings at the back, wondering if they would hold any clue to Abel's activities. There was a farmyard paved with loose oyster-shells. It was impossible to walk across it without making a noise, but the sea was beyond the further buildings and the sound of the waves drowned his footsteps.

The farm buildings seemed to be unused, and were in bad repair, but there was a tower behind them which attracted his attention. It was on the edge of the beach, solidly built of stone, standing in a shingle-bank. He went across to it and tried the door, which opened. Inside, a circular flight of stairs led upwards. It was dark and steep, and he had to feel his way carefully until he came to another door at the top which opened into a round room, lit by three small windows. I was nearly full of sacks, piled on top of each other. The sales man prodded them inquisitively. They might have contained grain or dried peas, but some of his pigeons who flew in after him displayed no interest in them.

The sound of the sea, which was now rolling in heavily, deadened all other noises, and the salesman did not hear the return of Abel's car. He pulled out his pocket-knife, and cutting the cord which tied one of the sacks, looked inside. It was full of large, pink pearls.

At this moment he heard a rasping voice from behind him which said:

'Hey, Abel. Abel! There's somebody in here. I can hear him feeling about.'

The salesman turned round and saw a fat man with a bald, shiny head, who was standing still with his head in a listening attitude. He seemed to be blind. Next instant Abel's face appeared over his shoulder.

'It's you, is it? poking about,' Abel said savagely. 'Well, I warned you to clear out before, but now you've gone too far and it's too late. Duke, bring that bit of rope up will you?'

A third man appeared, as tall as Abel, with a surly, brutish expression. He pulled out a rope without a word, and he and Abel closed in on the salesman. After a short struggle he was overpowered and they tied his hands.

'Now you can stay there for a bit,' said Abel, 'till we're ready for you. You're very clever to have found the pearls, and I dare say you've guessed that the oysters in this bay are pearl oysters, and that's the last guess you'll guess, because we're not fond of strangers poking into our affairs. When we've brought in tonight's haul we'll take you out and dump you in a sack to study the oysters close to, so you can be looking forward to that. I suppose that precious housekeeper of mine fetched you here – well, we'll dump her too, and her brat. I always said it was stupid to have them.'

'How are we going to run the teashop then?' grumbled the blind man.

'Duke will have to – he can cut bread and butter. And you can count the change,' Abel said sourly. 'Come on now – tide's getting down.'

They went off, slamming the door and bolting it on the outside, but reappeared in a few minutes shoving the housekeeper and Robbie in front of them. Their hands were tied as well.

'My cake's in the oven,' the woman kept crying. 'My cake!'

'Oh, bother your cake. You won't be there to eat it anyway.'

Abel's boy accompanied them this time, and he came over and gave the salesman a kick.

'That'll teach you to butt in when I'm talking to Rob,' he said vindictively. Then he gave a parting clump to Robbie and they went out, bolting the door again. Presently the three prisoners heard the chug of a motor boat starting up.

'How long do they take getting the pearls?' the salesman asked.

'A couple of hours,' the woman told him. 'Oh, why did you have to interfere?'

'Well, it's not hopeless yet,' the salesman said, though he did not feel too cheerful. He went to the landward window and whistled to his pigeons, who came flocking in. He showed them by signs that he wanted them to peck through his ropes, and in a few minutes they got the idea and began hammering away with their beaks. They were constantly bumping each other as they fluttered over him, and his hands became very sore and started to bleed, from the pecks that missed the ropes. By and by, though, he felt the ropes begin to give as they became more ragged, and at last, with a terrific effort he was able to break them. Then he untied the other two captives.

'Thirty feet to the ground – and anyway that window's too small for me to climb through,' he said thoughtfully. 'It'll have to be you, sonny.'

'He can't climb down the tower,' the woman said, going pale.

'No, no, I don't mean him to. He's going to wear my pigeon harness.'

He pulled a tangle of nylon webbing and cord out of his pocket and began fitting it round Robbie.

It was a delightful sensation

224

'I use this for crossing rivers, or if I get lost and want to take a sighting. The pigeons can't carry me very far, of course, too heavy, but they can manage a mile or so. They should be able to carry the boy a good long way. Where's your nearest police station?'

'Penbarrow,' she said dully. 'That's seven miles.'

'I think they could do that.'

'I'd sooner go and get Miss Samphire,' the boy said, wriggling himself more comfortable in the straps.

'No fairy-tales now, son. This is serious. You go for the police and tell them we're shut up here and if they don't get here by,' he glanced at his watch, 'eleven o'clock it'll be all up with us. Can you do that?'

The boy nodded.

'Pull the left-hand bunch of cords to go left, right-hand to go right, one jerk with both hands to go up, two to come down. Now help me harness these pigeons – that's more tricky.'

It was a long job, as each pigeon had to be securely buckled into her little harness, but at last it was done. The pigeons all flew out of the window at a signal from their master, and hovered outside, keeping the nylon cords just taut between them and the boy.

'Not frightened, are you?' asked the salesman.

He shook his head. He was rather pale, but he climbed up on to the window ledge. His mother hugged him goodbye with tears streaming down her face, and then he gave both bunches of rope a tug, and the birds rose a little and lifted him clean off the sill and up into the air. He swung in view for a moment and then was whisked away out of sight.

'Seven miles,' said the salesman reflectively. 'He ought to make it in an hour. Those birds can do thirty miles an hour easily without a load. I should think they could manage ten with the boy. I hope the police have a car.'

But Robbie had gone for Miss Samphire.

It was a delightful sensation being swung along by the birds, once he had recovered from the first moment's sick fright, as he saw the ground wheeling such a long way below

his feet. He took a deep breath and steered the pigeons down
to the sea. Beyond the house the ground rose into a cliff, which
formed one arm of the bay, and the beach came to an abrupt
end. Only at the lowest tides was the foot of the cliff exposed,
but an agile child could scramble across its face out to the
point, and this Robbie had done. Now he made the birds take
him the same way, out along by the black rocks and over the
heaving water. The pigeons disliked it very much.

Dusk was falling, and he had to strain his eyes to see the
place he was aiming for. Near the point of the headland there
was a dark crack in the cliff face. Robbie tugged twice when
they reached it, and the birds dropped until he was dangling
just above the water outside it. He leaned forward, grabbed at
a ledge and pulled himself up until he was kneeling on it.

'Miss Samphire!' he called urgently. 'Miss Samphire!'

'Yes?' a voice answered him – a very long-drawn, echoing
voice which seemed to come from somewhere deep, deep
inside the cliff. 'Yes, what is it?'

'Miss Samphire, Mr Abel and those other two men have
got Mother and a stranger shut up in the tower, and they are
going to drop them into the sea in sacks. And me too. Please
will you help us?'

'Well really,' said the voice, which was half a snarl, half a
yawn. 'These men are unbearable. First they take my pearls,
now they are going to start dropping people into my bay. I
shall have to put a stop to it, once and for all.'

She emerged suddenly from the mouth of her cleft, and the
pigeons rose cawing and flapping, dragging Robbie off his
rock most painfully. Many people would not have found Miss
Samphire handsome, but Robbie was fond of her, as she had
helped him on several occasions when he had been in difficulties.

She was eight feet high, or long, and her skin was bright
blue-green. Her hair was not hair, but a series of flutes or
folds something like a bat's wing, or an umbrella, which
hung down from her head round her neck and waved in and
out as she floated in the water. It was scarlet and white. Her
arms were very, very long, and her fingers were curved, more

like spines than real fingers. Her tail was covered, not with scales, but with thick, waterproof fur like that of a seal, grey-green in colour. She was rather phosphorescent.

'Where are those men now?' she asked Robbie, balancing herself with a downward thrust of her tail so that she bobbed in the swell underneath him.

'Across on the opposite rocks, getting the pearls. There would be time to go and rescue Mother and the man before they get back.'

'You go back to the shore and wait there. I shan't be long.'

The pigeons were only too glad to carry Robbie to the beach, and had started tugging him away before he gave the signal.

Miss Samphire disappeared in an arrowy flash of bubbles.

The three men and the boy had taken as many oysters as the boat would carry and were turning for home when they heard an echoing voice from the water which cried: 'Stop!' and Miss Samphire, green and glittering, appeared ahead. With one sweep of her tail she overset the boat, and that was the end of them.

Then she turned and made for the shore. Robbie had unloosed his pigeons and tried to unlock the door at the foot of the tower. The key was in the lock, but it was too stiff for him. Miss Samphire's long green talons turned it in a second.

'There's another one at the top,' said Robbie. 'I can't reach the bolt.'

She slithered up the stairs with the speed of someone used to crawling on slippery rocks, and bracing herself on her five-foot tail, undid the bolt at the top. The door opened inwards, and she practically fell into the round room.

Robbie's mother took one look at her and shrieked, but the salesman said:

'Ah! I thought there must be something of the kind about. Thank you, Miss.'

He helped the housekeeper down the stairs (she was having hysterics) while Miss Samphire shot on ahead like an eel.

The salesman very politely invited her in to have a bite of something, and she rather doubtfully accepted. They had

Robbie's birthday cake (which was just done) and a large omelette made from pigeon's eggs.

Robbie's mother kept on the house, which seemed to belong to nobody. Half the pearls went to the Crown, and the other half they were allowed to keep. The salesman always dropped in on them when he was round that way, and let them have a few dozen eggs for nothing, as compensation for having got them into such a tight corner. In return they gave him pearls, which he used to offer to the housewives on their doorsteps as an alternative to eggs.

If they saw a green shape at night, flashing across the bay, or heard a sad hoarse voice singing below the cliffs, they never mentioned it to anyone, knowing Miss Samphire's desire for privacy.

When Robbie was older he had a very beautiful pearl and silver necklace made, and left it in a little parcel beside the cleft in the rock.

The Mysterious Barricades

THE main thing about the mountains was their height. They were so high that they really did seem to join on to the sky; if you looked at them you had to tip your head back and back until your neck ached; then you were obliged to lie down so that your eyes might go on travelling up to the final snow-crowned summits which were like needles among the clouds.

The people in the village never looked up at them. They had had enough gazing at mountains when they were babies and lay on their backs in prams. As soon as they could walk they turned away from white peaks and dark forests and staggered off in the other direction, towards the plains. If they had to walk towards the mountains they kept their eyes on their boots.

One day a man on a bicycle came to the village. He was a stranger, and consequently everyone stopped work and looked at him, but furtively. The blacksmith put down his hammer, but picked up a piece of string and pretended to be untying it, with his eyes fixed on the traveller. The postman stood gazing at a letter that he had been about to slip into a box as if he had suddenly forgotten how to read. The innkeeper came out on to his balcony and began busily polishing and repolishing a glass, though everyone knew that half the time he didn't trouble to wash them at all.

The traveller pedalled slowly along, glancing from side to side. He saw that every house had someone standing in its doorway or leaning from its window. Only one house seemed to take no interest in him; it was a small bungalow with the name 'Mountain View' painted on its gate. All its windows were lace-curtained and the door was tight shut. He put on his brakes and came to a stop outside it. All the heads craned out a little further to see what he was doing. He leaned his bicycle against the garden wall, unlatched the gate, walked up the path, and rapped at the door.

After a few moments it was opened, and a voice snapped:

'Well, come in, come in. Don't keep me waiting in the cold.'

He hurriedly stepped into the dark interior. He could see hardly anything at first, except the glow of a fire. Both windows had ranks of dark, spreading pot-plants across them, as well as the lace curtains, and bird cages hung in front of the plants. It was very quiet inside; he could hear the clock tick, and the fire rustle, and the birds clearing their throats.

'Well,' said the old woman who had let him in. 'What have you come bothering me for? Aren't there enough busybodies in the village but you have to come and trouble someone who keeps herself to herself?'

'I thought I was more likely to hear the truth from someone who keeps herself to herself,' said the traveller. 'When was the last stranger seen in this village?'

'Ten years ago last Tuesday.'

'And where did he go?'

'He went up the mountains.'

'Did he have a canary and a roll of music with him?'

'As to a roll of music, I can't say; he had a big leather case. He certainly had a canary.'

As she said this one of the birds in the cages began to hop up and down, twittering in a very excited manner.

'Is that the one?' asked the man, looking at it attentively.

'Yes, that's him. Pip, I call him. The man gave him to me for a cup of tea.'

The traveller walked over to the cage, unlatched the door, and whistled a few bars of a tune. The canary continued the tune to its end, finishing with a triumphant trill, and then hopped out on to the man's shoulder.

'He seems to know you,' said the old woman. 'But he's mine for all that.'

The man pulled a cup of tea out of his pocket and handed it to her.

'I'll buy him back off you,' he said. 'Can you tell me anything more? What did this man look like?'

'He had glasses. And a tie like yours. He went off to the mountains and that was the last we saw of him. Ten years is a long time.'

She drank the tea, looking at him thoughtfully.

'I've been ten years tracing him,' said the traveller. 'He stole my canary and he stole my music. I'll go on now, and thank you kindly for the information.'

He tucked the canary into a pocket so that only its head showed, and moved to the door.

'Wait a minute,' said the old woman. 'In return for the tea I'll give you a warning. Those mountains are dangerous. No one who goes up them comes back again. They say there are animals up there with huge feet who can fly faster than the wind.'

'I can't help that, I have to go on,' the traveller said.

'The other man said that too,' the old woman muttered, shaking her head. 'He talked about some mysterious barricades he wanted to find.'

'Yes? In these mountains?' exclaimed the traveller, his face alight with interest and excitement.

'How should I know? It's only what he said. I've never heard of any mysterious barricades – nor do I know what they are, for that matter.'

'They are where the Civil Servants go when they retire,' he told her absently, and he thoughtfully fingered the black and red necktie he wore, which appeared to be made of typewriter ribbon. 'Well, many thanks once more.'

He walked down to the gate and threw one leg over his bicycle.

'You'll never get up the mountains on that,' she called. 'Better leave it here.'

'This machine has a thirty-three speed,' he called back. 'It goes up any hill that isn't vertical,' and he pedalled slowly off. The villagers watched him until he was past them, then they stopped looking in case they should catch a glimpse of the mountains, and went across to question the old woman about her visitor.

But – 'He's been in the Civil Service,' was all she would say, shortly.

'Civil Service!' They looked at their boots, spat, and went off to their own homes.

Meanwhile, the traveller had reached the foot of the great forest which cloaked the lower slopes of the mountains. He switched to the second of his thirty-three speeds, turned on his light, and pedalled boldly upwards. The road was good, although carpeted with pine needles as if it was rarely used. Far overhead the trees sighed to each other, and above them the out-thrust elbows of the mountain hung over his head.

Soon he came to snow, and the bicycle began to slip and stagger on the frozen crust. He took out chains from the saddlebag and painstakingly laced them round his wheels. This helped his progress, but he was now going more slowly, and night was falling; in the pinewood it was already almost pitch dark. He decided to halt for the night, and leaned his bicycle against a tree. Taking out a groundsheet from the bag he hung it over the bicycle making a rude tent, into which he crawled. From his pocket he drew out another cup of tea and a biscuit. He drank the tea, shared the biscuit with the canary, and then settled himself to sleep.

He had been sleeping for perhaps two hours when he was woken by a terrible howling in the woods above him. It sounded almost like a human cry, but a thousand times louder and more mournful.

He started to his feet, upsetting the bicycle and ground-sheet. He saw that it must have been snowing heavily while he slept, for all his footprints were gone and the groundsheet was covered several inches thick. All was silent again, and he moved cautiously a few feet from his encampment, turning his head this way and that to listen. Something caught his eye – a footprint – and he went over to look at it. It made him turn pale.

It was the print of an animal's paw, but what a size! He could have fitted his own foot into it four times over. When he looked for others he saw that they led in a single trail, fifteen feet apart, in a wide ring round his tent, and then away up the hill.

'Perhaps it has gone, whatever it is,' he thought hopefully, but in the same instant he heard the terrible voice again, nearer than before. It seemed to lament, and also to threaten; it echoed among the trees until he could not tell from which quarter it came, and he fled back to his tree and cowered by the bicycle, looking haggardly in all directions. His canary had fallen into a terrified cheeping.

Then his pride began to stir.

'Come,' he said to himself. 'I am a Civil Servant. What would the lower grades think if they saw me now? What would my Administrator think?' And he recited to himself the little rhyme which the juniors in the lowest grades are set to learn when they first join the ranks of the Service.

> 'Always helpful, never hurried,
> Always willing, never worried,
> Serve the public, slow but surely,
> Smile, however sad or poorly,
> Duty done without a swerve is
> Aimed at by the Civil Service.'

This encouraged him, and as he saw no prospect of further sleep he packed up his groundsheet once more, shared a few biscuit crumbs with the canary and wheeled the bicycle back to the path. He changed down to his thirtieth gear and started to ride up the hill.

Once again he heard the voice reverberating through the trees and seeming to cry: 'Woe! Oh, woe, woe.'

He ducked his head over the handlebars and pedalled on, reciting to himself:

'Grade I, Step I, ten pounds a year. Step II, ten pounds twelve shillings. Step III, ten pounds fifteen shillings. Step IV, ten pounds nineteen shillings. Step V, ten pounds nineteen and six. Grade II, Step I, eleven pounds a year. What a very peculiar tree that is over there. I wonder why there is no snow on it? Annual ex gratia allowances for married men, wife, ten shillings. First child, five shillings. Every subsequent child, two and six. There's another tree on the other side, just the same shape.'

He disliked the two trees which grew along the ground for some distance before turning upwards. They were so very black and so very symmetrical, on either side of the road. An unpleasant fancy came to him that they might be *legs* – but whoever heard of legs the size of pine trees? And if they were legs, where was the body that belonged to them?

He glanced up fearfully into the thickness of the branches above. The sky was beginning to pale with dawn around the edge of the forest, but overhead hung a dense mass of black, supported, it seemed, on those pillar-like trees. He put one foot on the ground and craned back, trying in vain to decide if it was merely the darkness of foliage or if there was something huge leaning over him? As he looked it seemed to move and draw downward, and all at once he saw two great pale eyes, mournful and menacing, descending on him.

With a frantic spasm of courage he flung the bicycle into twenty-second gear and pushed off. He felt a hot dry breath on his neck and struggled desperately up the hill, his heart almost bursting. The light grew ahead and in a few moments he was out of the trees, crashing across virgin snow with the rising sun striking warmly on the top of his head as he bent forward.

He could hear no sound behind, and finally ventured to stop and turn round. Nothing was visible except a distant agitation among the tree tops as if the creature was watching him from the cover of the forest but dared not come out. Encouraged by this he hurried on and was soon out of sight of the trees round a fold of the mountain.

All that day he climbed, and in the green light of evening he was nearing the top of a pass which seemed to cut right through the peak of the mountain. Huge rock walls, seamed with snow, reared up on either side of him.

The traveller was terribly tired. He had hardly halted all day and had eaten nothing save a cup of tea and a biscuit when he paused to pump up his tyres. He had sweated under the fierce heat of noon, but now it was beginning to freeze again and he shivered and longed to lie down and cover himself with the friendly snow.

It seemed to be only a few hundred yards now to the top, and making a final effort he struggled up in ninth gear, to stop aghast at what he saw. The right-hand wall of the pass dropped away at the top, giving a fearful vista of snowy and cloud-wrapped peaks; but the left-hand cliff continued sheering up more and more steeply until it was vertical, with its top veiled in obscurity. Across the face of the cliff ran a narrow ledge – all that remained of the path.

For a moment the traveller was daunted and his heart sank. He had been sure that the top of the pass was the end of his journey and that there he would find the Mysterious Barricades. But his courage only faltered for a short space, and soon he began doggedly working his way along the little path. At first it was wide enough to ride on, but presently he came to a sharp corner in the cliff and he had to dismount. He tried to edge the bicycle round but it slipped from his grasp on the icy rock, and fell outwards. He leaned sideways, holding on to a projection in the cliff and saw the bicycle falling down and down. It became as small as a moth, then as small as a tea-leaf, and finally vanished without the faintest sound coming back to him from the gulf.

He turned, sick and shaken, to continue his journey on foot, but to his unutterable astonishment found the path ahead blocked by another traveller. A short man, wearing spectacles and carrying a leather case stood gazing at him seriously.

The traveller stood silent for a long time.

'Jones!' he said, at length. 'I never expected to meet you here. I thought that you would have passed through the Mysterious Barricades many years ago, using my music as a passport.'

Jones shook his head.

'For ten years I have been wandering in these mountains,' he said sadly. 'I am beginning to believe that the Mysterious Barricades do not exist. I thought that your music would open all gates, but though I have played it daily upon my flute there has been no sign. Perhaps that was the punishment for my theft.'

'How have you lived?' asked the other, looking at him compassionately.

'Buns. They were all I was entitled to, as a Civil Servant Grade III. Would you care for one? I am sick of the sight of them.'

'I'll give you a cup of tea for it.'

'Tea!' Jones's eyes lit up. 'I didn't know you had reached the higher grades.' He drank it as if it was nectar, while the other man munched his bun, pleasantly filling after a prolonged diet of biscuit.

'Now what are we to do?' said Jones presently. 'We cannot pass each other on this ledge and if one of us tries to turn round he will probably be dashed to destruction.'

'Let us play my sonata for two flutes and continuo,' said the traveller, who had been looking at the leather portfolio for some minutes past.

Jones cautiously drew out some sheets of manuscript music and passed them over. The traveller turned through them until he came to the piece he wanted, which was inscribed:

'Sonata in C major for two flutes and continuo by A. Smith.'

The two men took out their flutes and Smith propped his manuscript on a ledge in the cliff face so that they could see it by looking sideways. They stood facing each other and played the sonata through, but when they came to the end nothing happened.

'It wants the continuo part,' said Smith sadly. 'Let us play it again and I will try to put it in.'

They began again, though Jones looked doubtful.

This time the canary suddenly popped its head from Smith's pocket, where it had been sleeping, and began to sing with its eyes fixed on the distant peaks and its throat filling and emptying like the bellows of an organ. The two players gazed at each other over their flutes in astonishment but nothing would have made them stop playing, for the music produced by the two flutes and the bird was of more than mortal beauty. As they played the mountains trembled about them; great slabs of

snow dislodged from their niches and slipped into the gulf, spires of rock trembled and tottered, and as the travellers came to the end of the sonata, the Mysterious Barricades opened to receive them.

Down below the villagers felt the ground quiver as they trudged homewards with the sugar beet harvest, and their tractors snorted and belched blue smoke. But the men never lifted their eyes from the ground, and the women turned their backs to the windows, so none of them saw the strange things that were happening in the mountains.

The music . . . was of more than mortal beauty

Nutshells, Seashells

IT was customary in the summer time for Miss Solliver's academy of dancing to remove itself to her farmhouse by the sea.

'Because,' said Miss Solliver, 'how can a lot of little cockneys express trees and grass and water in their dancing if they have never seen such things?' It was hardly true to say that her pupils were a lot of little cockneys – the members of her famous Ballets Doux had in their veins some of the bluest blood in Europe, but it was true that they were mostly city-bred and knew little about the country. Even the elegant Natasha Borodinova, whose father had once owned thousands upon thousands of acres, had never set foot in a real wood until she came to Miss Solliver's. The problem was soon solved, however, by hiring a large coach and taking them about on appropriate excursions – to a moonlit glade when they were doing *Sylphides*, a lake before a performance of *Swan Lake*, and so on.

This year there would be no need for the coach. The new ballet they were going to start rehearsing was called *Neptune*. It dealt with the sea, and there the sea was, ready to be studied, just at the foot of the cliffs. Several members of the corps de ballet looked at it carefully out of their bedroom windows as they unpacked; Natasha herself did so, and then glancing the other way into her mirror, performed some flowing, arching movements like those of a wave which at the last moment decides not to turn over.

Little Liz Miller, the youngest and smallest pupil, could not see the sea from her window. Her room, which she shared with two other girls was downstairs and looked out into the garden, which was surrounded by a thick, high hazel hedge. Nothing cloud be seen of the sea from the garden; it was warm and sheltered even on the windiest days, and had a wide, flat lawn, admirable for practice.

After tea they all went out and limbered up. Presently Miss Solliver appeared and told them her plans, allotting the parts of Neptune, Alcestis, Tritons, Nereids, Dolphins and the rest. The part of Neptune was being taken by Boris Grigorieff and that of Alcestis by Natasha. Already they were in a far corner of the lawn practising a *pas de deux* which Miss Solliver was describing to them, and looking more like two swallows than two dancers as they curvetted about. The rest of the cast flitted and bounded in the wildest confusion enjoying themselves in the evening sun. Serious work would begin tomorrow.

Little Liz Miller escaped from it all and ran down the lane which she had been told led to the sea. In a moment she could hear nothing of the laughter and voices – the road was deep sunk between banks, and shared its course with a stream which poured out of a hole in the bank and then cataracted down among tall grasses towards the sea.

Liz was so happy that she thought she would burst. For one thing it was her birthday, and her mother had given her a box to open on the train which proved to contain a large cake iced with pink icing and covered with silver balls. And then it was so wonderful to have come here. Liz had never been away from home before; never imagined places like this, like the sprawling white-washed farmhouse all tangled round with fuchsia, or the strange bumpy up and down hills surrounding it, or the sudden swoop of cliff to the sea, or the sea itself, as blue as a street light and going in every direction at once.

Liz was the only real cockney in the school; she had been born within the sound of Bow Bells and her mother, Mrs Miller, was the charwoman who polished the long, long expanses of glassy floor in the London classrooms. Miss Solliver had taken in little Liz out of kindness to Mrs Miller, who had difficulties with a sick father and no husband and very little money.

'Mrs Miller is convinced that the child is an infant genius,' said Miss Solliver, smiling indulgently, to the Assistant

Principal, Madame Legume, 'because she can skip and roller-skate. I am afraid it goes no further than that. But she will get good food with us and come to no harm, and be out of her mother's way. Poor little thing! She moves like a milkman's pony, all legs and joints. We shall never be able to make anything of her.'

'It is very charitable of you to take her in, chérie,' replied the ponderous Madame Legume.

Little Liz was not aware of this. She knew that her skipping and roller-skating were considered vulgar accomplishments, so she did not talk about them, but she had the purest and most loving admiration for all the other members of the school from Natasha downwards, and her only desire was to emulate them. She fully expected that in due time, if she worked hard, she would become a ballerina. She did not know that they were laughing at her and treating her like a mongrel puppy that had bounced in among a collection of aristocratic grey-hounds.

She had to stop half way down the lane and sit on the bank for a moment, hugging herself with happiness. Her birthday; and the cake; and having the privilege of sharing it with all these godlike creatures; it was almost too much. Even Natasha had eaten a piece, after delicately removing the silver balls and dropping them back into the little girl's hand.

'You eat them for me, Baby. They will break my teeth.'

The balls were in her pocket now, with some old hazel nuts found under the garden hedge as she came through.

But the last and almost unbearable happiness was that Miss Solliver had told her she could be a baby dolphin in the ballet. 'If you are good and do as you are told and don't get in the way.' To dance in a real ballet! She rolled round on to her stomach and lay kicking her legs. She did not know exactly what a dolphin was – some kind of a bird, perhaps.

There were harebells growing in the grass; she picked some and stuck them in her buttonhole, and then jumped up and ran on down the hill. Here was the sea, round this next corner, and a wonderful flat expanse of sand, just right for skipping on. Rather guiltily looking round to see that no one

else from the school was about – but no, they were all up
dancing in the garden – she pulled her skipping rope out of
her pocket. When Liz was happy she had to skip. But first
she must pick up those long pink shells and add them to the
collection that was beginning to weigh down her pocket.

'Nutshells, seashells – ' she sang, for she always made up
her own skipping rhymes.

> 'Nutshells, seashells,
> Silver balls, harebells,
> River lanes, waterfalls,
> Harebells, silver balls.'

And she began to skip.

When Liz skipped it was something quite special. Perhaps
Miss Solliver had never seen her do it? The rope that she
held seemed to become alive and partner her in a whirling
dance, thinking up things to do for itself. Other children,
back in the alley where Liz had learned to skip, could twirl
the rope under them twice while they were in the air. Liz
could do it seven times; and while she was in the air she moved
from side to side like a gull glancing about over the water.
Other children could skip a hundred times running, or a
thousand times, but Liz could probably have gone on for
ever if she had wanted to. She could toss the rope from her,
catch it in mid-air, cross it into a figure eight and skip forward
through the top loop and back through the bottom one; she
could dance a mazurka or a reel while the rope flashed round
her like a sword, she could dance a waltz or a minuet while it
wove a web round her as shining and insubstantial as the web
of ribbons round a maypole. She could swing the rope round
underneath her by one handle until it made a spinning circular
platform, while she spun round in the other direction above it;
sometimes the rope was a planet and she was the sun, or the
rope was Niagara and she was M. Blondin whirling down it in
a barrel with her legs hooked over her ears; sometimes it was
a tight-rope with its ends attached to nothing in particular
and she was skipping along it; sometimes it was a cradle and
she was rocking herself off to sleep in it.

As she skipped she sang her skipping rhyme, and at the end, when she had done all the different sorts of skipping that she could think of, she flipped out all the contents of her pockets and began to juggle with them. Pink shells, harebells, hazel nuts and silver balls tossed up and down over the rope, and Liz skipped underneath them, keeping them all in the air and herself as well. At last she flopped down on a rock, letting them scatter round her. To her surprise there was a loud burst of applause from the sea.

She looked round, rather pink and embarrassed, to see who had surprised her at her forbidden pastime. The whole sea appeared to be crammed with people.

In the midst of them all was a huge man, very like Mr Sammons who kept the whelk stall in Vauxhall Bridge Road. He was sitting on something that might have been a whelk stall, trimmed up a bit; it rose up and down on the waves and was pulled by two great fish like the stone ones on either side of the Mercantile Insurance Building doorway, only these were very much alive, plunging and bouncing, and the man had to keep pulling on the reins. All around the stall, which was encrusted with lobsters and crabs, cockles and mussels, was swimming every sort of fish that Liz had ever seen on a barrow – cod, skate, halibut, herring, mackerel, sole, plaice and rock salmon – and many that she hadn't; not to mention sea lions and walruses which she had once seen at the zoo. But in among these were much odder creatures; girls with tails playing on combs wrapped in paper, men with faces of fish, playing on mouth-organs; fish with wings, blowing trumpets; young ladies coming out of large whelk shells; birds with fins riding on oysters; lobsters blowing out long paper snakes that rolled up again with a click; fish with the faces of men, carrying shrimping nets; and so forth.

'Coo,' said Liz, shaken out of herself by this extraordinary scene. 'It's like Hampstead Heath on Bank Holiday.'

'Hello there, Liz,' shouted Neptune, waving a three-pronged toasting fork with an ice-cream cone on each prong. 'What can we do for you, dearie?'

'For *me*? Why?'

When Liz skipped it was something quite special

'You called us, didn't you? With your song about nutshells and seashells.'

'But that was just a skipping song I made up.'

'Any little song will do for an incantation,' said Neptune, 'if you're doing something important.'

'But I wasn't doing anything important.'

'Your skipping is important, my girl. It's Art, that's what it is.'

'Miss Solliver says it's vulgar.'

'Well, nuts to Miss Solliver, whoever she may be. But that isn't the point. The point is, you called for us, whether you meant to or not, and here we are, so what would you like? Anything you've a fancy for? Free cruise to Madeira? Streamlined modern kitchen installed in your home? Winning ticket for the pools? Pearl necklace? Strawberry or vanilla? Whelks in vinegar?'

'No, there's nothing at all, really, thank you,' said Liz, beaming all over again at the thought of her happiness, 'I've got all I want already.'

A long sigh, of admiration, envy and amazement went up from the sea.

'Still,' said Neptune rallying, 'we could give her a good time, couldn't we, boys and girls? How about a bit of deep-sea rock, eh? Or a mug with a Present from Neptune on it? You come for a ride in my chariot and look at the sights before you go back.'

So she skipped out over the heaving backs of dolphins into the chariot and they went careering off, everyone singing Cockles and Mussels and offering her ice-cream, potato crisps and prawns in jellyfish.

'There you are,' said Neptune, when at last they put her down again after she had seen the sights. 'Now don't forget, if there's ever anything you need, or if you're in any sort of trouble – I don't say it's likely, mind, but you never know your luck – don't forget your old pal. Ta, ta, now, don't lose the skipping rope.'

Liz had thought she was happy when she went down the lane, but she was ten times happier when she ran up it. She was longing to confide in someone: perhaps she could tell one of the girls she slept with, but not tonight, it was far too late; the moon was up, and the lane was in deep shadow between its banks. It was strictly forbidden to be out after dark and Liz wondered if she could crawl through the hazel hedge and climb in her window without being caught. She resolved to try.

But as she stole along behind the hedge she was alarmed to hear the voices of Miss Solliver and Madame Legume who were, apparently, strolling in the moonlight on the other side.

'Yes, the casting is none of it bad except for the dolphins. It is a pity that we have to have the little Miller girl in the show – it will give people a wrong idea of our standards. But it would look so invidious if she were the only one left out, and her mother would be upset.'

'Yes! That child!' sighed Madame. 'No one could ever teach her to dance gracefully; too much vulgar bounce. I wonder if it would not be kinder to tell her and let her leave.'

'No, we'll keep her a bit longer, till things are easier for her mother. Everyone in the school quite understands the position. It's a nuisance about *Neptune* though – we'll have to keep her well at the back of the stage –'

The voices moved away again.

Liz stood where she was, almost turned to stone. Her face, which had been flushed, became very white. After a little while she turned and walked slowly back into the lane. She was stiff, as if her arms and legs ached all over, there was no vulgar bounce about her now. Then she sat down and looked at the little stream which came pouring out of its hole in the bank, as if she could not understand what she had heard and needed time to take it in. The water tumbled down, making its gentle noise in the quiet night, and still she looked and looked, until presently tears began to run down her face and she stood up because she was too wretched to stay sitting still.

'I can't go back there,' she thought, 'they all laugh at me and know I'm no good. How silly I must have been not to see that before.'

She did not blame them; in fact she felt sorry for them because it must have been so tiresome. It was not their laughter that ached in her bones; it was that dreadful sentence: 'No one could ever teach her to dance gracefully.'

Where was she to go? Then she saw a couple of harebells nodding in the moonlight and remembered her skipping rhyme:

> Nutshells, seashells,
> Silver balls, harebells –

It was easy to find a couple of nutshells in the hedge. She ran down to the beach and picked up a handful of shells. But what about the silver balls? Then she remembered that her skipping rope had silver ball-bearings in the handles. She would have to break it to get them out. What did that matter when she was never going to skip or dance again – unless Neptune could help her? But suppose the song didn't work? She gave a little sob as she knelt down and cracked the handles on a rock.

Miss Solliver was very worried to hear next morning that Liz Miller was missing.

'It has occurred to me that we were rather near her window when we were talking last night,' she said to Madame Legume. 'Do you suppose she could have heard us? I don't know what I shall say to her mother if anything has happened to her.'

Later on a pair of sandshoes and a broken skipping rope, identified as belonging to Liz, were found at the foot of the cliff. As nothing more was seen of her she was presumed to have been drowned; the whole school was much upset, the plans for the Neptune ballet were laid aside and they all went back to London earlier than usual. Miss Solliver wrote a polite note to Mrs Miller regretting that her daughter had been drowned and suggesting that it would be best if she did not continue her employment as cleaner in the London school because the place would no doubt be painful to her; Miss Solliver enclosed a cheque in lieu of notice.

Seven years later a new ballerina took London by storm. Miss Solliver, full of curiosity, went to see her in the ballet

Atlantis, produced by a Mr Thalassoglu whom no one had ever heard of.

'She really is most strange,' said Miss Solliver to Madame Legume, in between two scenes. 'I suppose it's a trick of the lighting, but sometimes it's hard to decide whether she's swimming or flying. Do you suppose she's really hanging on wires?'

She leaned forward and stared intently at the silvery figure darting about the streets of the drowned city.

'It's odd, she reminds me of someone a little – who can it be?'

After the performance a journalist friend of Miss Solliver's offered to introduce her to the ballerina. They went round to her dressing-room.

In the far corner was old Grandfather Miller in a bathchair; knitting beside the fire was Mrs Miller; on the dressing-table lay a skipping rope. The ball-bearings were made from pearls, and round the coral handles was inscribed: 'A Present from Neptune.'

Some Music for the Wicked Countess

MR BOND was a young man who had just arrived in a small village to take up the position of schoolmaster there. The village was called Castle Kerrig but the curious thing about it was that there was no castle and never had been one. There was a large wood round three-quarters of its circumference which came almost to the door of the schoolmaster's little house, and beyond that the wild hills and bog stretched for miles.

There were only ten children needing to be taught; it hardly seemed worth having a school there at all, but without it they would have had to travel forty miles by bus every day, and a schoolmaster was far cheaper than all that petrol, so Mr Bond was given the job. It suited him very well, as he did not have to waste too much time in teaching and had plenty left for his collections of birds' eggs, moths, butterflies, fossils, stones, bones, lizards and flowers and his piano-playing.

There was a tinny old piano in the school, and when he and the children were bored by lessons he would play tunes and songs to them for hours at a time while they listened in a dream.

One day the eldest of the children, Norah, said to him:

'Faith, 'tis the way your Honour should be playing to the Countess up at the Castle for the wonder and beauty of your melodies does be out of this world entirely.'

'The Castle?' said Mr Bond curiously. 'What castle is that? There's no castle near here, is there?'

'Ah, sure, 'tis the Castle in the forest I mean. The wicked Countess would weep the eyes out of her head to hear the tunes you do be playing.'

'Castle in the forest?' The schoolmaster was more and more

puzzled. 'But there's no castle in the forest – at least it's not marked on the two and a half-inch ordnance survey.'

'Begorrah, and doesn't your Honour know that the whole forest is stiff with enchantment, and a leprechaun peeking out of every bush in it, the way you'd be thinking it was nesting time and they after the eggs?'

'What nonsense, my dear Norah. You really must learn not to come to me with these tales.'

But all the children gathered round him exclaiming and persuading.

'Faith, and isn't it the strange thing that your Worship should not be believing in these enchantments, and you playing such beautiful music that the very ravens from the Castle, and the maidens out of the forest are all climbing and fluttering over each other outside the windows to get an earful of it?'

Mr Bond shooed them all off rather crossly, saying that school was over for the day and he had no patience with such silliness.

Next day was the last day of term, and Norah was leaving. Mr Bond asked her what she was going to do.

'Going into service up at the Castle. They're in need of a girl in the kitchen, I'm told, and mother says 'twill be good experience for me.'

'But there *isn't* any castle,' said Mr Bond furiously. Was the girl half-witted? She had always seemed bright enough in school.

'Ah, your Honour will have your bit of fun. And what else could I do, will you be telling me that?'

Mr Bond was forced to agree that there were no other jobs to be had. That afternoon he started out into the forest, determined to search for this mysterious castle and see if there really was some big house tucked away in the trees, but though he walked for miles and miles, and came home thirsty and exhausted long after dusk, not a thing did he see, neither castle, house, nor hut, let alone leprechauns peeking out of every bush.

He ate some bread and cheese in a bad temper and sat down to play it off at his own piano. He played some dances from

Purcell's *Fairy Queen,* and had soon soothed himself into forgetfulness of the children's provoking behaviour. Little did he know that three white faces, framed in long golden hair, were gazing through the window behind his back. When he had finished playing for the night the maidens from the forest turned and went regretfully back to the Castle.

'Well,' asked the Wicked Countess, 'and does he play as well as the village talk has it?'

'He plays till the ears come down off your head and go waltzing off along the road. Sure there's none is his equal in the whole wide world at all.'

'I expect you are exaggerating,' said the Countess sadly, 'still he would be a useful replacement for Bran the Harpist, ever since the fool went and had his head chopped off at the Debateable Ford.'

She looked crossly over to a corner where a headless harpist was learning to knit, since being unable to read music he could no longer play.

'We must entice this schoolmaster up to the Castle,' said the Wicked Countess. ''Twill cheer up our dull and lonely life to have a bit of music once again. Ah, that will be the grand day when they have the television broadcast throughout the length and breadth of the country for the entertainment and instruction of us poor warlocks. I've heard they do be having lessons in ballet and basket making and all sorts of wonderments.'

'How will you entice him up?' asked one of the maidens.

'The usual way. I'll toss out me keys and let it be known that my hand and heart is in waiting for the lucky fellow is after finding them. Then we'll give him a draught of fairy wine to lull him to sleep for seven years, and after that he's ours for ever.'

So the Countess arranged for the message about the keys to be relayed through the village and the keys were left lying in a conspicuous place in the middle of the schoolmaster's garden path, visible to him but invisible to everyone else. Quite a number of people became very excited at the thought of winning the Wicked Countess's heart and hand, and the forest was almost as crowded as Epping Forest at Bank Holiday, but the schoolmaster was very preoccupied just at that time with his search for the Scarlet Striped Orchis, which blooms only during the first week in May, and he hardly noticed the commotion.

He did observe the keys lying on his path, but he knew they did not belong to him, and they came into none of the categories of things that he collected, so he merely kicked them out of the way, and then forgot them in the excitement of noticing a rare orange fritillary by his garden gate.

'The man's possessed,' exclaimed the Countess in vexation. It was mortifying to have her message so completely ignored, but she did not abandon her purpose.

'We'll try the snake trick – that'll be after fetching him in, and he interested in all manner of bugs and reptiles, the way it'd be a terrible life for his wife, poor woman.'

The snake trick was a very old ruse for enticing mortals. One of the maidens of the forest changed herself into a beautiful many-coloured snake with ruby eyes and lay in the path of the intended victim, who would be unable to resist picking it up and taking it home. Once inside his house, it would change back into the forest maiden's form again, and the luckless man would be obliged to marry her. She would become more and more exacting, asking for a coat made from rose-petals, or cherries in midwinter, until her husband had to go up to the Castle and ask them to supply one of these difficult requirements. Then of course he was in their power.

'Indeed, why didn't we try the snake trick before,' said the Countess. ''Twould have fetched him better than any old bit of a bunch of keys.'

Accordingly, when next Mr Bond went into the forest, looking for green-glass snails and the salmon-spotted hellebore, he found this beautiful coloured snake lying temptingly displayed in a wriggle of black, scarlet, white and lemon-yellow across his path.

'Bless my soul,' said Mr Bond. 'That is something unusual. Can it be *T. vulgaris peristalsis*? I must certainly take it home.'

He picked up the snake, which dangled unresistingly in his

hands, and rushed home with it. All the forest maidens and the ravens leaned out of the high branches, and the leprechauns pried between the stems of the bushes to watch him go by. He ran up the garden path, shoved open the front door with his shoulder, and dropped the snake into a jar of brine which was standing ready for specimens on the kitchen table. He was unable to find a picture or description of the snake in any work of reference, and to his annoyance and disappointment the beautiful colours faded after a couple of hours. The Wicked Countess was also very annoyed. One of her forest maidens had been demolished, and she had been foiled again, which was galling to her pride.

'Maybe we could give him a potion?' suggested one of the maidens.

'He's teetotal, the creature,' said the Wicked Countess in disgust. 'Will you be after telling me how you can administer a potion to a man that will touch neither drop nor dram?'

'Well, but doesn't he take in each day the grandest bottle of milk you ever laid eyes on that would make any cow in Kerry sigh with envy at the cream there is on it?'

'Very well, you can try putting the potion in the milk, but 'tis a poor way of instilling a magic draught into a man, I'm thinking, and little good will it do him.'

Two enthusiastic maidens went to Mr Bond's house at cockcrow the following morning and lay in wait for the milkman. As soon as he had left the bottle they removed the cardboard bottle-top, tipped in the potion (which was a powder in a little envelope, like a shampoo) put back the cap, and then hurried back to the Castle to report.

Unfortunately it was the schoolmaster's turn to be unwilling host to the village tits that morning. Shortly after the maidens had left, forty blue tits descended on to his doorstep, neatly removed the cap once more, and drank every drop of the milk. Mr Bond was resigned to this happening every eleventh day, and swallowed his morning tea milkless, before setting off to open up the school, as the holiday was now over.

Up at the Castle the maidens had a difficult time explaining to the Wicked Countess the sudden appearance of forty blue tits who flew in through the window and absolutely refused to be turned out.

'How are we to get this miserable man up here, will you tell me that?' demanded the Countess. 'I've lost patience with him entirely.'

'You could write him a civil note of invitation, that way he'd be in no case to refuse without displaying terrible bad manners in it?'

'I never thought of that,' admitted the Countess, and she sat down and penned a little note in her crabbed, runic handwriting, asking the schoolmaster for the pleasure of his company to a musical evening. She entrusted the note to Norah, who was now a kitchen-maid at the Castle, and asked her to give it into Mr Bond's own hands. Norah skipped off, much pleased with the commission, and presented the note to Mr Bond as he sat in morning school.

'Now isn't it herself has done you the great honour of requesting your worshipful presence at such a musical junketing and a singing and dancing you'd think it was King Solomon himself entertaining the Queen of Sheba.'

Mr Bond scrutinized the letter carefully.

'Now this is very interesting; the back of this document appears to be part of a version of the Cuchulainn legend written in a very early form of Gaelic. Dear me, I must write to the Royal Society about this.'

He became absorbed in the legend on the back, and clean forgot to read what was on the other side.

The Countess was very affronted at this, and scolded Norah severely.

'I've no patience with the lot of you, at all. I can see I'll have to be after fetching him myself, the way otherwise we'll be having no music this side of winter.'

It was now the middle of May, which is a very dangerous month for enchantment, the worst in the year apart from October.

The Wicked Countess set out her spies to inform her when Mr Bond next took an evening walk in the forest. A few days later it was reported that he had set out with a tin of golden syrup and a paintbrush and was busy painting the trunks of the trees. The Countess hastily arrayed herself with all her enchantments and made her way to where he was working. The whole forest hummed with interest and excitement and the leprechauns were jumping up and down in their bushes to such an extent that showers of hawthorn blossom kept falling down. Mr Bond noticed nothing of all this, but he was just able to discern the Wicked Countess with her streaming hair and her beauty. He thought she must be the District Nurse.

'The top of the evening to you,' she greeted him, 'and isn't it a grand and strange thing you do be doing there, anointing the bark of the trees with treacle as if they were horses and they with the knees broken on them? But perhaps 'tis a compliment you do be after paying me, and it meaning to say that the very trees in my forest are so sweet they deserve to be iced like cakes.'

'Good evening,' said Mr Bond with reserve. 'I'm out after moths.'

'And isn't it a wonderful thing to be pursuing those pitiful brown things when you could be stepping up to the Castle like a civilized creature and passing a musical evening with me and my maidens, the way our hearts and voices would be singing together like a flock of starlings?'

'Are you the Countess by any chance? I seem to have heard some vague tales about you, but I never thought that you were a real person. I hope you will forgive me if I have been guilty of any impoliteness.'

'Sure our hearts are warmer than that in this part of the world, and what's a trifle of an insult between friends? Do you be after strolling up with me this minute for a drop of something to drink and a few notes of music, for they say music be a great healer when there's hurt feelings in the case, and it smoothing away the sore hearts and wounded spirits.'

Mr Bond gathered that he *had* in some way offended this talkative lady, and his mind went back guiltily to the note

'Good evening,' said Mr Bond with reserve

Norah had given him, which he had sent off to the Royal
Society and forgotten to read.

He turned and walked with her, and was surprised to notice
a grey and vine-wreathed tower standing in a part of the
forest where, he would have been ready to swear, there had
been nothing before.

'Walk in this way,' said the Countess holding open a little
postern. 'We won't stand on ceremony between friends.'

They had to climb half a hundred steps of spiral staircase,
but finally emerged in the Wicked Countess's bower, a dim,
rush-strewn room full of maidens, leprechauns and wood-
smoke.

'Pray be taking a seat,' said the Countess, 'the while you
do be getting your breath. Fetch a drink for the poor gentleman, one of you,' she commanded the maidens, 'he has no
more breath in him than a washed sheet, and it clinging
together on the line.'

'Nothing stronger than tea for me, please,' said the schoolmaster faintly.

'Tea, is it? We must be after brewing you a terrible strong
poteen of the stuff, for how can you make music worthy the
name in a draught like that? Girls, put the kettle on.'

'It's all right, thank you, I'm better now. Please don't
trouble.'

'Do be after playing us a tune then, for since you came here
the village has hummed with your praise the way we've been
after thinking 'twas a human nightingale had come to live
among us.'

'I will with pleasure,' said Mr Bond, 'but I can't play
without a piano, you know.'

There was a disconcerted pause.

'Ah, sure, I'll send two of my leprechauns down to the
little house for it,' said the Countess rallying. 'They'll be back
in ten minutes, the creatures.' Two of them scuttled off, in
obedience to a ferocious look.

Mr Bond gazed round him dreamily, lulled by the atmos-
phere of enchantment. The arrival of the tea roused him a
little; he took one look at it and shuddered, for it was as black

as the pit and looked as if it had been stewed for hours. The maidens were not very expert tea-makers. The Countess was delicately sipping at a tall flagon of mead.

Fortunately a diversion was created by the two leprechauns who came staggering back with the piano in an astonishingly short time. While they were getting it up the spiral staircase amid cries of encouragement from the maidens, Mr Bond tipped his tea into the treacle tin.

'What shall I play for you?' he asked the Countess.

She thought for a moment. Musicians were notoriously vain, and the best way to get him into a flattered and compliant mood would be to ask for one of his own compositions – he was sure to have written some himself.

'Best of all we'd be after liking a tune you've made up yourself,' she told him.

Mr Bond beamed. Here was a true music-lover without a doubt – a very rare thing in this wilderness.

'I'll play you my new fantasia and fugue in the whole-tone scale,' he said happily, delighted at a chance to get away from the folk-songs and country dances which he was obliged to play for the children.

He brought his hands down on the keys in a prolonged, crashing and discordant chord. The leprechauns shuddered from top to toe, the maidens clenched their teeth, and the Wicked Countess had to grip her hands on to the arms of her chair.

Then Mr Bond really started to play, and the noise was so awful that the whole enchanted tower simply disintegrated, brick by brick. The Countess and her maidens vanished away moaning into the forest, the leprechauns retired grumbling into their bushes again, and when the schoolmaster finished his piece and looked round, he was astonished to find himself seated at the piano in the middle of a forest glade. He had to ask the people from the village to help him back with the piano, and was at great pains to try and think up some explanation for its presence in the forest.

They took no notice of what he said, however.

'Ah, sure, 'tis only some whimsy of the Countess's, the

creature, bless her. What would the man expect, and he wandering about the forest on a May evening?'

After that, if by any chance Mr Bond and the Wicked Countess met each other while walking in the forest, they said nothing at all, and each pretended that the other was not there.

A Room Full of Leaves

ONCE there was a poor little boy who lived with a lot of his relatives in an enormous house called Troy. The relatives were rich, but they were so nasty that they might just as well have been poor, for all the good their money did them. The worst of them all was Aunt Agatha, who was thin and sharp, and the next worst was Uncle Umbert, who was stout and prosperous. We shall return to them later. There was also a fierce old nurse called Squabb, and a tutor, Mr Buckle, who helped to make the little boy's life a burden. His name was Wilfred, which was a family name, but he was so tired of hearing them all say: 'You must live up to your name, child,' that in his own mind he called himself Wil. It had to be in his mind, for he had no playmates – other children were declared to be common, and probably dangerous and infectious too.

One rainy Saturday afternoon Wil sat in his schoolroom finishing some Latin parsing for Mr Buckle before being taken for his walk, which was always in one of two directions. If Squabb took him they went downtown 'to look at the shops' in a suburb of London which was sprawling out its claws towards the big house; but the shops were never the ones Wil would have chosen to look at. If he went with Mr Buckle they crossed the Common diagonally (avoiding the pond where rude little boys sailed their boats) and came back along the white-railed ride while Mr Buckle talked about plant life.

So Wil was not looking forward with great enthusiasm to his walk, and when Squabb came in and told him that it was too wet to go out and he must amuse himself quietly with his transfers, he was delighted. He sat gazing dreamily at the transfers for a while, not getting on with them, while Squabb did some ironing. It was nearly dark, although the time was only three. Squabb switched on the light and picked a fresh heap of ironing off the fender.

All of a sudden there was a blue flash and a report from the iron; a strong smell of burnt rubber filled the room and all the lights went out.

'Now I suppose the perishing thing's fused all this floor,' exclaimed Squabb and she hurried out of the room, muttering something under her breath about newfangled gadgets.

Wil did not waste a second. Before the door had closed after her he was tiptoeing across the room and out of the other door. In the darkness and confusion no one would miss him for quite a considerable time, and he would have a rare opportunity to be on his own for a bit.

The house in which he lived was very huge. Nobody knew exactly how many rooms there were – but there was one for each day of the year and plenty left over. Innumerable little courtyards, each with its own patch of green velvet grass, had passages leading away in all directions to different blocks and wings. Towards the back of the house there were fewer courtyards; it drew itself together into a solid mass which touched the forest behind. The most important rooms were open to the public on four days a week; Mr Buckle and a skinny lady from the town showed visitors round, and all the relics and heirlooms were carefully locked up inside glass cases where they could be gazed at – the silver wash-basin used by James II, a dirty old exercise book belonging to the poet Pope, the little pot of neat's foot ointment left by Henry VIII and all the other tiny bits of history. Even in those days visitors were careless about leaving things behind.

Wil was indifferent to the public rooms, though his relatives were not. They spent their lives polishing and furbishing and when everything was polished they went on endless grubbing searches through the unused rooms looking for more relics which could be cleaned up and sold to the British Museum.

Wil stood outside the schoolroom door listening. Down below he could hear the murmur of voices. Saturday was cheap visiting day – only two and six instead of five shillings –

so there were twice as many people, and both Mr Buckle and the skinny lady were at work escorting their little groups. Wil nodded to himself and slipped away, softly as a mouse, towards the back of the house where the tourists were never taken. Here it became darker and dustier, the windows were small, heavily leaded, and never cleaned. Little passages, unexpected stairways and landings wound about past innumerable doors, many of which had not been opened since Anne Boleyn popped her head round to say goodbye to some bed-ridden old retainer before taking horse to London. Tapestries hung thick with velvet dust – had Wil touched them they would have crumbled to pieces but he slid past them like a shadow.

He was already lost, but he meant to be; he stood listening to the old house creaking and rustling round him like a forest. He had a fancy that if he penetrated far enough he would find himself in the forest without having noticed the transition. He was following a particularly crooked and winding passage, leading to a kind of cross-roads or cross-passages from which other alleys led away, mostly dark, some with a faint gleam from a rain-streaked window far away down their length, and all lined with doors.

He paused, wondering which to choose, and then heard something which might have been the faintest of whispers – but it was enough to decide him on taking the passage directly fronting him. He went slowly to a door some twelve feet along it, rather a low, small door on his right.

After pushing he discovered that it opened outwards towards him. He pulled it back, stepped round, and gazed in bewilderment at what he saw. It was like a curtain, of a silvery, faded brown, which hung across the doorway. Then looking closer he saw that it was really *leaves* – piled high and drifted one on another, lying so heaped up that the entrance was filled with them, and if the door had swung inwards he could never have pushed it open. Wil felt them with his hand; they were not brittle like dead beech-leaves, but soft and supple, making only the faintest rustle when he touched them. He took one and looked at it in the palm of his hand. It was almost a skeleton, covered with faint silvery marks like letters. As he stood looking at it he heard a little voice whisper from inside the room:

'Well, boy, aren't you coming in?'

Much excited, he stared once more at the apparently impenetrable wall of leaves in front of him, and said softly:

'How do I get through?'

'Burrow, of course,' whispered the voice impatiently.

He obeyed, and stooping a little plunged his head and arms among the leaves and began working his way into them like a mole. When he was entirely inside the doorway he wriggled round and pulled the door shut behind him. The leaves made hardly any noise as he inched through them. There was just enough air to breathe, and a dryish, aromatic scent. His progress was slow, and it seemed to take about ten minutes before the leaves began to thin out, and striking upwards like a diver he finally came to the surface.

He was in a room, or so he supposed, having come into it through an ordinary door in a corridor, but the walls could not be seen at all on account of the rampart of leaves piled up all round him. Towards the centre there was a clear space on the ground, and in this grew a mighty trunk, as large round as a table, covered with roughish silver bark, all protrusions and knobs. The branches began above his head, thrusting out laterally like those of an oak or beech, but very little could be seen of them on account of the leaves which grew everywhere in thick clusters, and the upper reaches of the tree were not visible at all. The growing leaves were yellow – not the faded yellow of autumn but a brilliant gold which illuminated the room. At least there was no other source of light, and it was not dark.

There appeared to be no one else under the tree and Wil wondered who had spoken to him and where they could be.

As if in answer to his thoughts the voice spoke again:

'Can't you climb up?'

'Yes, of course I can,' he said, annoyed with himself for not thinking of this, and he began setting his feet on the rough ledges of bark and pulling himself up. Soon he could not see the floor below, and was in a cage of leaves which fluttered all round him, dazzling his eyes. The scent in the tree was like thyme on the downs on a hot summer's day.

'Where are you?' he asked in bewilderment.

He heard a giggle.

'I'm here,' said the voice, and he saw an agitation among the leaves at the end of a branch, and worked his way out to it. He found a little girl – a rather plain little girl with freckles and reddish hair hidden under some kind of cap. She wore a long green velvet dress and a ruff, and she was seated comfortably swinging herself up and down in a natural hammock of small branches.

'Really I thought you'd *never* find your way here,' she said, giving him a derisive welcoming grin.

'I'm not used to climbing trees,' he excused himself.

'I know, poor wretch. Never mind, this one's easy enough. What's your name? Mine's Em.'

'Mine's Wil. Do you live here?'

'Of course. This isn't really my branch – some of them are very severe about staying on their own branches – look at *him*.' She indicated a very Puritanical-looking gentleman in black knee-breeches who appeared for a moment and then vanished again as a cluster of leaves swayed. '*I* go where I like, though. My branch isn't respectable – we were on the wrong side in every war from Matilda and Stephen on. As soon as the colonies were invented they shipped a lot of us out there, but it was no use, they left a lot behind. They always hope that we'll die out, but of course we don't. Shall I show you some of the tree?'

'Yes, please.'

'Come along then. Don't be frightened, you can hold my hand a lot of the time. It's almost as easy as stairs.'

When she began leading him about he realized that the tree was much more enormous than he had supposed; in fact he did not understand how it could be growing in a room inside a house. The branches curved about making platforms, caves, spiral staircases, seats, cupboards and cages. Em led

him through the maze, which she seemed to know by heart, pushing past the clusters of yellow leaves. She showed him how to swing from one branch to another, how to slide down the slopes and wriggle through the crevices and how to lie back in a network of boughs and rest his head on a thick pillow of leaves.

They made quite a lot of noise and several disapproving old faces peered at them from the ends of branches, though one crusader smiled faintly and his dog wagged its tail.

'Have you anything to eat?' asked Em presently, mopping her brow with her kerchief.

'Yes, I've got some biscuits I didn't eat at break this morning. I'm not allowed to keep them of course, they'd be cross if they knew.'

'Of course,' nodded Em, taking a biscuit. 'Thanks. Dryish, your comfits, aren't they – but welcome. Wait a minute and I'll bring you a drink.' She disappeared among the boughs and came back in a few moments with two little greenish crystal cups full of a golden liquid.

'It's sap,' she said, passing one over. 'It has a sort of forest taste, hasn't it; makes you think of horns. Now I'll give you a present.'

She took the cups away and he heard her rummaging somewhere down by the trunk of the tree.

'There's all sorts of odds and ends down there. This is the first thing I could find. Do you like it?'

'Yes, very much,' he said, handling the slender silver thing with interest. 'What is it?'

She looked at it critically. 'I think it's the shoehorn that Queen Elizabeth used (she always had trouble with wearing too tight shoes). She must have left it behind here some time. You can have it anyway – you might find a use for it. You'd better be going now or you'll be in trouble and then it won't be so easy for you to come here another time.'

'How shall I ever find my way back here?'

'You must stand quite still and listen. You'll hear me

He found a little girl

267

whisper, and the leaves rustling. Goodbye.' She suddenly put a skinny little arm round his neck and gave him a hug. 'It's nice having someone to play with; I've been a bit bored sometimes.'

Wil squirmed out through the leaves again and shut the door, turning to look at it as he did so. There was nothing in the least unusual about its appearance.

When he arrived back in the schoolroom (after some false turnings) he found his Aunt Agatha waiting for him. Squabb and Buckle were hovering on the threshold, but she dismissed them with a wave of her hand. The occasion was too serious for underlings.

'Wilfred,' she said, in a very awful tone.

'Yes, Aunt Agatha.'

'Where have you been?'

'Playing in the back part of the house.'

'*Playing!* A child of your standing and responsibilities playing? Instead of getting on with your transfers? What is that?' She pounced on him and dragged out the shoehorn which was protruding from his pocket.

'Concealment! I suppose you found this and intended to creep out and sell it to some museum. You are an exceedingly wicked, disobedient boy, and as punishment for running away and hiding in this manner you will go to bed as soon as I have finished with you, you will have nothing to eat but toast-gruel, and you will have to take off your clothes *yourself*, and feed *yourself*, like a common child.'

'Yes, Aunt.'

'You know that you are the Heir to this noble house (when your great-uncle Winthrop dies)?'

'Yes, Aunt.'

'Do you know anything about your parents?'

'No.'

'It is as well. Look at this.' She pulled out a little case, containing two miniatures of perfectly ordinary people. Wil studied them.

'That is your father – our brother. He disgraced the family – he sullied the scutcheon – by becoming – *a writer*, and worse

– he married a *female writer*, your mother. Mercifully for the family reputation they were both drowned in the *Oranjeboot* disaster, before anything worse could happen. You were rescued, floating in a pickle barrel. *Now* do you see why we all take such pains with your education? It is to save you from the taint of your unfortunate parentage.'

Wil was still digesting this when there came a knock at the door and Mr Buckle put his head round.

'There is a Mr Slockenheimer demanding to see you, Lady Agatha,' he said. 'Apparently he will not take No for an answer. Shall I continue with the reprimand?'

'No, Buckle – you presume,' said Aunt Agatha coldly. 'I have finished.'

Wil put himself to bed, watched minutely by Buckle to see that he did not omit to brush his teeth with the silver brush or comb his eyebrows with King Alfred's comb in the manner befitting an heir of Troy. The toast and water was brought in a gold porringer. Wil ate it absently; it was very nasty, but he was so overcome by the luck of not having been found out, and wondering how he could get back to see Em another time, that he hardly noticed it.

Next morning at breakfast (which he had with his relatives) he expected to be in disgrace, but curiously enough they paid no attention to him. They were all talking about Mr Slockenheimer.

'Such a piece of luck,' said Cousin Cedric. 'Just as the tourist season is ending.'

'Who is this man?' creaked Great-Aunt Gertrude.

'He is a film director, from Hollywood,' explained Aunt Agatha, loudly and patiently. 'He is making a film about Robin Hood and he has asked permission to shoot some of the indoor scenes in Troy – for which we shall all be handsomely paid, naturally.'

'Naturally, naturally,' croaked the old ravens, all round the table.

Wil pricked up his ears, and then an anxious thought struck him. Supposing Mr Slockenheimer's people discovered the room with the tree?

'They are coming today,' Uncle Umbert was shrieking into Great-Uncle Ulric's ear trumpet.

Mr Slockenheimer's outfit arrived after breakfast while Wil was doing his daily run – a hundred times round the triangle of grass in front of the house, while Mr Buckle timed him with a stop-watch.

A lovely lady shot out of a huge green motor car, shrieked:
'Oh, you cute darling! Now you must tell me the way to the nearest milk-bar,' and whisked him back into the car with her. Out of the corner of his eye he saw that Mr Buckle had been commandeered to show somebody the spiral staircase.

Wil ate his raspberry sundae in a daze. He had never been in the milk-bar before, never eaten ice-cream, never ridden in a car. To have it all following on his discovery of the day before was almost too much for him.

'Gracious!' exclaimed his new friend, looking at her wrist-watch. 'I must be on the set! I'm Maid Marian you know. Tarzan, I mean Robin, has to rescue me from the wicked baron at eleven in the Great Hall.'

'I'll show you where it is,' said Wil.

He expected more trouble when he reached home, but the whole household was disorganized; Mr Buckle was showing Robin Hood how to put on the Black Prince's casque (which was too big) and Aunt Agatha was having a long business conversation with Mr Slockenheimer, so his arrival passed unnoticed.

He was relieved to find that the film was only going to be shot in the main public rooms, so there did not seem to be much risk of the tree being discovered.

After lunch Mr Buckle was called on again to demonstrate the firing of the 9th Earl's crossbow (he shot an extra) and Wil was able to escape once more and reach in safety the regions at the back.

He stood on a dark landing for what seemed like hours, listening to the patter of his own heart. Then, tickling his ear like a thread of cobweb he heard Em's whisper:
'Wil! Here I am! This way!' and below it he heard the rustle of the tree, as if it too were whispering: 'Here I am.'

It did not take him long to find the room, but his progress through the leaves was slightly impeded by the things he was carrying. When he emerged at the foot of the tree he found Em waiting there. The hug she gave him nearly throttled him.

'I've been thinking of some more places to show you. And all sorts of games to play!'

'I've brought you a present,' he said emptying his pockets.

'Oh! What's in those little tubs?'

'Ice-cream. The chief electrician gave them to me.'

'What a strange confection,' she said, tasting it. 'It is smooth and sweet but it makes my teeth chatter.'

'And here's your present.' It was a gold Mickey Mouse with ruby eyes which Maid Marian had given him. Em handled it with respect and presently stored it away in one of her hidey-holes in the trunk. Then they played follow-my-leader until they were so tired that they had to lie back on thick beds of leaves and rest.

'I did not expect to see you again so soon,' said Em as they lay picking the aromatic leaves and chewing them, while a prim Jacobean lady shook her head at them.

Wil explained about the invasion of the film company and she listened with interest.

'A sort of strolling players,' she commented. 'My father was one – flat contrary to the family's commands, of course. I saw many pieces performed before I was rescued from the life by my respected grandmother to be brought up as befitted one of our name.' She sighed.

For the next two months Wil found many opportunities to slip off and visit Em, for Mr Buckle became greatly in demand as an adviser on matters of costume, and even Squabb was pressed into service ironing doublets and mending hose.

But one day Wil saw his relatives at breakfast with long faces, and he learned that the company had finished shooting the inside scenes and were about to move to Florida to take the Sherwood Forest sequences. The handsome additional income which the family had been making was about to cease, and Wil realized with dismay that the old life would begin again.

Later when he was starting off to visit Em he found a little

group, consisting of Aunt Agatha, Uncle Umbert, Mr Slockenheimer and his secretary, Mr Jakes, on one of the back landings. Wil shrank into the shadows and listened to their
conversation with alarm.

'One million,' Mr Slockenheimer was saying. 'Yes, sir, one
million's my last word. But I'll ship the house over to Hollywood myself, as carefully as if it was a new-laid egg. You may
be sure of that Ma'am, I appreciate your feelings, and you and
all your family may go on living in it for the rest of your days.
Every brick will be numbered and every floorboard will be
lettered so that they'll go back in their exact places. This
house certainly will be a gold-mine to me – it'll save its value
twice over in a year as sets for different films. There's Tudor,
Gothic, Norman, Saxon, Georgian, Decorated, all under one
roof.'

'But we shall have to have salaries too, mind,' said Uncle
Umbert greedily. 'We can't be expected to uproot ourselves
like this and move to Hollywood all for nothing.'

Mr Slockenheimer raised his eyebrows at this, but said
agreeably:

'Okay, I'll sign you on as extras.' He pulled out a fistful of
forms, scribbled his signature on them and handed them to
Aunt Agatha. 'There you are, Ma'am, twenty-year contracts
for the whole bunch.'

'Dirt cheap at the price, even so,' Wil heard him whisper
to the secretary.

'Now as we've finished shooting I'll have the masons in
tomorrow and start chipping the old place to bits. Hangings
and furniture will be crated separately. It'll take quite a time,
of course; shouldn't think we'll get it done under three weeks.'
He looked with respect over his shoulder at a vista of dark
corridor which stretched away for half a mile.

Wil stole away with his heart thudding. Were they actually
proposing to pull down the house, *this* house, and ship it to
Hollywood for film sets? What about the tree? Would they
hack it down, or dig it up and transport it, leaves and all?

'What's the matter, boy?' asked Em, her cheek bulging
with the giant humbug he had brought her.

'The film company's moving away, and they're going to take Troy with them for using as backgrounds for films.'

'The whole house?'

'Yes.'

'Oh,' said Em, and became very thoughtful.

'Em.'

'Yes?'

'What – I mean, what would happen to you if they found this room and cut the tree down, or dug it up?'

'I'm not sure,' she said, pondering. 'I shouldn't go *on* after that – none of us would in here – but as to exactly *what* would happen –; I don't expect it would be bad. Perhaps we should just go out like lamps.'

'Well then it must be stopped,' said Wil so firmly that he surprised himself.

'Can you forbid it? You're the Heir, aren't you?'

'Not till old Uncle Winthrop dies. We'll have to think of some other plan.'

'I have an idea,' said Em, wrinkling her brow with effort. 'In my days, producers would do much for a well-written new play, one that had never been seen before. Is it still like that nowadays?'

'Yes I think so, but we don't know anyone who writes plays,' Wil pointed out.

'I have a play laid by somewhere,' she explained. 'The writer was a friend of my father – he asked my father to take it up to London to have it printed. My father bade me take care of it and I put it in my bundle of clothes. It was on that journey, as we were passing through Oxford, that I was seen and carried off by my respected grandmother, and I never saw my father or Mr Shakespeere again, so the poor man lost his play.'

'Mr Shakespeere, did you say?' asked Wil, stuttering slightly. 'What was the name of the play?'

'I forget. I have it here somewhere.' She began delving about in a cranny between two branches and presently drew out a dirty old manuscript. Wil stared at it with popping eyes.

THE TRAGICALL HISTORIE OF ROBIN HOODE
A play by Wm. Shakespeere

Act I, Scene I. Sherwood Forest. Enter John Lackland, De Bracy, Sheriff of Nottingham, Knights, Lackeys and attendants.

JOHN L.   Good sirs, the occasion of our coming hither
          Is, since our worthy brother Cœur de Lion
          Far from our isle now wars on Paynim soil,
          The apprehension of that recreant knave
          Most caitiff outlaw who is known by some
          As Robin Locksley; by others Robin Hood;
          More, since our coffers gape with idle locks
          The forfeiture of his ill-gotten gains.
          Thus Locksley's stocks will stock our locks enow
          While he treads air beneath the forest bough.

'Golly,' said Wil. 'Shakespeere's Robin Hood. I wonder what Mr Slockenheimer would say to this?'

'Well don't wait. *Go and ask him*. It's yours – I'll make you a present of it.'

He wriggled back through the leaves with frantic speed, slammed the door, and raced down the passage towards the Great Hall. Mr Slockenheimer was there superintending the packing of some expensive and elaborate apparatus.

'Hello, Junior. Haven't seen you in days. Well, how d'you like the thought of moving to Hollywood eh?'

'Not very much,' said Wil frankly. 'You see I'm used to it here, and – and the house is too; I don't think the move would be good for it.'

'Think the dry air would crumble it, mebbe? Well, there's something to what you say. I'll put in air-conditioning apparatus the other end. I'm sorry you don't take to the idea, though. Hollywood's a swell place.'

'Mr Slockenheimer,' said Wil. 'I've got something here which is rather valuable. It's mine – somebody gave it to me. And it's genuine. I was wondering if I could do a sort of swap – exchange it for the house, you know.'

'It would have to be mighty valuable,' replied Mr Slockenheimer cautiously. 'Think it's worth a million, son? What is it?'

'It's a play by Mr Shakespeere – a new play that no one's seen before.'

'Eh?'

'I'll show you,' said Wil confidently, pulling out the MS.

'The Tragicall Historie of Robin Hoode,' read Mr Slockenheimer slowly. 'By Wm. Shakespeere. Well I'll be gosh-darned. Just when I'd finished the indoor scenes. Isn't that just my luck. Hey, Junior – are you sure this is genuine? – Well, Jakes will know, he knows everything; hey,' he called to his secretary. 'Come and have a look at this.'

The dry Mr Jakes let out a whistle when he saw the signature.

'That's genuine all right,' he said. 'It's quite something you've got there. First production of the original Shakespeare play by Q. P. Slockenheimer.'

'Well, will you swap?' asked Wil once more.

'I'll say I will,' exclaimed Mr Slockenheimer slapping him thunderously on the back. 'You can keep your mouldering old barracks. I'll send you twenty stalls for the première. *Robin Hoode by Wm. Shakespeere*. Well, what do you know!'

'There's just one thing,' said Wil pausing.

'Yes, Bud?'

'These contracts you gave my uncle and aunt and the others. Are they still binding?'

'Not if you don't want.'

'Oh, but I do – I'd much rather they went to Hollywood.'

Mr Slockenheimer burst out laughing.

'Oh, I get the drift. Okay, Junior, I daresay they won't bother me as much as they do you. I'll hold them to those contracts as tight as glue. Twenty years eh? You'll be of age by then, I guess? Your Uncle Umbert can be the Sheriff of Nottingham, he's about the build for the part. And we'll fit your Aunt Aggie in somewhere.'

'And Buckle and Squabb?'

'Yes, yes,' said Mr Slockenheimer, much tickled. 'Though what you'll do here all on your own – however, that's your affair. Right, boys, pack up those cameras next.'

Three days later the whole outfit was gone, and with them,

swept away among the flash bulbs, cameras, extras, crates, props and costumes, went Squabb, Buckle, Aunt Agatha, Uncle Umbert, Cousin Cedric and all the rest.

Empty and peaceful the old house dreamed, with sunlight shifting from room to room and no sound to break the silence, save in one place, where the voices of children could be heard faintly above the rustling of a tree.

About the Author

Joan Aiken was born in Rye, Sussex, in 1924. Her father was the American writer Conrad Aiken, of New England and 'Mayflower' ancestry. Miss Aiken has engaged in a variety of work, including ten years with the London office of the United Nations. For five years she was a feature editor for *Argosy*, and more recently has worked as a copy-writer for a large London advertising agency. She has always written a great deal, mostly short stories, but now she devotes all her time to free-lance authorship. Her hobbies are painting and gardening at her home, an ex-pub in Petworth.

Also by Joan Aiken

The Wolves of Willoughby Chase

Bonnie and her cousin Sylvia were left in the charge of wicked Miss Slighcarp, who intended to banish them – but she didn't know what exceptional little girls she had to deal with.

Black Hearts in Battersea

Simon (hero of *The Wolves of Willoughby Chase*) goes to London to find Dr Field. He finds Dido Twite however, and their adventures include fire, wolves, kidnapping, an escape in an air balloon, explosion and even shipwreck. Joan Aiken's 'playing about with history' makes a funny, exciting, outrageous story.

Night Birds on Nantucket

A new lease of life for Dido Twite – she wakes up after being asleep for over ten months to find herself in one of the strangest vessels that ever sailed the seas, chasing a pink whale. But she helps to foil another Hanoverian plot, this time to blow up the Houses of Parliament.

The Cuckoo Tree

Dido Twite, brisk and capable as ever, returns to England and lands straight in a hotbed of witches, smugglers, kidnappers and reckless Hanoverian conspirators.

The Whispering Mountain

The story of a stolen harp, a wicked Marquess, a lost tribe of dwarfs, who live inside the whispering mountain, and a lonely boy full of courage and wisdom who saves all situations and resolves all dangers.

A Small Pinch of Weather

A book of short stories. The sad ones are spiced with wit, and the funny ones have a tinge of sadness, but you're never too sure what will happen next.

The Kingdom Under the Sea

Beautiful, haunting East European fairy stories with Jan Pienkowski's hauntingly beautiful illustrations to match.

If you have enjoyed this book and would like to know about others which we published, why not join the Puffin Club? You will receive the club magazine, *Puffin Post*, four times a year and a smart badge and membership book. You will also be able to enter all the competitions. For details send a stamped addressed envelope to:

The Puffin Club, Dept. A
Penguin Books Limited
Bath Road
Harmondsworth
Middlesex